PRAISE

LAKE OF DESTINY

Also By Martina Boone

Compulsion

Persuasion

Illusion

LAKE OF DESTINY

—A CELTIC LEGENDS NOVEL—

MARTINA BOONE

MAYFAIR
PUBLISHING

MAYFAIR
PUBLISHING

712 H Street NE, Suite 1014,
Washington, DC 20002
First Mayfair Publishing edition April 2017
Copyright © 2017 by Martina Boone

Jacket design by Kalen O'Donnell
Interior Design by Rachel & Joel Greene

Published in the United States of America
ISBN 978-1-946773-00-5 (paperback)
Library of Congress Control Number: 2017905183

To Erin and Sandra, without whom this book would not exist.

LAKE OF DESTINY

BAND-AIDS AND CHOCOLATE

Let us go, lassie, go tae the braes o' Balquhidder
Where the blaeberries grow 'mang the bonnie Highland heather

ROBERT TANNAHILL, "BRAES OF BALQUHIDDER"

ANNA CAMERON HAD spent too many hours in an airline seat tighter than a respectable dress, and that had done nothing to improve her mood. Used to being impeccably groomed, she felt crumpled, grubby, and even more like a failure as she stepped off the jetway with a wine-stained blouse and naked face. But flying business class was not in her future anymore. As an unemployed lawyer—aka fired with no hope of ever practicing law again—she needed to manage on a tighter budget.

Honestly, she was lucky to be in Scotland now at all. If her Aunt Elspeth hadn't been desperate for help with the Beltane Festival and willing to pay her way, Anna would have been stuck in the Cincinnati suburbs instead, hiding out in the kitchen she'd worked so hard to escape, while her mother delivered yet another lecture on the topic of her middle daughter's many failings. With two broken engagements and a colossal screw-up behind her, Anna was officially a "disappointment."

Mostly to herself.

But enough. She was determined to be positive. Her old life in Washington, D.C.—and Mike and his new fiancée—were three thousand miles behind her on a different continent. She had dreamed of coming to the Scottish Highlands all her life. Now she was here for an entire month, visiting with her favorite aunt. As a bonus, there was the possibility of turning her knack for organizing events into a new career—one she badly needed.

Shrugging the straps of the four-year-old Louis Vuitton Keepall she'd gotten as a law school graduation present into a more secure position, she set off on long, slim legs toward the baggage claim, her dark tumble of curls bouncing around her shoulders. She even refrained from stopping at the duty-free shop to buy a Toblerone.

But then it happened. An ocean away, and she still could not escape.

The television at the United Airlines gate cut over to a White House briefing, and there was the press secretary, the woman who had just announced her engagement to Anna's ex-fiancé less than four months after he had walked out on Anna. The beautiful and successful woman who, unlike Anna, could apparently focus on Mike and a high-pressure career without managing to sink both in disaster.

To heck with budgets. And to heck with calories.

Anna plowed a U-turn in the middle of the terminal and waded back to the duty-free shop to buy that candy bar, almost mowing down a pair of British Airways flight attendants who were walking side-by-side. Bypassing the Baileys Truffles and the overpriced Godiva Connoisseur collections, she snatched up the single candy bar—large size—and queued up at the cash register behind a woman arguing into her cell phone. Which reminded Anna that she needed to let her Aunt Elspeth know that she had landed safely.

Switching on her cell, she ignored the three new voicemails from her mother and used the cheap-phone app she had installed before leaving her apartment to dial Elspeth's number.

"Hello?" Elspeth Murray picked up breathlessly after the seventh ring and spoke with her lilting Scottish accent. "Is that you, Anna?"

Anna smiled just hearing Elspeth's voice. "Yes, I'm just heading over to collect my luggage. With a little luck, I should be there to fix your dinner."

"Och, don't you worry about that. Take your time. I've had help today, and I've had my feet up. You're the one who's likely to be exhausted. I don't suppose you've managed to get any sleep since you left, have you?"

It was so like Elspeth to worry about everyone except herself. During her annual Christmas visits, she'd always wrapped Anna in acceptance like a well-worn blanket, offering up the perfect word of comfort or a plate of fruited gingerbread along with a cup of tea as she took charge of the kitchen for the duration of her stay.

"You can't possibly know how happy I'll be to see you," Anna blurted out.

"Likewise, love, but mind you're careful on the road. You're sure you'll be all right driving on the wrong side? I could still send someone to come and get you."

"That's too much trouble. I'll manage," Anna said, squashing down a twinge of doubt. But the thought of driving on the left in rush-hour traffic was daunting as she hung up. She still wasn't sure whether to cut through Edinburgh or try to go around. After four days of little sleep, the long trek to the remote glen where Elspeth lived was going to be hard enough, and Anna didn't want to add any more time than necessary.

She was considering redialing Elspeth's number, so when the phone rang as she sidled up to the cash register, she tucked it between her cheek and shoulder. "I was about to call you back," she said, plunking a couple of two-pound coins onto the counter. "I meant to ask you, is it worth taking the M8 instead of the M9 at this time of day?"

"Why on earth would you want to take the long way around?" Anna's mother asked from the other side of the Atlantic.

Anna gave a mental groan.

"Not that I understand why you're going there in the first place," Ailsa Murray Cameron continued. "You'll be bored to tears an hour after you arrive, and don't get me started on that ridiculous excuse Elspeth gave you about a Beltane festival. Since when does the village need help organizing the Sighting? That stupid superstition has been going on at least a thousand years, and it's always caused more damage than it's worth."

If there'd been a wall beside her, Anna would have banged her head against it. Instead, she accepted the plastic sack with her candy bar from the cashier and peeled away from the counter. "I told you already. They're making it bigger this year to pay for the Village Hall reconstruction, and Elspeth's fallen behind with her knee not healing as quickly as it should. Anyway, I'm looking forward to finally seeing the place where you grew up."

"There's nothing there worth seeing, but suit yourself. It's not like you ever listen to me anyway. Otherwise you'd be married and gainfully employed like both your sisters. What has your so-called independence and following in your father's footsteps ever gotten you? Two broken engagements and a Harvard law degree you'll probably never use again, that's what. Now, on top of that, you're running away to the end of nowhere to take care of the last person on the planet who will ever talk sense into you. Come here instead, Anna." Her mother's voice softened, and the faintly Scottish cadence left over after thirty-odd years as an American lawyer's wife grew more pronounced. "Come home, and let me help you find a way to fix this. That new girl, what does she have that you don't? You can win Mike back. Compromise a wee little bit, set a wedding date. I've no doubt at all he's marrying her on the rebound because you hurt him."

"I didn't hurt Mike—I delayed him," Anna said, "which is different. And I don't want him back."

In the brief ensuing silence, she was shocked to discover the words were true.

She missed Mike. But she didn't want to marry him.

She missed his company. She missed his acid wit and sharp intelligence, and the way he smelled of coffee and vanilla and spicy soap. The way his arms wrapped around her and made her warm. She missed the parties they had loved to throw, the way their Watergate apartment had filled with friends on the weekends. The way the two of them had used to cook together before settling down to watch a movie after an exhausting, high-pressure day. The way they used to laugh together. But she'd honestly thought that his leaving was temporary. That they would work things out once her monster of a case had ended.

And now? Clearly, given his whirlwind engagement, she'd realized he wasn't coming back, but she hadn't taken stock of how that made her feel. The shock and humiliation of hearing the news at work had been too raw. Then there'd been the aching, stomach-clenching sense of rejection that had led to her meltdown and the fatal mistake that had gotten her fired.

Where, though, was the heartbreak and longing that she'd felt after Henry . . . after her first engagement? The sense that her life—the whole world—had lost some of its sparkle, and become, like the first gasp of darkness after the sun had gone but before the beauty of the stars emerged, a place she couldn't navigate?

Confused, Anna shook her head. Out in the terminal, the long white corridor was crowded with passengers disembarking another flight, and she slowed to let a young mother rush past, trailing a child and two carry-on rolling bags behind her. The child, a tousle-headed girl of about four or five, wobbled beneath the weight of a pink backpack, half dragging an oversized stuffed rabbit by one ear as she jogged to keep up. Anna knew the feeling, like she was losing her grip on everything that was familiar while the world swept her along.

"Anna Cameron, are you listening to me at all?" On the other end of the phone, Ailsa's voice had grown louder and more shrill.

"What?" said Anna, who—out of habit and self-defense—had succeeded in tuning her mother out. "Of course, I am."

Her mother huffed a long-suffering sigh. "I asked when you plan to stop trying to run from your problems. You do this every time. Something gets difficult or awkward, and you give up."

Outrage over that statement formed a hard lump in Anna's stomach. She never gave up. She wouldn't have gotten through law school if she gave up.

"Helping Aunt Elspeth isn't running away," she said. "It's fulfilling a family obligation. *You* aren't going, and someone needs to help."

"If Elspeth claims she needs help at all, much less with whatever she's calling a festival, you can bet she's up to something. You've always adored her, but trust me when I say she always has at least sixteen different reasons for everything she does. And at least fifteen of them are about what *she* is going to get out of it. Her surgery was two weeks ago. She's gotten along fine so far. Why does she need you now?"

"Do you even hear yourself, Mother? She's your sister."

"Since when have you thought that was important? How long has it been since you last spoke to Katharine?"

Anna's throat threatened to squeeze itself shut. This entire conversation was why she needed to be anywhere other than Ohio.

"Katharine and I are different," she wheezed. "Aunt Elspeth didn't steal *your* fiancé away from you two weeks before *your* wedding."

Shaking, literally shaking, Anna mashed the END button with her thumb and hung up on her mother for the first time in her life. Just thinking about Henry married to Katharine, every emotion she hadn't felt with Mike suddenly churned in her chest, all the despair and colorlessness and hurt. Which, she couldn't help acknowledging, were vastly different feelings from disappointment and humiliation.

She switched off the phone before it could ring again and stared down at it in horror. She would pay for hanging up; she knew that. Soon, and for the rest of her life. Her mother was worse than an elephant when it came to never forgetting. Any. Darn. Thing. And coping with additional stress was beyond Anna's capacity at that moment.

What she ought to do was buy herself a local SIM card and conveniently forget to give the new phone number to her mother.

Hand still trembling, she slipped her cell back into her purse and took a deep, calming breath as she hurried down the corridor. In front of her, the girl with the pink backpack dropped her rabbit. Tugging her small hand out of her mother's grasp, the child rushed back to pick it up, but a businessman emerging from a coffee shop couldn't step aside fast enough to avoid knocking into her. The girl landed chin-first on the gray linoleum tiles and, stunned, began to wail.

The mother had to wrestle the two rolling bags to turn around, so Anna scooped up the rabbit and knelt beside the girl, offering a hand to help her up. "That was some spectacular fall. Good job on saving your rabbit, though. You wouldn't want to leave him behind. Or is it a her? I had one named Violet when I was about your age."

"He's P-peter, like the s-story," the girl said with a sob. She took Anna's hand and climbed to her feet, snuggling the rabbit as if she'd been afraid she'd lost him forever. Her chin bled, and she'd skinned her knees, and while her mother arrived and fussed with antiseptic wipes and Band-Aids, Anna handed the girl a tissue and the Toblerone. Then she took charge of one of the two rolling bags and helped mother and daughter down to the baggage claim carousel, wishing that all wounds were as easy to soothe with a stuffed rabbit and a chocolate bar.

Life would have been so much easier if that was how healing worked.

SHEEPISH

"My name is not spoken," she replied with a great deal of haughtiness. "More than a hundred years it has not gone upon men's tongues, save for a blink. I am nameless like the Folk of Peace."

ROBERT LOUIS STEVENSON, *CATRIONA*

DRIVING WITHOUT GOOGLE MAPS yielded unexpected benefits. To save on data charges and avoid her mother, Anna kept her phone turned off and used the directions she had hastily written down to navigate. That combined with intermittent bucketloads of rain, and the confusion of driving on the left, led her to make five wrong turns that cost her at least an hour. On the other hand, it was impossible to stay depressed when something surprising and delightful popped out at her everywhere she looked.

She was finally *here*.

The reality of being in Scotland thrilled her all over again. This was *Outlander* country, *Braveheart* country, the home of heroes like Robert the Bruce, William Wallace, and Rob Roy MacGregor. The stuff of Aunt Elspeth's stories, Sir Walter Scott's books, and Robert Burns's poetry—along with every adolescent dream Anna'd ever had of men in kilts.

Not that she was likely to find men in kilts or bagpipers piping out the tune to "MacGregor's Gathering." But Balwhither, where Anna's mother had grown up and Elspeth still lived, had always been MacGregor land, the place where Rob Roy himself lay buried. Anna wanted to take in everything on the way, experience everything. Unfortunately, her eyes kept trying to close, and her stomach growled with growing insistence.

She tried singing to keep herself awake.

She opened the window.

She stopped for coffee and an onion-laced meat pasty in Callander at the border of the Highlands. The food only made her sleepier.

Meanwhile, the road grew narrower. She drove more slowly, squeezing over to make room whenever faster cars whipped around her shoebox-sized Chevy rental. By the time the odometer advised her that the cutoff for Balwhither Glen was coming up, she was traveling at a turtle's pace. Even so, she would have missed the turn if she hadn't spied the black-and-white signpost for Rob Roy's grave and slammed on her brakes.

In the glen itself, a single-track road led past scattered farms and houses, past the ruined church and the cemetery where Rob Roy's tombstone read, "MacGregor Despite Them," showing the same defiance with which he'd lived.

According to Elspeth, Anna's own family had been MacGregors, too, before the name had been banned for almost two hundred years. Since then, they'd used the name of Murray, and all of them were buried in that graveyard. The thought sent goosebumps over Anna's spine, but ignoring the impulse to stop, she drove on toward the loch that began at the end of the tiny village.

Calling it a village was a bit of a hopeful overstatement. Together with a handful of white houses, a smattering of businesses each did double duty: The Last Stand Inn and Tavern, Grewer's Sweets and Groceries, and a face slap of a pink building with a sign that proclaimed it was the Library and Tea Room. Beyond those, the long opalescent strip of Loch Fàil unfurled, more spectacular than Anna could have imagined. The last spun-silk rays of sunset pierced the clouds and turned the water gold and red as it faded into a diminishing rank of hills.

Seen like this, Anna could almost believe that the legend about people seeing images of their true loves reflected in its waters at the Sighting was more than a romantic bedtime story. But she had little opportunity to admire its beauty.

Alongside the loch, the road gave up any pretense of being paved. Or free of obstacles.

Rounding a bend, Anna found a flock of black-faced sheep milling across the puddle-soaked gravel beneath an overhanging rowan. She wrenched the car to the verge to avoid plowing into them. They scattered, half of them running in front of her, and it took her fifty yards before she got back on the road. The sheep didn't seem to care. According to the rearview mirror, they were all back in the road again, half of them turned in her direction, watching her taillights fade.

Lights.

A flash of headlights hit her head on, and a car barreled at her around a second bend. She jerked to the right before she remembered she was supposed to be on the left—not that there was much of a left or right; the road scarcely offered room for a single car. Anna yanked the wheel over and caught a bump—a rock or wretched log—and, flustered, missed the brake and jammed the accelerator.

Her car shot toward the loch. Adrenaline tightened Anna's chest. She fought a skid. The car fishtailed and finally slid to a stop some twenty feet off the road.

Hands strangling the wheel, Anna sat gulping air and wondering how deep the water in the loch was in front of her—and whether her rental insurance would have covered submersion through stupidity. On the bright side, if she'd drowned herself, at least she'd have been out of her misery.

Which was not a cheerful thought. Hadn't she promised herself that she'd be more optimistic?

Forcing her lips into a smile and the car into reverse, she mashed the gas. Mud and grass spat from beneath the tires, and she turned to look back over her shoulder. It was only then that she noticed the tall, muscled figure approaching behind her.

The man jumped aside, swearing. Anna didn't hear him, but she didn't need to. By the glow of her taillights, the gesture and the facial expression that marred what was otherwise a handsome face were clear enough. To remove all doubt, he pounded a fist against the driver's window as he stooped beside it.

Anna fumbled with the power controls.

He'd stopped knocking by the time the glass slid down, but his hand still hovered in the air. He stared at her, his blue eyes narrowed beneath wiry dark hair, as if she'd shocked him.

Anna felt just as stunned. With the sunset behind his shoulders, he shimmered, all gold and gleaming around the edges, like a hopeful memory. The impression vanished the moment she blinked, but then disbelief set in. Because she recognized him. Throughout most of their teenage years, her sister Katharine's bedroom had been plastered with posters of his face, and Katharine had obsessed over every bit of tabloid speculation when he'd disappeared after the accident that had killed his wife.

"Aren't you Gregor Mark?" Anna barely managed to keep the surprised squeak out of her voice.

"The hell I am," he snapped in an accent decidedly more Scottish than Gregor Mark's cut-glass British accent, "and what do you think you're doing, driving like an idiot on this road? Or off the road, to be exact. My daughter's in the car. You could have killed us both."

Anna winced at the tone of his voice and at her own stupidity. "I'm sorry. It was the sheep—"

"The bloody sheep are part of the reason it's daft to drive that fast through here."

Daft? Hold on. Even the sheep had practically laughed at how slowly she'd been driving. Why was it that no one gave her the benefit of the doubt lately, not for a single second? Not Mike, not her boss, not even her own darn mother. Yes, she'd made mistakes, but was it necessary for everyone to overreact?

"I wasn't even close to speeding," she said through gritted teeth, "and I already told you I was sorry, so you don't have to yell—"

"You think this is yelling?"

"I can hear perfectly well that it is, so go back to your daughter, and let me get my car back on the road."

"Best of bloody luck to you if you want to try. You'll only dig yourself in deeper." The man straightened and shook his head. A muscle ticked in his cheek. "Look, sorry, but since you've already managed to splatter me in mud, I'd be grateful if you'd at least wait until I'm out of range before you try again. Meanwhile, I'll go phone for someone to come and dig you out."

The dark mud had blended into the dull green waxed jacket he wore open over a well-tailored white shirt and jeans, but it stood out on the lighter clothing. Anna hardly had time to register the mess before he'd turned away to stalk off on long, angry legs.

Even the way he crossed the boggy ground made her think of how Gregor Mark had used to stride across a movie screen, claiming the landscape and every inch of attention. Not that the resemblance was perfect. His

Rudeness's hair was shorter and darker, not Gregor Mark's famous windblown style, and Gregor had always been clean-shaven or with a light scruff of five o'clock shadow. His Rudeness'd also had more of a chiseled-out-of-rock sharpness to his features. Of course, who knew what Gregor Mark would look like now? Even though his blockbuster films were still all over the television, the newest were a decade old. His disappearance had simply frozen him in time.

Unable to help herself, Anna watched the stranger until he'd reached the silver Audi station wagon that stood with its driver's door open and dome lights shining. From the passenger side of the car, a small pale face strained to look around him in Anna's direction, but the man swung himself onto the seat, slammed the door, and drove away.

Anna threw her own door open. Beneath her feet, the grass was torn, and cold mud squelched into her loafers while she slogged around to check her wheels. It didn't help that His Rudeness had been right: the rear tires had burrowed down three inches. That wasn't insurmountable. If she was careful, she might still be able to ease the car out and get back onto the road without having to subject herself to additional humiliation. She'd had enough of that for one day, one week—one lifetime, for that matter— hadn't she? The universe couldn't be this cruel.

Except, it could. Back in the car, she alternated between forward and reverse, but the harder she tried to rock the Chevy out of the mud, the deeper the wheels dug in. That left her the choice of searching for a tow truck to pull her out in the dark, or abandoning the car there and hiking the last mile to the house with her suitcase and carry-on bag. The thought of trudging that distance, when all she wanted to do was flop into a comfortable bed, made her want to scream.

Head buried in her hands, she almost missed the first flash of headlights on the road. By the time she looked up, more lights had pierced the darkness and cars were pulling up onto the grass behind her, doors slamming as people got out. Then a man in a kilt—an actual kilt—black military-style tactical boots, and a well-worn leather jacket strode up, grinning. His mop of wavy chin-length hair fell deeply auburn across his forehead, and his cheekbones were as sharp as knives above a white flash of teeth.

Anna wondered whether she'd hit her head on the steering wheel and was, in fact, hallucinating or dreaming, or whatever it was one did when one was unconscious. Or was Scotland naturally full of gorgeous men? Which would figure, because a man of any kind was the very last thing she needed.

The new arrival reached her window and leaned down, grinning more broadly. "You've gotten yourself into a wee pickle, haven't you?" he said in a Scottish burr even lovelier than her Aunt Elspeth's. "Himself phoned the house, and your aunt rang me, and here I am to help—along with half the village. I was down at the pub, mind, so you'll have quite the welcoming party here in a minute."

"Himself?" Anna blinked at him.

"Connal MacGregor. The laird—the one you ran off the road."

"I ran *him* off the road? That's rich since I'm the one sitting here in the muck—also he was rude."

"Well, he would be, wouldn't he, with you coming to help with the festival?" The man laughed, a deep rumble in his chest. "I'm Brando, by the way. We've all been expecting you." He glanced behind him to where an ever-larger crowd was emerging from their cars. "Elspeth's that excited about your visit. She's talked of nothing else since the moment you agreed to come; she's missed you so much these past few years."

Anna swallowed an automatic twinge of guilt. Between Mike and her workload, she'd missed going home the last three Christmas holidays, and it had been ages since she'd seen Elspeth. Still, she pushed the guilt aside. She'd earned enough of that on her own lately without dwelling on things beyond her control. It was time for a New Year's resolution, even if it was two days before April Fools' Day. No more gratuitous guilt.

The oddly-named Brando wasn't waiting for her to acknowledge what he'd said. He'd turned to shout instructions to the people straggling toward them while simultaneously warding off a huge golden retriever who lunged at him with muddy paws and an ecstatic bark. Then a sturdy middle-aged woman in a dull-green sweater and her more handsome husband came to haul the dog away, and a man in a Royal Mail truck started rounding up the sheep along the road. A little gnome-like man with merry blue eyes gave Anna a shy tip of his cap before he sloshed through the churned-up mud to attach a chain from the back of her car to the back of Brando's Land Rover.

Still more people arrived, and in the resulting slurry of introductions and car-extricating activity, Anna had little opportunity for guilt or even embarrassment. With their smiles and a bit of gentle teasing, the villagers of Balwhither managed to make her laugh at the situation and feel genuinely welcome.

Disaster-to-Disaster Delivery

Many miles away there's a shadow on the door
of a cottage on the shore of a dark Scottish lake.

Sir Walter Scott

DESPITE THE EXHAUSTION that claimed her in waves, Anna put on a brave face while Brando towed her filthy green Chevy rental into the driveway at Breagh House. A sign at the edge of the road pointed visitors for the BREAGH HOUSE HIGHLANDS MUSEUM around to the side of the rambling Gothic-style construction that, sometime in the nineteenth century, had replaced the Murrays' earlier home.

The museum was another overly-hopeful title. As Elspeth described it, the former ballroom of Breagh House now held an ever-rotating collection of Highland history and memorabilia, most of it acquired at bargain prices from local estate sales, or on eBay and various online sites, before receiving fanciful backstories that Elspeth changed whenever she got bored. Elspeth had no shame about that at all.

"It's the stories people enjoy, not the rusting junk. Who cares about a sword? Tell them who owned it and whom he stabbed with it. A flask? Describe the man who sipped from it as he lay dying on the battlefield. Who drank from it before he bedded the lass who would become his wife? That's what people want to know."

Anna and her sisters, Margaret and Katharine, had always loved the museum stories whenever Elspeth came to visit. For the length of Elspeth's stays, the whole family gravitated to the kitchen, and for once in the hectic and perpetually-dieting Cameron household, the smell of baking wafted from the oven. Everyone sat and laughed together. Even Anna's mother would allow herself a sliver of Ecclefechan butter tart or Montrose cake along with a "wee dram" of the whiskey Elspeth had brought for Anna's father. But inevitably Ailsa would remember herself again. Her face would stiffen and her voice go shrill while she lectured Elspeth on the evils of taking in unsuspecting tourists with her Highland flimflam.

Anna had never thought there was much harm in Elspeth's stories. If the tourists came and had a good time, they'd gotten their money's worth and helped Elspeth keep a roof on the family home.

That roof was more sizable than it had appeared in photos, Anna realized once Brando had stopped the Land Rover. Still, despite the almost ostentatious structure, the front floodlights provided a cheerful glow to the weathered gray stone, and the smell of woodsmoke curling out of the chimney promised a warming fire.

Brando flicked off the ignition. The front door of the house flew open and, backlit by the chandelier hanging from the foyer ceiling, Elspeth emerged onto the stoop. Leaning heavily on a walker, she waited in the doorway instead of coming to greet Anna with her usual energy and enthusiasm. The sight of her conjured up the best memories of Anna's life.

Anna raced up the steps. Elspeth released one arm from the walker to tuck her into just the kind of hard, unconditional embrace Anna needed. The kind that didn't care whether she was more or less pretty or dutiful than her sisters, whether she had a stain on her blouse, whether she didn't smile on cue at beauty pageant judges as her mother instructed, no matter what they said or did to her, or whether she had a man or a job or a future.

"Aren't you a sight, now?" Elspeth stood back and looked Anna over. "You have had a tough time of it, haven't you? Poor love, but no matter. We'll soon get you sorted. Are you hungry? You must be famished."

"I stopped for a meat pasty in Callander. Mostly, I'm half-asleep."

"Well, and no wonder. You'll get a hot bath, a nice cuppa, and some scones to nibble on while you soak, then it's straight off to bed with you. And no arguing. We can catch up in the morning. Plenty of time for all of that."

Anna couldn't help smiling. "I'm supposed to be taking care of *you*, remember?"

"The day Elspeth lets anyone take care of her, that's a day I'd love to see." His tread light and graceful for such a large man, Brando came up the stairs behind them, carrying Anna's suitcase in one arm and her Keepall in the other. Pausing beside Elspeth, he shook his head at her and bent to kiss her cheek. "You're not fooling anyone, old woman, you know that? You'd better hurry up and tell her before she susses it out herself."

"Mmmh. Watch that 'old' business, Brando MacLaren. You're not getting younger yourself."

"Aye, and the rate I'm going, I'll catch up with you before too long."

Elspeth raised both eyebrows at him. It was a look Anna had seen her mother direct at people a million times, but Elspeth's eyes sparkled with humor and gave the expression a different meaning. Intrigued, Anna studied her aunt's face, which was so similar to her own mother's countenance, but at the same time so very different. Where a facelift and years of expensive skincare had left Ailsa's skin unlined beneath black hair she touched up twice a month like clockwork at the most expensive salon in town, Elspeth appeared a decade older, her chin-length curls left to gray attractively, and her complexion weathered by laughter and sun and wind. Even now, deep lines scored the corners of her eyes as she let Brando pass into the foyer.

"Thanks for bringing our girl home in one piece," she said.

"What do you want me to do with the car?" Brando set Anna's baggage down at the bottom of the wide, carpeted steps and glanced from Elspeth to Anna and back again.

"No point unhooking if you'd like me to take it back for you. I'm heading to Edinburgh in the morning, so it'd be no trouble, and she'll have your Volvo to use in the meantime."

A bit of strain lifted off Anna's wallet, and she gave him a grateful nod. "If you really wouldn't mind . . ."

"Brando's always the first person to be there when you need anything. Before you know you need it, half the time," Elspeth said, directing a fond smile at him and patting his arm as he slipped out past her. "Not half-bad to look at either, is he?"

"Enough flattery now, you." Kilt fanning out around his knees, Brando turned to wave good-bye then waded down the front steps without seeing Anna's reddened face. "I'll try to come back by tomorrow afternoon," he called over his shoulder. "That light on the far side of the house has gone out again, and you'll want to start thinking 'bout security if we're going to get more visitors." He strode down and jumped into the Land Rover to drive away down the circular drive with Anna's rental car still chained up behind him.

"Lovely man." Elspeth cleared her throat and turned to go back into the house. "You could do worse, you know. Although at this rate, I'm afraid we'll never manage to get him married off. Even Duncan at the inn has given up trying to find a woman for him. There was a time when Davy the postman had the whole glen laying bets on a different girl each week, but we've all gotten tired of losing money."

"Sorry. Not interested," Anna said firmly, trailing Elspeth inside. "I'm leaving in a month, and he doesn't seem like he'd transplant very well. Everything except his name seems very Scottish."

"Aye, isn't that the truth? His mother watched *On the Waterfront* and *A Streetcar Named Desire* a dozen times too many, and now he's stuck with it. Don't let the kilt fool you, though. Brando's only been wearing it since he moved back from London. Swears it's more comfortable, a lot of men do, but I suspect it started off for the tourists as much as for any other reason. Now you take your bags up to the bedroom—third door on the left—and then come down to get your tea. The kitchen'll be that direction." Elspeth gestured toward the right.

Anna looked around. The whole house gave the impression of belonging in a different time, and she had the odd sense that it was reaching out to welcome her, folding her inside itself. The intricate wood of the hardwood parquet gleamed beneath the chandelier that spilled cascades of color across a Victorian stained glass window on the landing, and the carved staircase with thick, square newel posts spoke of solidness and security. Warm yellow light shone down the corridor from the kitchen.

Anna couldn't help thinking her mother must have loved John Cameron very much, at least at first, to give up all this for a modern faux-chateau in Indian Hill on the outskirts of Cincinnati. But she'd long ago given up despairing about her parents. If they wanted to spend their time arguing with each other, that was their business.

The thought of their polite fights led her back to the rude man with the Audi, and partway up the staircase she paused and turned. "Who was the man who called you to say I'd run off the road, Aunt Elspeth? The one who looks like Gregor Mark. Brando said he was rude because I was coming to help with the festival."

"Did he now?" Elspeth looked away. "Brando ought to keep his tongue in his head."

"But who is he? And why does he object to the festival?"

Elspeth pursed her lips. "Connal MacGregor. He lives down at Inverlochlarig, the big house at the end of the loch there, though he owns half the glen. The Sighting and the bonfire are both on his property, and he's none too happy about us making the festival bigger."

"Can he stop it?"

"He could—but listen, all this is a longer conversation than we've time for tonight. Connal's bringing his daughter 'round for dinner tomorrow night, and we'll settle everything then."

Anna's heart gave an unexpected thump. "Settle what?"

"Well, not so much settle as negotiate. That's where your lawyer skills come in—and now that's more than enough for tonight. Away upstairs with you. You're so tired you'll fall asleep in your bath if you're not careful."

Warning bells pealed loud and long in Anna's head as she studied Elspeth. Even so, just hearing the word bath brought up a yawn that rippled up from the bottom of her exhausted body.

Whatever fresh disaster was heading in her direction, she was going to have to wait and face it in the morning. After a good night's sleep.

MEET THE PRESS

The best laid schemes o' mice an' men gang aft agley.

ROBERT BURNS, "TO A MOUSE"

T HE BATHROOM WAS EQUIPPED with a heater and a deep, claw-footed tub. Soaking in the water, Anna had a view of the night sky filled with stars splattered bright and moonlight that turned the loch to liquid silver. She lay back surrounded by lavender-scented bubbles, every one of her muscles unknotting. Tired as she was, though, after she set the alarm on her nightstand and crawled beneath the soft comforter with her hair wet, she didn't sleep for long.

In the middle of the night, her worries all roared back at her as if a storm had churned up the sediment. She tried to coax herself back to sleep. Tried to forget. Even something as simple as thinking of the time difference between Scotland and Washington, D.C. was a reminder that, for her, there was no such place as home anymore.

The lease on the apartment she had once shared with Mike was up in just two months.

When she finished here in Scotland, she'd have less than four weeks to move and get her life back in order. No one was going to hire her as a lawyer after she'd missed an EPA filing and cost her firm's client a small fortune in penalties. She had savings, but they wouldn't last forever. All the way around, helping Elspeth organize the Beltane Festival for May Day was a heaven-sent opportunity. If she could pull it off, it would give her a new event to add to the many she had helped organize for her mother before she'd left for law school, and the combination might be enough to get her a foot in the door with one of the companies that planned the big D.C. events.

But that meant she had to pull it off. No matter what Connal MacGregor wanted or didn't want.

The thought propelled her out of bed an hour before the alarm was set to ring. Immediately, she felt better. The walls of the airy room upstairs were covered in a cheery damask Victorian wallpaper that she hadn't had time to appreciate the night before. The sun filtered through a haze of clouds, casting a glow over the polished hardwood floor and refracting off the antique mirrored dresser.

Outside, beyond the windows, Loch Fàil came to a head at a narrow peninsula where the Sighting took place and slipped into the smaller, oval lake, Loch Daoine. After that, the valley narrowed, wild and lonely, and vanished into steep-sided braes and taller Munros.

The view fired Anna's imagination. Rob Roy's house had stood at the end of the smaller loch before the Duke of Montrose had evicted him, branded him an outlaw, and forced him to hide within the untamable Highland hills. The original dwelling had been burned at the time, but an enormous house, almost large enough to be called a castle, stood there now. Built of gray stone, baronial, turreted, and surrounded by a high stone wall that ran all the way down to the peninsula, it was also vaguely intimidating.

Very much like its owner.

On that thought, and the reminder that His Rudeness was coming to dinner that night, Anna's craving for coffee went from need-it-now to what-the-heck-are-you-waiting for. Why on earth would Elspeth have invited Connal MacGregor to dinner if he was angry about the festival? More importantly, why was he so upset?

She turned on her phone just long enough to send an email to her mother saying she'd arrived safely, then powered it off again and shoved it in the nightstand drawer. After shimmying into faded jeans and a comfortable cashmere sweater that had seen better days, she let herself out into the carpeted hallway and tiptoed down what had once been the servants' stairs at the back.

Intending to get a jump on breakfast in bed for Elspeth, she mentally ticked through the list of ingredients for cinnamon donut muffins. All of them were basics that Elspeth was sure to have on hand, and the recipe would make the house smell like warmth and comfort. Smiling, she reached the open doorway to a bright kitchen papered in old-fashioned yellow roses. But instead of going in, she stopped dead on the threshold.

Elspeth was there ahead of her, humming as she removed a kettle from the modern, stainless steel cooktop set in among the white cabinetry. Taking the kettle to the counter near the sink, she poured steaming water into a waiting Wedgwood teapot. However, this was not the frail Elspeth who had greeted Anna the night before.

This Elspeth still wore the post-surgery elastic stocking and limped a little, but she'd left the walker abandoned beside the Welsh dresser that displayed china and a collection of photographs on the far side of the room. Abandoned also was Elspeth's earlier slumped and weary posture. She might have put on a few pounds since the last time Anna had seen her, but she was still clearly fit and as full of energy as ever.

Standing in the doorway, Anna thought back to her mother's accusation. Which was not something she wanted to think about.

Still humming, Elspeth got down a delicately-patterned cup and saucer from the cupboard and poured herself some tea before turning with it toward the table that sat near the door. On seeing Anna, she gave a startled jump. Tea sloshed over the rim of the cup onto the scrubbed oak floor.

Anna rushed to clean it up. Only when she straightened with the cloth hot and damp in her hand did she meet Elspeth's eyes.

They looked guilty and more than a little frightened.

Anna gave a sigh. "What are you up to, Aunt Elspeth? Why have you been pretending your knee is worse than it is?"

"Would you have come if I hadn't?" Flushing a mottled red, Elspeth turned back to the cupboard beside the sink, got down a fresh cup and saucer, and poured out tea for Anna. She handed it to her ceremoniously, like a peace offering. "I am sorry for misleading you, but I didn't want you going home to your mother when you've already been through so much. I won't apologize for that."

Anna took the tea, but it was coffee that she craved. She suspected she was going to need to be wide-awake for whatever Elspeth was going to tell her. "What about the festival?" she asked. "About making it bigger and rebuilding the Village Hall? Was any of that true?"

"Aye, it was. After I told you."

"What?" Anna's stomach sank.

"The truth is, I've gotten the village into a pickle." Elspeth blew out a breath, as if getting the confession out had freed air trapped inside her lungs, and then rushed on. "It's your mother's fault, really. She kept going on about Mike and your job, and all I could think about was you back in that house of hers, having to listen to her badgering. And back in September, when the Village Hall burned down and we realized the insurance had lapsed, we did all talk about expanding the bonfire and the Sighting into a festival and bringing in more tourism. Some of the businesses here are desperate. Only—well, we can't ever make a decision for all the arguing. Then when I was on the phone with you, I remembered how much you always loved organizing your mother's charity events. So why not kill two birds? Ailsa always bragged how you had a talent for planning."

Anna glanced up. "She did?"

Elspeth's smile kindled with mischief in a way that made her look a decade younger. "It's one of the few times I've ever heard her give anyone their due."

It was stupid how much that one little bit of praise distracted Anna, how much it made her realize how rarely her mother had ever praised her. She forced herself to concentrate. "I don't understand, though, Aunt Elspeth. Why is Connal angry about the festival if it doesn't even exist yet?"

"I'm afraid that's where I went and did something stupid." Elspeth shifted in her seat, looking even more uncomfortable. "As soon as you said you would come, some of us in the village got together and came up with a list of ideas a mile long for events and ways to raise money. I told them I would talk to Connal about it in the morning, but by the time I got back here that night, I'd gotten to worrying that you'd think I'd invited you here on a pretext—"

"Which you did—"

"—and I thought if I could at least organize a few things before you arrived, it would seem more like we were further along in the planning. You know how I get. I started looking online, and I found one of those press release services, and the next thing I knew, it was four in the morning, and I'd sent notices out to half of Scotland, and I'd emailed all the travel agents and websites and hotels that send us visitors besides. All without saying a peep to Connal. Now we'll look like right idiots if we back out— and people could show up even if we try to cancel."

34

Anna could picture it as Elspeth talked, the way Elspeth would get swept away on a wave of enthusiasm, wrapping herself within a story until she half-believed it herself. Embellishing it with more and more details until the line between fact and fiction blurred. It was only the Connal piece that made no sense. Elspeth had talked about the village May Day traditions for as long as Anna could remember. Anna's mother had been May Queen the year she'd left the glen, and Elspeth had been Queen the next two years. No one even knew how far back the tradition of the Beltane bonfire and the Sighting went.

"What is it that Connal's objecting to?" Anna asked. "The Sighting's always been in the same place, hasn't it? Is it just the extra people? Litter? Noise? What?"

"Nothing like that." Elspeth pushed back her chair and crossed to the refrigerator. "But listen to me going on and on when you must be famished. Do you want a savory breakfast or something sweet? I can do you a full Scottish, or a full English, or eggs and sausage by themselves. There are scones left, too, and I baked up some of that fruited gingerbread you like. I figured you'd be needing a bribe before I finished with you."

"Bribe away," Anna said with a faint shake of her head. "You know how much I love your gingerbread, but that won't get you off the hook. You have to tell me everything."

Elspeth brought a dessert plate and a small platter of gingerbread to the table. The gingerbread glistened with dried apricots and dark currants, and Anna cut a piece with her fork and closed her eyes as it melted on her tongue. "I've missed this."

"You wouldn't have needed to miss it if your mother believed in calories. Or joy, or anything to do with where she came from, when it comes to that. Just because she chooses to ignore facts doesn't make them go away."

That was harsher than Anna'd ever heard Elspeth speak about her sister, and she looked up in surprise. As far back as Anna remembered, it was always Elspeth who made the effort to come to Ohio, never Ailsa going back to Scotland. None of the rest of them had been allowed to visit Elspeth, either. Summers had always been crammed with pageants and camps and extra ballet lessons, or trips to visit their father's side of the family in Chicago.

Anna thought back to how upset her mother had been on the phone and the way she'd talked about the festival. "Does the Sighting have anything to do with the reason she won't come back here?"

"She won't come back because she's pig-headed and too selfish to see what's right in front of her nose." Elspeth brought the teapot over and refilled first Anna's cup then her own before sinking into a chair at Anna's elbow. "Not that she's alone in that. People don't always like what the Sighting shows them. That's part of the reason we've always kept the tradition close, just us here in the glen. I know you think my stories are nothing but flimflam, and more of them are than not, but the Sighting is as real as the fact that every glen in the Highlands is filled with braes and lochs and heather, not to mention inns and caravan parks. It's the one thing we have going for us besides Rob Roy

MacGregor's grave, and if you ask me, it's high time we use it to help the folks around here do more than scrape out a living. That's why I need you to work out a solution with Connal."

"Me?" The idea of getting Connal MacGregor to work with her on anything struck Anna as less than likely. "I'm an outsider here. Why should he listen to me? I don't even understand the problem."

"The problem is, half the village will side with him no matter the question, and the other half will side against him. The fact that you don't have a history in the glen works in your favor. We'd make no headway at all, left to ourselves, and there's only a month before Beltane as it is. Look, Connal's afraid, that's the long and the short of it. He's afraid the festival will bring attention to him and Moira and end up hurting her the way it hurt his wife."

Anna stopped in the act of reaching for another square of gingerbread. "His wife?"

Elspeth turned away. "Isobel Teague."

"So then he *is* Gregor Mark?" Anna asked softly, as if just saying the words aloud was taboo somehow. In her mind's eye, she saw Connal MacGregor again: the deep blue eyes, the high cheekbones, the walk that had captivated her as he'd hurried back to where his daughter waited. How rude he'd been when Anna had recognized him, and the pale, odd face she'd seen looking back at her from the car.

There had been public hysteria after Isobel Teague had crashed her car while she was eight months pregnant. Eight months pregnant and too drunk to avoid driving head-on into a truck. The baby had been born before Isobel died of her injuries, but there'd been something wrong that had sent the tabloids into a frenzy of speculation about everything: what was wrong with the child, Isobel's drinking and mental health, her high-profile marriage to her equally high-profile husband. The tabloids had accused Gregor Mark of everything from abuse to cruelty to engineering Isobel's death.

"So is this where he's been all this time?" Anna asked. "How on earth has he kept that secret?"

Elspeth set her teacup down after taking a long, slow sip. "It's been no secret to any of us, but he's a MacGregor from the glen. The MacGregors and MacLarens may have been squabbling here since the massacre of 1558, but there isn't one of us—MacGregor or MacLaren or anything in between—who doesn't love that little girl of Connal's. We'd all go a long way to make sure the tabloids don't make Moira's life miserable, poor mite, but we do need the tourism and the Village Hall rebuilt, and that's the truth. That's why we need your help making Connal see sense. It's what you did at your law firm sometimes, wasn't it? Broker settlements when there didn't seem to be solutions?"

Anna had worked on plenty of land use cases, blocking people wanting to drill for oil in national parks, blocking a pipeline that threatened to degrade the environment. On the flip side, she'd argued cases for public use of private conservation areas. This was Scotland, and she didn't know the first thing about the laws, but Elspeth was right. The basics weren't too far out of her comfort zone. How hard could it be?

SHIFTING BOUNDARIES

The love of books, the golden key, that opens the enchanted door . . .

ANDREW LANG, "BALLADE OF THE BOOKWORM"

AFTER WANDERING THROUGH THE MUSEUM and touring the rest of the house, Anna spent the day in the kitchen working through the manila file of press releases, emails, and festival preparations that Elspeth had given her. She'd forgotten, she realized halfway through the task, how much she loved doing this. Breaking one huge task into smaller pieces, making to-do lists, schedules, charts, and spreadsheets on her laptop.

Organizing a big event was like conducting a piece of music or creating a piece of art from thousands of tiny brushstrokes. And the press release Elspeth had put together was perfectly phrased to bring in tourists by the busload. Too bad it hadn't gone out sooner. It hit all the right notes: a range of events that included Highland

Games and a bagpipe competition, a craft fair with vendor stalls, the crowning of the May Queen and Winter King chosen by the village, the decorating of the May Bush that would be carried around the glen before it was burned in the traditional fire on Beltane Eve.

There was even a community production of Shakespeare's *A Midsummer Night's Dream* to tap into the fairy stories created by the sober Presbyterian minister, Robert Kirk, who had preached at the old stone Balwhither church in the seventeenth century.

Included also was the translation of the original Gaelic poem about the Sighting:

On the bright day
in the morning dew
to the pure of heart
the Lake of Destiny
will reveal the true love who
will warm the winter of your life
and the Lake of Enchantment
will turn sight to truth.

The morning's faint-hearted sun had given way to a driving rain, and sitting in the warm kitchen with delicious scents bubbling from the stove reminded Anna of all the Christmas holidays she'd spent in the kitchen in Ohio helping Elspeth cook. This time, Elspeth refused her help rolling out dough for home-baked bread, stirring up a rich cream soup, and peeling the apples for chicken Bonnie Prince Charlie with Drambuie sauce and the apple butterscotch pie that Elspeth claimed was Moira's favorite.

"She's got a sweet tooth on her, that child," Elspeth said as she put the finishing touches on the salmon for the fish course and dusted stray oats off her hands. "You've never seen the like, and she's a little slip of a thing. Looks identical to her mother, at least on the half of her face that isn't damaged. That same haunting fragility of Isobel's."

Anna couldn't resist pulling up an Internet search for Isobel Teague and the accident that had claimed her life. Not that she needed a reminder of how beautiful Isobel Teague had been. The year Isobel had left television and made her first big blockbuster film, Katharine had worn her hair like Isobel's and imitated her makeup and elegant, ethereal style. Seeing *The Royals of London* had helped spark Katharine's interest in community theater and set her on a collision course with Henry.

For all the thousands of images the Internet had of Isobel, though, there was nothing about her daughter. Nothing apart from the initial speculation around her birth.

"What did you mean about Moira's face being damaged? Is there something physically wrong?" Anna finally asked as Elspeth browned the flour-dusted chicken in a pan.

"The doctors call it facial palsy. The nerves in half of her face were injured, either at birth or in the accident. She's had three surgeries already, so it's much better than it was, but I don't think it will ever completely match the other side. Och, heavens, look at the time! They'll be here any minute, and I have grease on my blouse and slippers on my feet! Would you be a love and soften the apples in butter for me and keep an eye on that chicken, Anna? Mind it doesn't burn."

Dropping the wooden spoon into Anna's hand, Elspeth hurried out, her limp light but more pronounced than it had been earlier, as if she'd already been on her feet too long. Anna glanced down at her own casual jeans and sweater and realized she hadn't put on so much as a smudge of lipstick or eyeliner that morning. And her hair. Stooping to look at herself in the glass door of the oven, she groaned. She looked about twelve years old, eyes huge and tired in her narrow face, her hair curling every which way since she hadn't made any attempt to tame it with a blow-dryer or flatiron.

On the other hand, the fact that Connal MacGregor was Gregor Mark was oddly freeing. He'd already seen her looking her worst, and he'd been married to Isobel Teague. Nothing Anna did to herself was going to impress him, not when women had no doubt been dressing up for him since the instant he'd hit puberty. Anna had already had her trust crushed to sand by one man like that—Henry—and she was done playing those sorts of games.

Shifting her attention back to the stove, she pushed all thoughts of Connal MacGregor from her mind. A moment later, she had lapsed into autopilot, humming the same tune Elspeth had been humming all day and losing herself in the delight of preparing food for someone else, of working to make someone happy. The sweet, tangy scent of caramelizing apples mingled with the skin-crisping scent of frying chicken, and the light tang of roasted onion potatoes drifted in the air. She filled a glass with wine and took a long, deep draught. A bracing draught. But it had been a good idea of Elspeth's to invite Connal and Moira to dinner. How unreasonable could Connal MacGregor be with his daughter in tow?

At the very least, he would have to remain polite.

Despite her efforts to reassure herself, Anna's optimism faded when she opened the door a few minutes later. Connal loomed on the stoop, his hands protective on his daughter's shoulders and his eyes wary and cold on Anna.

His smile must have been pure acting. Even so, it packed an unexpected punch. "You got here all right last night, then," he said. "No worse for the accident, I take it?"

"Um, no. Thank you." Anna smiled right back at him, and then her expression grew genuine as she turned to the child who stood looking up at her, wide-eyed and solemn.

Elspeth had been right: Moira was beautiful. Slight for her age, with waist-length blond hair that had the perfect amount of wave, bright eyes in her father's unusual, stormy shade of blue, a high, straight nose, and cheekbones that, even covered in the last fullness of childhood, showed the promise of being high and sculpted. She resembled, as Elspeth had said, her very beautiful mother, except that the left eye didn't quite close when she blinked, and the slight droop to that side of her face was just pronounced enough to trick Anna's mind into being unsure what she was seeing when she looked at her.

"Hi, Moira." Anna stepped aside to invite them in, careful not to stare as she offered a hand for Moira to shake. "I've been eager to meet you ever since last night. I wanted to apologize for scaring you with my horrible driving."

Moira shook her hand and smiled but didn't say anything. She scooted past Anna into the foyer at the same moment that Elspeth arrived at the top of the stairs.

"Here you both are," Elspeth said, holding the handrail with one hand and maneuvering the walker onto the stair below her as she stepped down. "I'll be with you as soon as this leg of mine will get me there. Anna, would you mind getting their coats in the meantime?"

Anna bent close to Moira's ear as Moira shrugged out of a purple jacket that was still cool to the touch from the soon-to-be-April chill. "I hear I have you to thank for tonight's dessert," she whispered. "Elspeth told me apple butterscotch pie is a particular favorite of yours."

Moira nodded, but again she didn't speak.

"Well, I can't wait to try it. I've never met one of Elspeth's desserts that I didn't want to dive into face-first." Anna turned to Connal who had already removed his own coat and stood holding it. Beneath the glittering chandelier, the light all seemed to dance around him, and unfortunately, he hadn't gotten any less gorgeous overnight. Really, a photo of him and Brando together would have been all the advertising the glen ever needed to bring tourists in by droves.

The thought made Anna pause. Because, of course, Connal himself would be a draw, wouldn't he? Moira's disfigurement would have been difficult for any child, but for the daughter of Isobel Teague and Gregor Mark, the standard would be different.

"Is something wrong?" Connal asked.

Anna exhumed her smile again. "Nothing at all. Shall I take your coat as well?"

A hint of genuine laughter lit his eyes. "Forcing yourself to be polite, are you? Yes, by all means, take my coat."

Anna blinked like an owl at that hint of humor. That faint smile. Because that smile was clearly Gregor Mark. Not quite at full wattage, but it didn't lose a thing translated off the screen.

No. She didn't need to be thinking thoughts like that. Practically snatching the coat out of his hands, Anna hurried to the front sitting room to throw it with Moira's across a wingback chair upholstered in faded blue brocade.

By the time she returned to the foyer, Elspeth was already downstairs and leading Moira and Connal straight through to the dining room where Anna had set the gatelegged Jacobean table earlier. The contrast of the dark wood in the room made Moira look even more delicate and fey.

Anna went out to the kitchen to get the soup, and when she came back, Connal had seated himself under the portrait of some long-dead kilted Murray ancestor opposite the only empty place setting. Slipping into her chair, Anna avoided looking at him by setting herself the task of coaxing Moira into conversation.

"So what's it like growing up in a fairytale castle in a fairytale valley, Moira? I hope you at least managed to snatch up that tower for your bedroom."

"She would have if it hadn't meant moving three stories of overflowing bookshelves. The whole tower is a library," Connal said, "which we both share, except that Moira is flooding it with so many of her own books that she seems determined to boot me out."

"A literal tower of books?" Anna smiled at Moira. "That sounds like my idea of heaven. Do you know, I used to adore Andrew Lang's fairy books when I was about your age? I still do, but I haven't read any of the fairy stories from Reverend Kirk. Have you?" She cupped her hand over her mouth and leaned close to Moira, saying in a lowered voice, "I don't suppose there are any actual fairies here in the glen, are there? Because I've spent my whole life trying to see one in America, and I haven't had any luck at all."

"Moira knows nearly every bit of fairy lore ever told. Don't you, duck?" Connal gave Moira an encouraging smile. "She helps Elspeth make up the stories about Reverend Kirk's fairies for the museum."

Moira gave a quick nod and bent to concentrate on spooning her soup into her mouth.

"The stories with the clever pencil drawings?" Anna asked, remembering the placards she'd seen in the museum earlier with sketches of sprites and pixies and fairies and short fanciful descriptions about the thimbles, cups, and walking sticks that supposedly had once belonged to the

Reverend Kirk. "Are those made-up stories? Because sometimes with what Aunt Elspeth says it's hard to know what might be true."

Moira studied her longer this time, one small brow puckering toward the other while the other remained fixed in place. She gave another quick, jerking nod.

"What about other books?" Anna prompted. "I love Harry Potter, but I expect you're probably past all that, aren't you?"

Spoon pausing in midair, Moira gaped at her. "I love Harry," she said, her words a little soft around the edges because her mouth didn't quite open the same way on the left as on the right. "I've read the first book seven times."

"Seven? Goodness." Anna hid a smile. "And here I thought that with an entire library full of books to choose from . . . "

"It wouldn't matter if I had all the books in the world, I'd still love Harry."

"Me, too, but can I tell you a secret? I've always loved Hermione better."

"She *is* better!" Moira's eyes shone. "Not just because she's a girl. She's smarter, and works harder, and she's nicer."

"All true. And she punches Malfoy in the face," Anna said, glancing across at Connal.

"Not that we encourage punching people in the face," Connal said sternly, though his eyes were filled with laughter.

Anna couldn't resist quirking a brow at him. "Unless they bully other people and there are no policemen around—in which case, all bets are off."

Connal's smile turned rueful—and no less dangerous to Anna's equilibrium. "I suppose I deserve that. I should have apologized the moment you met us at the door, but I was saving it for later."

"Why do you need to apologize, Daddy?" Moira tipped her head to look at him.

"Because I was very rude to Anna last night when she had her accident."

Anna found it hard to stay angry with him, no matter how much she wanted to. Although why she wanted to didn't bear examining. Except that it was easier to resist a Connal MacGregor who wasn't both kind and gorgeous.

She needed to resist him.

In fact, she was meant to charm him. Not the other way around.

She needed to remember how rude he'd been, and that he didn't want to have the festival on his property. Also, there was something about the way he was hiding here in the glen that bothered Anna, the way he kept Moira hidden away.

Far from the damaged child Anna had pictured given what Elspeth had said about how Connal and the entire glen protected her, Moira was more like Rapunzel in her tower, locked away from strangers. The poor girl might seem close to happy and normal now, or as close as she could be to normal when the palsy made it a little hard to speak, but how long would she stay that way if no one gave her the confidence to face the world?

Connal MacGregor, however charming he might be when he wanted to put in the effort, was misguided, Anna decided. She didn't realize she was staring at him until Elspeth kicked her beneath the table and bugged her eyes out.

Right. She was supposed to be smiling. Charming.

For the sake of the festival. For Elspeth's sake.

First rule of negotiation. Don't let your opponent get inside your head.

A Thousand Stars

*he . . . remembers and cherishes the memory of his forebears,
good or bad; and there burns alive in him a sense of identity with the dead
even to the twentieth generation.*

ROBERT LOUIS STEVENSON

T HINKING OF CONNAL MACGREGOR as an opponent
grew harder as the night wore on. He seemed
determined to be fun and gracious, and the conversation
circled around light topics and stories about people and
places in the glen.

During the fish course, Anna tried to steer the subject
toward the festival. Connal glanced at Moira and back again
with a faint pucker between his brows and a pleading look.
Then he went back to cutting his salmon without having
answered.

With a clink against the porcelain, Elspeth set down
her fork. "Moira, I have a new box of artifacts that arrived

for the museum. Do you think you could help me sort and label them after dinner?"

Moira's face lit up. "Can I write stories for them? And JoAnne can draw the pictures? Maybe that will make her less mad."

"Of course you can, mite. The box is sitting right beside the computer. We'll go have a look after dessert, shall we?" Elspeth said.

Watching Moira, Anna couldn't help wondering if this was how she'd sounded at the age of ten. There'd been a time at that age when she'd had a romantic streak an ocean wide. She'd hung on every legend Elspeth had ever told her, imagining the landscape the way Elspeth described it. Imagining that knights always rescued maidens and that honor and valor were the most important things a man possessed.

She'd fallen in love with this glen and Scotland through Elspeth's stories, and she still couldn't quite believe that she was here at last. For a moment, watching Connal and Moira, she felt a sense of unreality, everything blurring around the edges. The feeling grew more pronounced as she brought in the main course and heard the two of them tell Elspeth about having spotted a piper playing his bagpipes beside the loch.

"It was while we were walking over here," Moira said in her slightly softened but careful pronunciation. "One of the MacLarens, we could tell by his kilt. Only he wasn't very good."

"But then they're never going to be as good as the MacGregor pipers, are they, duck?" Connal winked at his daughter with his eyes dancing.

Moira shook her head, giving him back a lopsided smile.

The mental image of the piper at the edge of the loch sent goosebumps along Anna's arms. At least, she hoped it was the piper and not Connal's rich, low laugh or that smile of his that did odd things to her stomach. He had a trick, too, of watching whoever he was talking to like they were the only person in the entire room. She found it hard to look away.

"Whoever your piper was," Elspeth said, "he's in for a long month, poor laddie, if his wife's kicked him out already."

Anna passed Moira the platter of Elspeth's delicious, home-baked bread. "Why would his wife kick him out?"

"MacGregor pipers have been famous for centuries—a MacGregor was Prince Charlie's own piper at the Battle of Culloden. But the MacLarens like to take away our victories wherever they can. They practice day and night when there's a competition coming up," Connal said, taking the platter as Anna offered it to him in turn.

"So, of course, the MacGregor pipers practice harder," Elspeth added.

Connal flashed a grin while he slathered a slice of bread in creamy butter. "And MacLaren and MacGregor alike, their wives get tired of the noise and the children not being able to sleep, so they boot them outside."

"Aye, but then it's a nuisance for the rest of us," Elspeth said, nodding.

"I like hearing them practice outside," Moira said. "It's almost the only chance I get because Daddy won't let me go to the Highland Games at Lochearnhead."

"You might like hearing them, but half the cows in the glen gave sour milk last time there was a competition." Elspeth exchanged a glance with Connal.

He avoided looking at Moira and turned to Anna instead with a slightly wistful grin. "I imagine the atmosphere at home would be even more sour for the poor lads than it is outside."

That grin had a kick like a mule, and Anna gave herself a mental shake. She focused her attention on cutting her chicken and spearing a bit of softened apple coated in the Drambuie-flavored cream sauce to go with it. It was a relief to escape back out to the kitchen when she went to get dessert and tea. Then two slices of pie later, the sweetness of the creamy butterscotch drizzled apples, plum jam, and frothy meringue along with the soft drone of comfortable conversation punctuated by Connal's deep laughter had begun to make her acutely uncomfortable. She jumped up again to clear the table.

Elspeth stood, too, holding out her hand to Moira. "Ready to go look at that box of new things? Maybe we can finish one or two stories, and you can take them back to JoAnne with you."

Moira scraped her chair back and skipped away from the table, her limbs moving with uncanny grace and her hair flying like a banner behind her until she spun on the threshold to wait for Elspeth. The two disappeared down the hall together, leaving Anna and Connal all alone.

They stood looking at each other across the table as if neither knew what to say.

Anna busied herself gathering up the plates, cups, and saucers. "I assumed JoAnne was a local artist," she said, thinking not only of the fairies and pixies on the museum placards but also the real historical figures the drawings brought to life, people who had—according to Elspeth's wild imagination—had something to do with various artifacts. "Does she live with you?"

Connal nodded. "JoAnne Campbell—she's Moira's nanny. That's why she's furious about the festival. For Moira's sake."

"I thought she was a professional. She's very talented."

"Aye, she should be doing more to make a name for herself, but I'm hoping she'll stay with us a few more years. I'm selfish." Connal twisted his lips into a rueful smile. "Moira adores her, and I hate the thought of changing their relationship until Moira herself is ready for it to change."

Anna stacked Moira's cup and saucer with her own. She reached for Elspeth's cup, but Connal beat her to it. She hadn't even heard him moving.

"I'll take half of this in for you, shall I?" He stacked his cup with Elspeth's and slanted a smile at Anna. "And I'm sorry for waving you off talking about the festival earlier. I didn't want to discuss it in front of Moira, but now that Elspeth has done her best to sweeten me up with that dinner and cleared Moira off, she's left you to do the heavy lifting of talking sense into me. Is that about the size of it?"

Charm again. Anna suppressed a sigh.

"Did the sweetening work?" she asked.

"My concerns haven't gone away, let's put it that way. It may seem like I'm unreasonable, but now that you've met Moira, I hope you can at least empathize with what I'm trying to do."

"Of course." Responding to the wave of his arm, Anna tucked the cups beneath her chin and, grabbing the plate of leftover pie, preceded him through the doorway. But there must have been something in her expression that she hadn't intended for him to see.

He hurried to catch up. "Look, I am sorry we got off on the wrong foot yesterday. I swear to you, I'm not generally prone to bellowing at women the first time I meet them."

The cups rattled against the saucers, and Anna readjusted her chin to steady them. "We were both shaken by the accident."

"That wasn't the—never mind." Connal looked past her as if seeing something else. "For whatever it's worth, I *am* sorry, and I didn't mean to lie to you. I haven't been Gregor Mark in a decade, and I have no desire to be. I was angry at letting myself be recognized, and I didn't realize who you were at first."

"You knew to call Elspeth."

"I was thinking straighter by the time I reached the car, and I remembered she was expecting you to arrive last night." Connal trailed Anna into the kitchen. "Please try to understand. It might seem odd to you, but the glen has been a refuge for us. For Moira. I don't want that to end.

Can't you imagine what the attention would do to her? We're already careful because of the hikers who use the right of way across the upper part of my land outside the wall. I don't want to have to keep her locked indoors with hundreds of people on our doorstep. How would I tell her she couldn't participate in the fun? She's as much a part of the glen as anyone—I don't want her thinking otherwise. She looks forward to the procession and the bonfire and the Sighting every year."

His voice had gone tight, and Anna's heart squeezed at the thought of seeing hurt or disappointment in Moira's eyes. What was Connal supposed to say that wouldn't make Moira feel self-conscious or rejected—or signal to her that people weren't to be trusted?

"No one would know who she is," she said.

"Not this year, maybe, but she looks more and more like Isobel as she gets older. Like it or not, we're setting a precedent. If this first Festival is successful, what happens two years from now when Moira's the same age as Isobel was in *Coronation Square*?"

"You could take her away somewhere. Visit a friend for a week."

"I've never taken Moira with me when I do that. Except for her surgeries, she's never left the glen, and she wouldn't want to leave with the festival going on. The Sighting is the biggest excitement we have here the entire year."

It was a horrible, no-win situation for Connal, and Anna felt awful for him. She set the pie plate on the counter beside the sink and lowered the stack of cups, saucers, and dessert plates beside it. "I sympathize," she said, "believe me, I do, but I have to play devil's advocate. Elspeth says some of the businesses here are desperate for money from tourism. I researched some of the other Beltane festivals, and if we do this right, we could bring in a thousand people, not to mention press coverage that would help advertise the glen all year long. You're asking the village to sacrifice a lot."

"Don't you think I'm aware of that?" Connal stopped beside Anna and put down his own stack of plates and cups. His arm brushed hers and gave her a jolt of static electricity. "I'm not an idiot. I realize full well that half the farmhouses in the Highlands have been turned into B&Bs, and any pile of stones that has, or ever had, any pretension of being called 'stately' has been turned into a hotel. There's no shortage of competition for tourism, and I'd be blind not to see there are people here in the glen who are having a hard time scraping by. I try to help wherever I can. I've offered to pay to rebuild the Village Hall myself if it will keep us from having to turn the glen into a circus. That pig-headed Brando and his MacLaren mates turned me down."

"It would be generous for you to pay for the reconstruction," Anna said, bristling at the insult to Brando, "but it wouldn't increase tourism. Which is what they need."

"I know that, too. I'm just hoping you can see my position enough to be willing to help me find a solution Moira and I can live with." Connal's voice had gone softer, gentler, but his jaw was no less determined.

Anna felt for him and Moira. She did. Which didn't help anything.

"I'm sorry, but I don't understand what you and Elspeth expect from me. Isn't this something you and the village would be better off working out between yourselves?"

"Scots will discuss an issue to death. Highlanders will argue any point, small and large. Here in the glen, that argument will go on a hundred years without reaching a conclusion. But they're more likely to listen to you since you're an outsider. They know you've planned big events before, and you don't have a history here aside from being Elspeth's niece. They'll assume you're going to be on her side in any dispute between her and myself, and since you came here to organize the festival, you have no reason to try to help me. But I hope you will. I do have a compromise to propose. If the village will agree to turn the procession back at the hotel instead of cutting through Inverlochlarig to go all the way around the glen, and if they'll have the bonfire back at the village instead of on my property, I'll open the gate and let the public in for the Sighting on Beltane morning. Just help me convince Brando and the others. Otherwise, Brando will object to anything I suggest, and half the village will follow where he leads."

Connal stood at Anna's elbow, close enough that she had to step back to look up at him. But meeting his eyes . . . The kitchen walls shrank in around her.

Clearing her throat, she turned to run the water for the dishes, which involved rummaging under the sink until she found the drain stopper. The dishwashing liquid was dark green and came in a bottle that, appropriately enough for Balwhither, had the name FAIRY SOAP printed on the label. Connal took the bottle from her and squeezed a bit of the liquid into the sink as he submerged the plates. The soap sent bubbles drifting around his head, making him look as though he was surrounded by a thousand winking stars.

As if the universe hadn't already provided enough reasons for women to look at Connal MacGregor and pay attention.

SHAMED

As long as the Fates permit, live cheerfully.

SIR WALTER SCOTT, *ROB ROY*

OVERLOOKED BY A SURLY red Highland bull watching from beneath a shaggy forelock in a nearby pasture, Anna bumped Elspeth's old Volvo station wagon along the single-track road toward the village. Loch Fàil, the long, narrow loch, sparkled on her right, and puffs of white clouds drifted above the braes that ringed the valley.

"Mind the sheep ahead," Elspeth said as they passed the bright turquoise Braeside Hotel on the hill and approached the bend by the rowan tree. "Davy Grigg never can seem to keep them contained. In part because they're smarter than he is, and in part because he takes the entire day delivering the mail and gabbing. Most of all because he's got paralysis of the trousers and can't abide a lick of farm work."

Anna sat there shaking, and she wasn't the one on the side of the Volvo that had hit the other car. "I'm sorry. Yes, I'm fine. I'm an idiot, but I'm fine. You? Are you hurt?"

"I didn't mean you were the idiot. It's Shame—Seumas—the blasted dog that belongs to Duncan Macara." Elspeth gestured at the retriever who now sat in the center of the road with his head cocked, staring at the car as if waiting to see if it would do something else as interesting as the crash. "I swear, Davy's sheep are smarter. And easier to keep corralled."

Someone tapped on Anna's window. Intent on the dog, she jumped in her seat and found Brando standing at her window. Still wearing his kilt and tactical boots, he had no jacket this time, only a pale blue T-shirt stretched taut across his arms, chest, and shoulders. Beyond him, people spilled out the door of the inn, many of them familiar to Anna already from her encounter with the sheep, including Davy Grigg and the innkeepers, Flora Macara and her husband Duncan, who owned the dog.

With a sigh, Anna rolled the window down. "I don't suppose you'd believe," she said to Brando, "that I'd never had an accident in my entire life before I got here?"

His green eyes laughed at her. "I'll be happy to pretend I believe you." He leaned down to address Elspeth across in the passenger seat. "You want me to take the car into town or let Brice have it? Either way, he's likely got a car you can borrow in the meanwhile."

"No car," Anna said. "From now on, I'm walking everywhere. Or I'll take a cab—if you have cabs here."

"For you? I'm always good for a lift." Brando grinned again, waggling his eyebrows at her.

Elspeth groaned and leaned her elbow on the Volvo's center console to shake her head at him. "Whose Toyota is that? Tell me it's not Rhona's new one. What in the world's the bloody woman doing driving here when she lives a hundred yards up the road?"

"Trying to make sure everyone sees what she's bought," Brando said.

"And now she'll be demanding a new one at the expense of my insurance."

"*My* insurance," said Anna.

"Not on your life—it ought to be Duncan's insurance if it's anyone's, but we'll worry about all that later." Elspeth let out a hiss of breath. "Aye, take the car to town tomorrow, please, Brando. If you can spare the time. Park it for now so we don't miss the meeting."

"The meeting's moved out here, it seems to me." He waved a hand to indicate the gathering crowd and opened Anna's door, stepping aside to let her out.

Red-faced, Anna considered insisting that she was perfectly competent to park on her own, but who was she kidding? She'd already proven her *in*competence the past few days. Really, it was time to crawl back into bed for a week and pull the covers over her head.

She climbed out of the car and had to stand watching, furious with herself, while Brando slid into the driver's seat without so much as ruffling his kilt. He backed the car away from the Toyota with another ear-jarring screech of metal. A well-preserved woman with an hourglass figure and streaked blond hair emerged from the pub. Shrieking at the sight of the car, she rushed forward on precarious stiletto heels, the flowing fabric of her red dress wrapping around her legs in the wind. Two surly and identical teenage girls followed in her wake.

"What did you do to my car?" she demanded.

"Only a little scrape, Rhona," Elspeth called out the window as Brando set the car in drive again and lurched it forward. "Terribly sorry, but I'll make it right—"

"You'd better." The woman glared as Brando drove away, then she turned to gape at the damage to her car, clutching her small black cashmere cardigan around herself more tightly in the cold. Her expression hardened, and she set off after the Volvo with a determined stride and her daughters trailing behind her.

Anna stood at the side of the road, uncertain what to do. Cheeks burning, she didn't want to turn to face the assembled crowd.

Flora Macara came over and squeezed her shoulder with a beaming smile of reassurance. "Don't you worry about Rhona. Elspeth and Brando will sort her out."

"I should at least go and admit that it was my fault," Anna said.

"Don't you feel one whit bad about any of this. There isn't a soul in this glen that Seumas hasn't gotten into trouble at one time or another." Flora's gaze shifted to where her husband had seized hold of Shame by the collar and was wrestling the retriever back inside the inn from whence, presumably, he'd escaped.

Tall and big-boned, with no makeup and a shapeless dress that had seen too many washings, Flora might have been considered plain except for the fact that her smile was clearly a force of nature. She was the type of woman, Anna suspected, who could wield kindness like a weapon.

"I keep threatening Duncan I'll give him away one of these days," Flora continued. "The dog, I mean, not my husband. Though no one'd take either one of them off my hands, and that's a fact. But come on inside. I'll get you a drink. You're shivering."

Anna didn't dispute the need. She waded through the villagers in Flora's wake, murmuring an embarrassed "hello" to the people she recognized—the people who had managed to witness the aftermaths of both her accidents—and nodding and smiling at the unfamiliar faces who pressed in to introduce themselves. They were universally amused, but not unsympathetic.

A sandy-haired barrel of a man with a wind-burned face opened the door to the inn for them as Flora and Anna approached. Inside, the lobby was off on the right, while to the left a wide doorway revealed the half-timbered pub fitted with booths and tables, many of them already occupied. Flora slipped behind the bar. "What can I get you, Anna?"

"My dignity back?" Anna suggested, prompting a laugh from the people who'd come in behind her.

"How about a Scottish coffee instead?" Flora asked. "It's like Irish, except with Scotch, and I throw in a dash of citrus liqueur."

"Sounds lovely, but it's barely noon. A bit early for me to start drinking."

"Nonsense. Never too early to start when you've been Shamed."

Shamed.

It was, Anna thought, the perfect way to describe the last week of her life. And after her two accidents, how was she supposed to stand up in front of all the people who were watching her with equal parts curiosity and amusement to explain the plans she and Elspeth had spent half the night working out?

Turning to look for Elspeth, she found Connal MacGregor instead, entering the pub to the accompaniment of bells and ducking his head to keep from banging it on the low lintel above the door. He was backlit with a faint shimmer around the baseball-style cap he'd pulled low over his forehead, and he was already staring back at her as he started across the room. As if she wasn't already mortified enough, Anna felt her cheeks heating. She raised her hand in a lukewarm greeting.

Eyes still locked on hers, Connal made his way through the crowd, stopping here and there to exchange a few words with people along the way. Anna couldn't help watching him, and not just because the light V-neck sweater he wore made it clear he hadn't let himself go one bit since giving up his acting career. He had the same compelling presence, too, the way he offered a smile each time someone stopped him, the way he leaned down to listen in the noisy room, the way he tipped his head in concentration when people spoke and clasped a shoulder or a forearm or a hand in greeting as if he was genuinely glad to see someone. He was *nice*.

He was trouble. No two ways about it.

Anna turned away, answering a couple of questions herself and trading a few jokes at her own expense with the villagers who had gathered around her. Despite not looking at him, though, she couldn't help being aware of Connal approaching, as if the air around her had charged itself up, molecules exciting, pushing her toward him.

He slipped in beside her at the bar. "I hear we're going to need to hire a chauffeur to keep you out of trouble. I'm not sure there's any other way to safeguard the livestock."

"Ha," Anna said. "I've already told Elspeth I'll be walking from here on out."

"I've just arranged to take you both home when the meeting's over, but you're all right? You didn't get hurt in the accident?"

Anna shook her head and accepted the glass mug of coffee Flora slid toward her, taking an overly-enthusiastic sip. The coffee was hotter and stronger than she'd expected, but also as sweet and smoky and creamy as Connal MacGregor's voice, with that deep, sexy quality to it.

No. She wasn't going to think about Connal MacGregor like that. She wasn't going to notice his sexiness. She'd work with him to find a compromise about the festival—for Moira's sake and for the sake of the village—which was what she'd agreed to do. Strictly in a professional capacity. Because he was trouble, and if she thought about him in any other way than professionally, she might as well hang a sign above her head: trouble welcome here.

That wasn't going to happen.

Connal was watching her, staring at her mouth. "You like it?"

She wiped a smidge of cream off her top lip and blinked at him in confusion before realizing he meant the coffee. "It's delicious." She whipped around to Flora. "This drink might be my new best friend," she babbled. "You may need to pry me away from here with a crowbar after the meeting."

"I can offer a tire wrench and a willing shoulder if you like," Connal said, smiling down at her again. That smile. "But I'm fresh out of crowbars."

She blinked at him like an idiot. "It was a joke."

He leaned closer. "I know that," he said, his breath fanning across her cheek. "So was mine."

This was flirting. He was flirting with her, wasn't he? Or was he?

Maybe, like Henry, he said things like this to every woman.

See? This was why it was treacherous to be around a man like Connal.

Anna couldn't come up with a single word to say. Mercifully, the bell jangled again above the door, and he glanced across the room. "Here's Elspeth," he said, sounding relieved. "I suppose we should go through and get the meeting started."

Anna blinked again and took another long, slow sip of spiked coffee that scalded her tongue, seared warmth down into her stomach, and left her disoriented. At least, it must have been the whiskey's fault. Another explanation would have involved admitting that it was Connal as much as the Scotch, and that was inconceivable. Men hadn't had this kind of an effect on her since high school. Since college.

Since Henry.

She'd grown up since Henry. Grown more rational since Henry. And she'd learned a thing or two about not taking actors at face value.

Actors lied. Their charm, their seeming sincerity and devoted attention, those were all an act. Underneath the pretense, they were always looking out for their own best interests, and the moment a better deal or opportunity came along, they would drop you like a bomb and turn their back on every promise they'd ever made.

NEGOTIATIONS

And there begins a lang digression about the lords o' the creation.

ROBERT BURNS, "THE TWA DOGS"

THE LARGEST OF THE INN'S several dining rooms was packed and growing loud as the villagers drifted in to start the meeting. Already, the booths along the perimeter overflowed with bodies, and people sat crammed at tables in the center. Brando and about twenty others had squeezed into the empty spaces along the paneled walls.

The wooden paneling and high ceilings amplified the many conversations and quiet arguments that had already broken out in clusters. Facing the room, Anna sat in her seat between Elspeth and Connal, trying to imagine what it would have been like to grow up in a place where everyone was comfortable enough with each other to argue like this. In her experience, people who disagreed hid behind icy smiles—or lectured and bludgeoned each other with words until one gave in and walked away.

She slid a sideways glance at Connal. In the brighter light of the dining room, he looked unfairly better than he had in the bar, the stormwater blue of his eyes and that sure jaw beneath the beard and those lips that could stretch into the most unexpected and warmest smiles . . . He glanced over as if he felt her watching and arched a brow at her. She turned and stared anywhere except at him, until Elspeth leaned over and whispered, "I think about everyone's here. Do you want to start us off? Introduce yourself."

"Go ahead." Connal nodded.

Anna dug in her purse for the clipboard and pen she had brought with her, then stood to get everyone's attention. She might as well have been invisible for all the effect that had.

"Not like that," Elspeth said. "No one stands on ceremony here. You want their attention, you have to be louder than they are." She took a last sip of the still-steaming—and deeply spiked—toddy that Flora had fixed for her before setting it on the floor. Rising to her feet, she shouted, "Quiet, you lot! Most of you have already met Anna, my niece. She's come to save us from ourselves, and she's fair magic at organizing things, so try not to make your usual objections while you listen to her. We wouldn't want to scare her off."

Duncan Macara, Flora's ruddy-cheeked bear of a husband, laughed at that from the table where he'd settled beside his wife. "She doesn't scare too easy, or Seumas and the sheep would have already sent her packing."

Elspeth leaned toward Anna and prodded her with an elbow. "Start talking quick now, or you'll never get a word in edgewise."

"Thank you all for trusting me to help you with this," Anna said, shocked at how nervous she suddenly felt, aware of Connal and the crowd both watching her, all of them wanting different things. As crowded as the room was, there were probably only seventy people present. But she was used to arguing in packed courtrooms and presenting at meetings full of Washington power brokers, lobbyists, and the political glitterati. Or at least, she had been, before she'd had her Mike's-getting-married meltdown.

Getting dumped, fired, and being on the way to broke hadn't—as it turned out—done wonders for her confidence. Especially when half the people in the crowded room had gone back to talking to each other instead of waiting to hear what she had to say.

She dragged her spine up straighter and pasted on the smile she'd learned to fake early in her childhood. Confidence was ninety percent appearance, her mother had always said, but if you didn't look a hundred percent in control, no one was going to trust you.

Briefly, Anna waved the clipboard like a flag. "I've brought along a signup sheet for the various committees we're going to need," she continued, "one for each of the main events listed in the press release Elspeth sent out the other day. If you're willing to help out, sign your name under the event you most want to work on, and if you're able to work on more than one, please put an asterisk beside your name. Elspeth and I will group everyone from there. Also, if you have any special skills, write those down. We'll use some of the money from the Village Hall Fund where we need to, but the more we can do on our own, the better. Painting signs, helping set up the craft booths, building sets for the play, anything at all. Also, speaking of the play, try-outs for that will begin here promptly at six o'clock tomorrow night."

Stepping to the nearest table, she handed the clipboard to Flora Macara to start passing around. Sitting at Flora's right, Duncan Macara leaned forward in his seat. "So the festival is going forward, then? Connal, you're all right with that?"

Connal stood and moved up alongside Anna. "Elspeth, Anna, and I have worked out a compromise that— hopefully—will work for everyone."

Without any visible shift, he'd suddenly turned into Gregor Mark as he spoke. He hadn't so much as raised his voice, but he commanded the room, drew the audience in with a force as clear and palpable as if he'd stepped into one of his most famous roles.

"I've agreed to have the Sighting go ahead as part of the festival," he said, "as long as we can move the bonfire to the village somewhere. Also, I'd like the procession to turn back at the hotel instead of going all the way around the loch so I don't have to unlock my gate until Beltane morning. That will keep the focus of the activities centered on the village and the craft booths anyway, which is where you want them."

Brando peeled himself away from the wall where he'd been leaning. "Are you giving us a choice, or are you saying outright you won't allow the bonfire on your property?"

"I'd like it to be your choice." Connal shifted his stance, about as close to uncomfortable as Anna could imagine him. "That's the point of a compromise, and if it will help, I'm still willing to pay for the Village Hall to be rebuilt."

"That seems very generous to me," Anna said, nodding at Brando and practically willing him to agree.

He shook his head. "Aye, it's generous, but we'll have changed tradition—everything the festival was built around." His eyes swept the room, appealing for support. "We all love Moira, but it's not right to throw away a thousand years of what's always been done for her sake."

"If you're worried about not having as many people to stay at the hotel, I'll—"

"I don't need your help with the hotel," Brando snapped at Connal, "and there are other businesses besides mine who aren't situated right here in the village and may miss out if the procession doesn't go all the way around the glen. But that's not my only point. What if the Sighting doesn't work if we change the traditional celebration?"

"Traditions change organically over the centuries. We can't even be sure the bonfire was always held on the peninsula. It would make more sense for it to have been on Tom-nan-aigeal originally," Connal said in a level tone.

Anna shifted close to Elspeth. "What's Tom-nan-aigeal?"

"The knoll behind the present church," Elspeth said. "Hearth fires in the glen have been re-kindled there since Druid times, and Duncan usually lights the torch there and carries it to the bonfire site on Connal's peninsula where the Sighting takes place."

Arguments had broken out around the room, everyone talking to be heard above their neighbors, and no one listening to anyone but themselves.

"Seems reasonable to me," someone shouted.

"Aye, it would—seeing as you're a MacGregor," someone else shouted back. "But Brando said it: What's the point of having traditions if we throw them away so easy?"

"I say it's worth trying if himself will pay to rebuild the Village Hall," a woman in the back responded. "Otherwise, we could do all this work and still not raise the money we need."

"What if moving the bonfire means the Sighting doesnae work?" yelled another, older, voice from off to the left somewhere. "Then people come this year, see nothing, and we'll get no one coming back next year."

"No one will come expecting to see anything anyway. No more than they would going to see a fortune teller at the circus," Rhona Grewer yelled from near the front.

"Just because you didn't see anything doesn't mean the rest of us don't want to," a young woman in the middle shouted.

"Want all you like, Saundra." Rhona turned to glare at her. "Wanting won't make it happen."

Saundra crossed her arms. "We'll see. Maybe my heart is purer than yours."

"Och, Rhona's heart ain't been pure since she were a wee barra no higher than my knee," the older man on the left retorted.

The room erupted in laughter. Even Rhona gave a brittle laugh. Then an instant later, the arguments had started up again, growing in volume as even more villagers chimed in.

Connal sat back down and watched Anna, his intent expression a reminder that he was counting on her to help craft a solution. She had no idea what to say. Neither he nor Elspeth had mentioned the village truly believing the Sighting was real—or fearing that it might stop working if they moved the bonfire. How was she supposed to know how to counter arguments she didn't understand?

"They can't mean to turn Connal down, can they?" she asked close to Elspeth's ear. "What do you think, Aunt Elspeth?"

"I think arguing's a local sport, and everyone's determined to have their say. Nothing for it except to nudge them along and wait."

They'd be waiting all night, at this rate. Anna couldn't negotiate a compromise if she didn't even know who she was compromising with or how many were on what side. She could at least find out that much.

Climbing onto the seat of her chair, she attempted an awkward whistle. "How about if we take a vote? Maybe it'll turn out we don't have anything to argue over."

There was a mutter at reduced volume and a rustle of fabric as people glanced around at their neighbors. Anna took advantage of the lull.

"All right. All those in favor of moving the bonfire and changing the procession route, raise your hands."

Hands went up eagerly. Additional hands rose more slowly. Still more were prodded up with sharp elbows administered by neighbors, and a few other people pulled their hands down in response to glares from friends and family.

Standing on her chair, Anna counted the votes one by one.

"That's thirty-five in favor," she said with a sinking feeling.

"Thirty-seven if you count me and Elspeth." Connal did not sound pleased. "And you didn't raise your hand."

"I shouldn't take sides, or I'll lose credibility for the negotiation," Anna said, not daring to turn around and look at him.

The vote had been a mistake, she realized with her stomach turning sour. A vote implied a democratic decision, which this wasn't. She shouldn't have allowed the village to think it would be—that wasn't fair to Connal.

"Aren't you going to ask for the votes against?" someone shouted at her.

Anna gave a sigh. "Fine. All those against Connal paying for the Village Hall in exchange for moving the bonfire?"

Hands shot up again. She felt queasy as she counted them.

Brando beat her to it. "Good. That's thirty-nine against and thirty-seven for, so that's it then."

"It's still Connal's land," Anna said, "and we can't force him to unlock his gates. That means we need a different compromise. Anyone have suggestions?"

Connal sat stiff with shock or anger, or perhaps a bit of both. He scrubbed a hand across his jaw and rose to his feet. Catching Anna's hand as she climbed down from the chair, he drew her toward him instead of letting go. "I thought we'd agreed to work together."

"Negotiations usually go several rounds," she said, working to project confidence at him. "This is only the beginning."

"But you just gave away the endgame."

"I can't make them agree, Connal. I don't live here, and they don't know me—much less trust me."

"That's the point. I do live here, and so does Moira."

"Which is why you voted, and I didn't." Anna took a breath and prepared to gamble that he would have flat refused to have the Sighting on his property if he was absolutely set against it. She hoped she was reading him right.

"Tell them no, then, if you want to. But you'll have to be the one to do it."

"Are you always so bloody-minded?" Connal muttered beneath his breath.

Anna tilted her chin at him. "Are you going back to being rude?"

"For the love of heaven, you two." Elspeth stepped between them. "There are enough of us disagreeing without you both going at each other. Find a solution. We still have the play to settle, not to mention all the other events."

"Yes, the play!" Rhona cried. "What about it, Connal? Will you direct?"

Elspeth shifted around to glare at her. "If he ever meant to consider it, he'd hardly be likely to now, would he? I want the festival as much as anyone, but we have to be fair to him."

Flushing, Rhona shook her head. "What's wrong with asking him? I'm not saying we'd have to publicize he's directing, but we don't want the play to be a complete disaster. He knows the play. He did it with Julian Ashford in London between filming *Steal the Night* and *Cry of the Falcon*."

Connal winced as if the sound of his films was physically painful, or maybe he was uncomfortable at the thought that Rhona knew his resume so well. Without having moved an inch, he was very distant at that moment, distant and alone and worried. His shoulders had bunched themselves into knots.

"It's not a bad idea," Anna said to him quietly. "A possible compromise. You could offer to help direct the earliest rehearsals and turn it over to someone else before people start arriving for the festival."

Raising his head and staring out across the room, Connal cleared his throat, a small sound that with the sweep of his gaze drew attention as much as if he'd shouted. "I'll direct the play if you will all agree to move the bonfire and the procession. It takes two sides to compromise."

"And there are two of you and a hundred of us." Brando stepped forward again, and though he didn't raise his voice either, it sliced like steel through the murmur of the crowd. "This isn't the Middle Ages, Connal. Why should you have more say in our livelihoods than we do? How many times are we supposed to go to you hat in hand, waiting for you to pull out your checkbook or give us your cooperation so we can solve our problems?"

"It's still his land, ye daft man," someone shouted from the rear of the room. "Like it or not, ye're asking him for all those things."

"It may be his land, but for the rest of us, this glen is our home and our livings besides. I've poured everything I have into the hotel these past years, just like Flora and Duncan have with the inn, and everyone else who's relying on visitors to make ends meet. We don't any of the rest of us have the luxury of walking away, locking our gates, and ignoring the world." Brando turned back to Connal. "You're part of the glen, aye, but not like the rest of us. We're all rolling up our sleeves, and you're pulling out your wallet."

"This is my daughter we're talking about! Don't you understand—" Connal cried. Then he shook his head, and for once there was silence in the room.

His eyes met Anna's, half-defiant, half-apologetic. He lowered his voice. "I won't have people staring at Moira, the tabloids distorting photographs and telling lies to line their pockets. They've already killed her mother. I won't let them hurt Moira, too."

The despair and fury in his expression were so stark that Anna swallowed a lump that slid coldly down her throat and raised goosebumps along her skin. Not from fear. From some far less noble emotion, something base and green and ugly. From the knowledge that no one, not even her own mother—especially not her own mother—had ever fought for her the way Connal was fighting for Moira. Even when she'd been Moira's age and had desperately needed to be defended.

"Then tell them no," she said, her voice vibrating hoarsely with long-buried memories.

"And Moira and I would become even less a part of the glen." He stared at Brando across the room, and Brando stared back, the tension between the two of them thick and throbbing until Connal raised his voice again. "You want me to roll up my sleeves? All right. Meet my terms, and I'll direct the play, and I'll make up any funds for the Village Hall that aren't earned from the festival. I'll even ring a few friends who've done *A Midsummer Night's Dream* and see if they'd be willing to take the major roles so there will be more publicity. That's my final offer."

"The procession stops at the museum," Brando countered. "Not the hotel."

"Fine, the museum," Connal agreed with a sharp, brief nod.

"There. Everyone wins. Can we all live with this?" Anna nodded emphatically at Brando and narrowed her eyes at him.

"What about the Beltane Ball?" Rhona called out. "Can we have that at Inverlochlarig again instead of the museum so long as you approve the guest list?"

"No," Connal said without looking at her. With an expression like an approaching clap of thunder, he strode away through the crowd, which parted silently to let him pass.

Anna watched him go, and for the first time, it occurred to her that avoiding trouble might be very hard.

THREE-STEP PROGRAM

*I wish I were with some of the wild people
that run in the woods, and know nothing about accomplishments!*

JOANNA BAILLIE, *THE ELECTION, A COMEDY*

EVERYONE MELTED AWAY after the meeting, leaving
Anna, Elspeth, and Brando to track down the signup
sheet and help the Macaras put the chairs back in place.
The three of them left the inn together and found Connal
waiting for them outside.

Arms folded across his chest, he stood braced against
one of the empty outdoor tables in the courtyard, and he
was brooding. There was no other word to describe the way
he scowled down at the gray flagstones furred around the
edges with soft green moss.

"So you haven't forgotten us after all?" Elspeth
stopped in front of him and poked him in the chest with
her index finger. "Over your snit, are you?"

"I do not *snit*," he retorted, but then his eyes kindled with humor in response to Elspeth's smile, and he straightened away from the table with his trademark athletic grace. "I may huff a little now and then. But I promised you a ride, so forgive me for making you think I'd forgotten."

"I told Elspeth I'd take them home," Brando said.

"I pass the museum anyway, and you've got the Volvo to tow away."

They were of a height, their eyes level. Brando's hair was longer and redder with a deeper curl than Connal's dark mahogany that was mostly hidden beneath his hat. Brando was bulkier, his muscles bunched and thick where Connal's were hard and lean and elegant, but at that instant, it was Connal who gave the impression of wildness below the surface, a force not quite contained. Neither seemed willing to compromise on another thing. Brando stared at Connal a while longer before he slid a look at Elspeth.

She shook her head at him. "Be an adult, Brando. Play fair."

His jaw tightened then relaxed. "Aye, fine." Raising both eyebrows, he tipped his head in a gesture of surrender and held his hand out to Connal with a sigh. "I meant no insult to Moira in there. I hope you know that."

Connal studied the hand Brando held out, then he stepped forward and gave it a cursory shake.

Brando clasped his forearm, holding him in place. "No hard feelings, right?"

"So long as word doesn't get out that I'm directing." Connal's voice was gruff.

"We'll keep it close among ourselves."

"You don't know what the paparazzi are like. But if I'm going to suffer through this, you're going to suffer with me. I'll need an assistant director. Someone I can count on once I have to turn control over."

"Me?" Brando shook his head and stepped away. "Aw, no, mate. That's where I bow out."

"You do it, or I won't. You never gave me the option of bowing out." Turning his back on Brando without waiting for an answer, Connal offered Elspeth his elbow and supported her as they crossed the courtyard to walk the short distance down the side road to where he'd left the Audi. Brando, striding beside Anna, muttered something beneath this breath that didn't sound in the least bit flattering.

It wasn't until Connal had dropped them at the museum that Anna was able to ask Elspeth the questions that had been bothering her since the meeting. "What was all that about between Connal and Brando? And why didn't you tell me Brando owned the hotel? I thought he was the local handyman."

"Handyman? Och, no." In the foyer beneath the glittering chandelier, Elspeth stopped and laughed. The sound echoed through the empty house and raised the temperature as if the heat had kicked on in welcome. "Brando has no family left here," Elspeth said, "so he likes to make himself useful. His parents were killed coming up from Edinburgh in the rain one night when he was twelve, and his sister raised him by herself before she ran off and married a man from Cornwall. A friend of Connal's as it happened, which is why there's always been a bit of tension between those two. Brando was only nineteen then, and Janet wanted him to move along with her, but he wasn't past his rebellious streak, and he felt like that would have been letting Connal run him out of town. Instead, he worked his way through culinary school in London and came back to turn the family farm into a smart hotel. Small but posh and trendy, and he's making a name for himself with the restaurant. Just opened a bakery in Callander, too. Braes Bread right there on the High Street, in case you noticed it when you passed through."

Anna remembered it well. "I picked up a pasty there. It was delicious, and I can't believe he bakes on top of everything else."

"There's not much that man can't do, and that's the truth. Not to mention looking fit to eat himself in his kilt, don't you think?"

"I haven't thought," Anna lied primly, and she and Elspeth both laughed at that as they headed off to the kitchen and spent the evening over the volunteer signup sheet.

Anna's head ached by the time Elspeth had given her the rundown on everyone who'd offered help. It was impossible to remember who was in the habit of overestimating their abilities, who was going to be more trouble than they were worth, and who would do their own share and more. She wrote it all down and promised herself she'd memorize it and destroy the notes.

"Rhona'll be your biggest problem," Elspeth said. "Her and those daughters of hers, and Erica MacLaren.

They're all thick as thieves and slick as snakes. Now that they know Connal will be directing, you won't be able to turn around without finding them underfoot."

"Can they act, at least?"

"I've no idea, but mark my words, roles in the play won't be the only juicy bits Rhona has her eyes on."

Anna choked back a laugh. At the same time, the suggestion left an uncomfortable tightness in her chest.

She had no business letting it bother her.

It should have been Brando she was thinking of as she drifted off to sleep that night beneath the down comforter with the starlight sifting through the mullioned window. He was the one who'd been nothing but kind to her. He was considerate of Elspeth and intelligent and hardworking and, Elspeth was right, he did look delicious in a kilt.

So why was it Connal who raised her temperature, as if the comforter were snuggling her deeper into its folds the moment she thought of him?

Really, it was ridiculous to let herself think about either man—or anyone here in the glen. She was leaving in a month. Going home. Wherever home would turn out to be.

The thought brought another moment of tightness to Anna's chest, and this one was harder to will away. Her entire life was so uncertain, and while there would be other chances for her if the festival failed—she would create other chances for herself—she didn't want to let Elspeth and the village down. She didn't want to let Moira down. She had to make it a success. For everyone.

She needed to stop thinking about Connal and concentrate on the job at hand. Focus. It was time to reaffirm the three-step program she'd set out for herself when Henry had left her a month before the wedding.

One, she wasn't going to let any man limit or decide her future ever again. Two, she was going to carve out a successful career and a place for herself in the world—on her own terms without setting aside her values to get ahead. And three, once her future was secure, she would marry a man she loved, one who would be a true partner in every aspect of her life, without all the arguments and uncertainty that had defined her parents' marriage.

Just because she'd failed twice at the first step, and let that failure derail the second, didn't mean it wasn't a solid plan. She needed to learn from her past mistakes. She wasn't going to become her mother, brushing things aside for the sake of appearances, letting men take away her choices instead of standing up to do what was right.

Anna had been about Moira's age the first time she'd learned that lesson, and seeing the way Connal had fought to protect Moira had been a raw reminder. A pageant judge had tried to touch her backstage, and her mother had told her not to overreact, to keep quiet and use it to her advantage. She'd promised to stay with Anna every moment if Anna would stick with the pageant, but Anna had refused. Refused not only to return to the stage that night, but also to compete in any other pageants. Her mother's arguments hadn't swayed her, so she'd stopped having the pageant experience in common with the female members of her family. She'd stopped being one of the three beautiful Cameron sisters. She'd stopped belonging in her mother's world the way Margaret and Katharine belonged.

In self-defense, she'd become her father's daughter. That hadn't done her any favors with her mother either. Or her sisters.

The first time Anna had mentioned law school, years later, Ailsa had stood up from the breakfast table and carefully smoothed her skirt. "Ignore my advice if you want to," she'd said, "but cutting off your nose to spite your face won't make you happy in the end. Relying on your brains isn't going to get you half as far as you think it will, my girl. You'll only end up working three times as hard as any man, and when it comes time for a promotion, you still won't be the one to get it. The world is a man's place if you don't use every tool you have. And the Lord didn't give you a face like yours so you could waste it."

"How did you get so cynical? When did you ever try to compete with a man in the first place?" Anna had retorted, kicking her legs under the table and watching as her mother slammed down a cookie sheet and the big, blue mixing bowl she only used to make Elspeth's sweet oat biscuits. "Upset oaty biscuits," Anna's father had always called them, because they meant that Ailsa was upset enough to overlook the calories in favor of the comfort.

Anna remembered waiting in the kitchen that day, hoping her mother would answer her. Hoping for a clue that would explain why Ailsa was the way she was, why she'd given up on Anna so easily. But Ailsa never had responded.

It occurred to Anna now, as she drifted off in the moonlight that streamed in through the window of her room at Breagh House, that she had long ago stopped wondering about her mother's *whys*. Maybe Elspeth could explain. Or maybe it wasn't worth the words.

Whether or not it had been the lesson her mother had meant to teach her middle daughter, the one thing Anna had learned from her childhood was that too many people tried to define the power of girls and women. They pigeonholed it, required it to look a certain way, made it seem small or pointless, or they tried to steal it away by force. Women could either let them do that or refuse.

Anna had already given up too much. First with Henry and now with Mike. Well, she wouldn't make that mistake again. Which was why she needed to keep herself from thinking about any man here in the glen, especially Connal, as anything other than a casual acquaintance. Connal MacGregor was pretty to look at from a distance but definitely not safe to play with.

LORD, WHAT FOOLS

If a farmer fills his barn with grain, he gets mice.
If he leaves it empty, he gets actors.

SIR WALTER SCOTT

T HE RESIDENTS OF BALWHITHER undoubtedly had
many talents. Acting was not among them.

Sandwiched as a buffer between Connal and Brando at
a table in the most elegant of The Last Stand's several
dining rooms, Anna had been wearing a fixed smile for so
long her cheeks ached. The fact that Flora Macara
continued to send her alcohol in the form of a delicious
new coffee concoction with honey and Drambuie liqueur
was the only saving grace. But now on her third one, Anna
found herself having to work to keep from giggling at the
sarcastic comments Brando muttered after each
performance.

Connal, meanwhile, with another of his baseball-style hats pulled low to shadow his face, sat stoically through the succession of bad auditions. Until now, he had nursed the same glass of single-malt the entire time, but when he saw Davy Grigg, the grizzled postman—and owner of the meandering sheep—approaching, he threw back the remaining contents of his glass in a single swallow.

Davy, enveloped in a cloud of cheap whiskey fumes and obviously the worse for drink himself, dropped the printout of his performance piece onto the table in front of Connal and waddled to the front of the room.

Positioning himself on the "stage" in the small alcove where the French doors led onto the terrace, Davy rubbed his belly soothingly, like a pregnant woman. With a hiccup, he darted a look around the room and licked his lips. Judging by his red-veined nose and bloodshot eyes, Anna suspected he was no stranger to drinking at the best of times, but she couldn't help wondering if he'd given himself a few extra shots of courage to get over stage fright.

"I'll be doin' Philostrate, Master of the Revels," he said, emitting a second hiccup.

"If there's anything Davy Griggs knows how to do," someone shouted, "it's revel."

Laughter rippled around the tables in the room, which were filled by everyone who'd already auditioned, the few still waiting, and random villagers who hadn't wanted to miss the fun.

"Been reveling a bit too much tonight if you ask me," Brando murmured.

A giggle escaped Anna, though considering how much spiked coffee she had drunk herself, she had no right to be judging Davy.

"That's fine." Connal picked up Davy's audition sheet. "Just be warned that we may still have a professional actor coming to play the part of Philostrate, Davy. There are plenty of characters to cast, though, so go ahead and begin when you're ready. Start with 'Here, mighty Theseus.'"

Davy nodded. Clutching his stomach with both hands now as though it pained him, he lifted his eyes to the back of the room and waved a meaty paw in a vague pantomime that, Anna supposed, was meant to suggest he was handing over a sheet of paper. "Here," he said, still not looking at Connal, "mighty Theseus."

Connal, pretending to take the paper, delivered the lines from Theseus, Duke of Athens, back to him. "Say, what abridgment have you for this evening? What masque? What music? How shall we beguile the lazy time, if not with some delight?"

Connal's voice had gone low and resonant again, reaching deep into Anna as it had every time these past couple hours when he'd read to help someone with an audition, as if he were tugging some unseen thread she hadn't known existed. He made it seem so effortless, that ability to command every breath of attention from everyone around him.

Unaware or uncaring of Connal's effect, or the starkness of the contrast, Davy Grigg continued speaking to the back of the room. "There is a brief how many sports

. . . are ripe: make choice . . . of which Your Highness will see first."

Connal, though he knew all of Theseus's lines by heart, stared down at Davy's wrinkled audition sheet. "The Battle with the Centaurs," he pretended to read, "to be sung by an Athenian eunuch to the harp." Pausing, he frowned up at Davy and shook his head. "We'll none of that: that have I told my love, in glory of my kinsman Hercules."

One by one, Connal read off and dismissed the other possible entertainments that were supposed to be written on the list Philostrate had given him. Then he came to the final entry. "A tedious brief scene of young Pyramus and his love Thisbe; very tragical mirth," he read, his voice bemused. Lowering the paper again, he peered at Davy across the top. "Merry and tragical? Tedious and brief? That is hot ice and wondrous strange snow. How shall we find the concord of this discord?"

Davy puffed himself up and coughed. "A play there is, my lord, some ten words long, which is . . . as brief as I have known a play; but by ten words, my lord, it is too long which makes it tedious; for in all . . . the play there is not one word apt, one player fitted . . . "

"Which about sums up these auditions, never mind Shakespeare's play within the play," Brando whispered to Anna. "We haven't had a half-decent performance the entire night."

Anna failed to suppress another giggle. Connal sent her a quelling look and soldiered on until Davy's piece had reached its end. "Thank you, Davy. That was . . . interesting. We'll get back to you tomorrow night."

"I was good, wasn't I? Or I can do it again." Davy gave a rueful nod. "Aye, I could probably do it better. Let me try again."

"No, no," Connal said hastily, sending Anna a sideways glance that hinted at amusement. "I think we've seen everything we need to see."

With a beatific smile, Davy hitched up his pants and stumbled unsteadily out of the recessed stage area. He wound between the crowded tables and stopped halfway across the room near the fireplace to have a loud exchange with someone about a wager. Money changed hands.

"I hope he's not betting on himself to get the part," Anna said.

"That's one bet he'd lose outright," said Connal.

Anna marked a number four beside Davy's name on her copy of the audition signup sheet and circled it. Four out of ten. Unfortunately, that was on a theoretic scale, not an indication that they'd seen any performances worthy of a ten. Or even six performances better than Davy's. More unfortunately still, there were only four names left on the sign-in sheet, which made the odds of avoiding having to cast at least some of the people they'd already seen impossible.

Anna nodded. "You're going to have your work cut out for you, that's all I have to say."

As if to underscore the point, Rhona Grewer hurried up to Connal carrying her audition piece, her steps small in her tight red skirt and mile-high heels. Brando gave a low, quiet groan. "Can't we take a break? I need a break."

"Brilliant idea." Connal stood up. "Let's take fifteen minutes, shall we, everyone? Rhona, hold tight, and we'll call you the moment we're ready to start up again." He smiled at Rhona in a way that made her blink, and she made a U-turn back to where her daughters were sitting with Erica MacLaren at a table beside the wall.

"This is going to be pure disaster," Connal said, slumping back down into his chair. "Whose brilliant idea was it to do a play in the first place?"

"Rhona's. Whose do you think?" Brando said.

Anna rolled her shoulders, trying to ease some of the tension away. She debated sneaking into the pub to get another coffee. Without the liqueur. Or maybe with.

She turned to Connal. "All I can say is, I hope you're planning to ask a lot of friends to help."

"They won't be my friends for long if I saddle them with this lot." He rubbed the back of his neck and frowned down at the audition sheets.

"I don't suppose they'd believe you're being meta? Making the whole thing awful on purpose to spoof the way Shakespeare wrote the play-within-the-play for the Mechanicals to be so bad that they were funny?"

"Shakespeare couldn't have envisioned the low bar these auditions have set," Brando said.

"Hold on. That's not a bad idea." Connal's head came up. He cocked it slightly and stared at the empty stage area, lost in thought. "With a bit of a rewrite here and there, some modernizing and gender flipping . . . it could work. We could make the bad performances funnier and easier to understand, and if a few of my friends will agree to do the larger roles, we could pull it off."

"We'd still have the problem of too many women," Anna said.

"Since when is that a problem?" Brando asked, laughing at her.

She cast him a dark look and shook her head at Connal. "Who would have an ego big enough to rewrite Shakespeare? That's begging for trouble with anyone who comes to see the performance."

"Maybe." Connal smiled over at her, a smile like a little boy, full of mischief. "I know someone who might be willing to try."

"Of course you know someone," Brando said.

"Who?" Anna jabbed an elbow into Brando's ribs.

Connal ignored Brando entirely. "Graham Connor," he said to Anna. "He's a screenwriter not a playwright, but he's used to working under pressure. The rewrite shouldn't take much time, and if we double up some of the bigger roles, which was what Shakespeare intended in the first place, it would make it easier for Julian Ashford and Victoria Holmes and the others I've asked to agree to help us. What do you think?"

What was there to think? Even Anna had heard of Graham Connor, who had won an Oscar for best screenplay two years back. And the actors whose names Connal had been throwing around so casually were household names, almost as big as Connal had been at the height of his career. Victoria Holmes had been Isobel Teague's best friend offscreen and also her closest rival.

Shifting in her seat at the thought, Anna looked up to find Connal watching her, his expression expectant and intimate and oddly vulnerable.

"That would be fantastic," she said. "As long as it's all right with Elspeth and the rest of the village."

"I can't see that it wouldn't be. Let me go make a few more calls." Connal surged to his feet, creative energy sparking in the air around him. "If I'm not back in ten minutes, you two start Rhona, Erica, and the twins on their auditions. I'm not expecting a miracle from any of them, but it would be a relief to end up with halfway reasonable versions of Hermia and Helena. I don't have a clue what we'll do with Rhona."

"She signed up to audition for Titania and Hippolyta."

"Which she'll play over my dead body." Connal snatched his cell phone off the table along with the scratchpad onto which he'd been making notes and strode from the room.

Brando turned to watch him leave. "Typical, isn't it? Himself forces us into sitting through this misery with him then finds the first excuse to get out of having to deal with Rhona. She won't be half-pleased, I'll tell you that much."

"To be fair, Connal wouldn't be directing if you hadn't forced him into doing the play in the first place." Anna rubbed the spot between her eyes where her head had begun to ache. "Really, I'm the only innocent bystander here. Anyway, Rhona can't honestly be throwing herself at him, can she? Isn't she a bit too old?"

"Try telling her that; I dare you. And why does everyone defend Connal all the time? You should see how much grief I've gotten since yesterday. Don't tell me you're already on his side. You'll break my heart."

"I didn't think your heart was breakable."

"You malign me." Brando threw his hand onto his chest, tipped his chin in the air and assumed an overwrought expression. "'Oh, why rebuke you him that loves you so?'"

Anna laughed, and it felt good to let the giggles out. "I suspect you're far more likely to be the heartbreak*er* instead of the break*ee*."

"If only that were true," Brando said.

Anna thought he was joking at first, but the creases of laughter in the corners of his eyes had grown a little shallower, and his smile had dimmed. It was only a minuscule change of expression, almost invisible, as if the general air of amiability he wore had slipped just enough to reveal that it was, in fact, a disguise. Anna wondered, suddenly, how much of his inner self, his true self, Brando ever let others see.

"I'm sorry," she said. "I didn't mean to imply—well, anything really. Elspeth mentioned the village taking bets on the women you've dated since you've been back from London."

"True, which is why I make a point of falling in love at least once a month for practice." Brando smiled with effort, and again she had the impression that beneath the affable exterior there was a deep well of sadness.

He had an actor's face, Anna realized abruptly, that same deceptive mobility of expression as Henry. And like Henry, too, he used it to cover up what he was truly thinking and feeling. How had she never seen that until this moment? She also hadn't realized how much she'd bought into the stereotype and the muscles and the kindness—she kept misjudging Brando. Maybe people in general. She'd gotten complacent about her ability to read people, and apparently she was failing at it. Maybe she'd always failed at it.

"I wonder how often we talk ourselves into believing that falling in *like* is the same as falling in *love*," she said. "Liking someone is painless. Less risky. Falling in love, though, that requires trust and hope—or a deep streak of masochism. But I'm sorry. It must be frustrating to have the village meddling in your love life."

"Much as I love most everyone here, they don't know half of what they think they do. It's hard when they've all watched me grow up from a child in dirty nappies, felt sorry for me when my parents died, and watched my sister drag me across the glen by the ear for smoking and drinking at the bothy across the loch. I went to London to make something of myself and came back, and no one ever noticed that I'd grown up in between."

Anna thought of her own family, where the dynamics had been realigned when she was ten and hadn't changed much since. Margaret and Katharine had gotten married, and Katharine had moved to Hollywood with Henry while Anna had gone off to D.C., as far on the other side of the country as she could get. Until last week, she'd had a successful career at one of the top law firms in the world, but that had never mattered when she went home.

Always when she saw her family, she still felt like a child. Even before her meltdown, the only person who had been impressed when she'd graduated magna cum laude from Harvard Law was her father. To her mother and sisters, that achievement didn't come close to Margaret snagging a job anchoring a local morning program in Cincinnati or the handful of speaking roles in B+ movies that Katharine had landed out in Hollywood while waiting for her "big break."

"I'm sorry you got hurt," Anna said to Brando softly, "and I'm sorry about the village. The people who know us best sometimes don't look hard enough to see who we really are."

He smiled in a way that no longer fooled her. "First love is a training wheel romance. It's full of extremes, the best feelings in the world and the worst, but you have to live through that. You have to find your balance so you're ready when the next love, the real love, comes along."

Anna wondered if that was true. But what happened if the next love never came? Did you spend your whole life waiting?

Brando looked so wistful that she wanted to tell him she understood, that he wasn't alone. Except he wasn't the one alone, was he? He seemed to be ready and waiting for that real love to come along. Meanwhile, she'd been making bargains with herself since Henry had left her, making plans and three-step programs about when and how she would allow herself to live and fall in love. Had she been guarding her heart so carefully that she hadn't given love a chance to set down roots?

With a sudden wrench in the pit of her stomach, she clamped her lips together. That's what she'd been doing, wasn't it? Making plans instead of living.

With Mike, deep down, she'd never wanted the time to be right to set a wedding date. That had been an excuse for not making the commitment. Her relationship with Mike had been safe, easy, but never right. Staying with him, she'd been protecting herself against falling all the way in love.

His expression concerned, Brando turned in his chair and studied her. "Are you all right? I didn't mean to upset you."

Anna shook her head. "The idea of one perfect love for every person is a romantic notion, isn't it? That's what makes the legend of the Sighting so compelling. But what if the love of your life passes you by? What if you never get a second chance?"

"The Sighting's not about promising someone for everyone. Some people never see anything. Other people wait so long for the person they're meant to be with that they give up hope. But my sister used to say the loch would find a way to make things happen even when the head wouldn't listen. Maybe that has less to do with the loch than it does with fate or destiny or God having plans for us. I won't pretend to know why the Sighting works or what's behind it. I only know it's as real as the fact that you're sitting here beside me."

"What if what you see isn't what you want to see?" Anna asked, thinking about what Elspeth had told her.

"I've known people who've walked away from what they saw and ended up miserable all their lives, and plenty of others who've managed to sabotage the love they were meant to have. Maybe love's like anything else. You have to be willing to accept it when you're lucky enough to have it cross your path."

Anna frowned down into her empty cup. Her head swam, and her chest felt tight. Maybe the alcohol had gotten to her more than she'd thought, or maybe the dizziness came from the fact that the word *sabotage* felt too right, the way sometimes the universe rang out with a clear, echoing note in answer to a question she hadn't even known she'd asked.

Consciously or unconsciously, maybe she had sabotaged her relationship with Mike. She'd put off setting a wedding date so long that he'd finally stuffed a suitcase full of boxer briefs, socks, and t-shirts, and carried it away along with an armload of shirts in dry cleaner plastic when he stormed out of their apartment the last time she'd tried to push things back.

"Maybe some people aren't good at being in love," she said. "No matter how much they wish they were."

Brando's expression softened. "I may not know much about you at all, Anna, *mo chroí*, but anyone who's not a sad, blind fool can see that there's love and joy inside you."

Anna didn't know what to say to that. What to do with the sudden inexplicable hope and longing and brittleness she felt in her chest and the thickness developing in her throat.

A chair scraped on the right and Rhona, with impeccable timing, stood up from her seat at the nearby table and tapped her watch. "So where's Connal got to, then? The twins have school in the morning, and it's getting late."

"He's outside making a call, I think. Let me go and find him," Anna said, feeling a sudden, desperate need for air.

DANGEROUS AIR

He who kisses joy as it flies by will live in eternity's sunrise.

WILLIAM BLAKE

T HE LAST STAND INN was a warren of rooms spanning what had once been a handful of separate buildings connected through the centuries with step-ups and step-downs, odd angles, crooked walls, and scattered courtyards in between. Anna left the small dining area where the auditions were being held and wove through several cozy side rooms, each occupied by one or two scattered groups of people. When she reached the pub, she found Flora and Duncan moving at double-quick speed behind the bar, a well-orchestrated dance of beer foaming into glasses, light refracting on bottles of amber whiskey, ice clinking. A small crowd clustered near the television watched a soccer game, their occasional cheers or groans punctuating the hum of conversation. A goal shortly after Anna entered brought three-quarters of the fans to their feet.

Connal wasn't in the main pub, but she finally spotted him on the far side in a quiet alcove of the adjacent room. Seated alone by the fireplace, he had his phone wedged against his shoulder while he scribbled notes.

The sight of him caught Anna unexpectedly. Caught her in the pit of her stomach like an ache she'd been trying to ignore.

Still listening to whoever was on the other end of the phone, Connal took off his hat and ran a hand through his hair. He looked vulnerable in that moment, the way he had at the first village meeting, and the distance shrank between them, the air growing warm and lighter, as though parting to let her reach him faster. To push her toward him. Which was a ridiculous notion, brought on—clearly—by one or possibly two too many of Flora's Highland coffees.

Cheeks hot, Anna stopped halfway down the bar to collect her thoughts. She couldn't let her imagination overrule her common sense.

It wasn't just that he was pretty. Brando was pretty. Brando was also smart, considerate, more complex than she'd imagined, and—as Elspeth had repeatedly pointed out—looked darn good in a kilt. Brando had a sense of humor. For all she knew, Connal MacGregor had none of those things, and while Brando had an actor's ability to mask his feelings, Connal *was* an actor. That made him doubly dangerous. So what was she doing, standing here gaping at him with her stomach tied in knots and her heart beating too fast?

Being an idiot, that's what.

She really needed air.

What was it that Brando had said? The loch would find a way to make things happen even when the head wouldn't listen. But Anna had already been kicked into a thousand pieces once by the kind of romance that made her dizzy. Henry had made her palms sweat the first time he'd passed her a handout in AP Bio their sophomore year of high school, and she'd never stopped feeling that way about him. Not until the moment when, the summer after college while she was back home finalizing the arrangements for their wedding, he'd thrown away his job managing his father's furniture factory and run off to Hollywood with her sister Katharine.

He'd given Anna no warning at all, none that she had seen anyway. Maybe none that she'd been willing to see. Apparently, he'd always been a better actor than she'd believed him to be.

She'd spent the rest of that summer sending back wedding gifts and trying to politely hold her head up while her mother told her to pretend it didn't matter, that she couldn't let people see she minded. Of course, Anna *had* minded. So much she'd ached with it.

In her cold bed every night, all the moments of their time together had played like a song stuck in her head— every touch, every word, every last glance between her and Henry, between Henry and Katharine. She had spent months searching her mind for clues she could have missed, and she'd never found any answers.

Getting out of bed in the mornings had been even harder. Every new day meant eating in the kitchen with her mother watching, eagle-eyed, to make sure Anna didn't let herself get fat on greasy food and Ben and Jerry's ice cream. It meant more long hours mired in the scandal of it all while her mother paraded her around the country club. Smile, Anna, smile.

Law school had been a merciful escape, but Anna hadn't gone out on a single date in those three years. Even after law school, apparently, she'd played it safe and let herself get engaged to a man who made her feel little more than friendship for him.

Connal MacGregor was not the sort of man to inspire lukewarm emotions. Not in her. Perhaps not in anyone. Which made him a complication Anna didn't need in her life.

So why couldn't she make herself stop staring?

"Did you lose something, doll? I'd be 'appy to help you find it." From beside the bar on Anna's left, a voice addressed her. Seated there with two mates, all three of them clearly the worse for drink, a tall man in an Aran sweater and leather jacket got up and headed toward her.

Smiling at him vaguely, Anna shook her head and whipped around to her left. She marched toward the inn's main entrance and let herself out amid the jingling bells.

The night was cold. The wind smelled of mountain thyme, greening heather, and something like fear, acrid and bitter and suffocating. Anna had left her coat inside, and the chill raised goosebumps on her skin. Around the side of the courtyard, the loch was visible, the dark water rippling with moonlight and the ranks of shadowed steep-sided Highland braes standing guard over both sides down the long length of the glen.

Hugging herself for warmth, Anna stopped on the moss-edged flagstones by the fence, trying to still the confusion that made her itchy and unsettled, like pins and needles, like a limb that was waking up after having lost circulation for too long.

It was ironic: At home, focused on work and day-to-day activities, she had rarely stopped to think about relationships or love or emotional needs. She'd met Mike soon after moving to D.C., and he'd been charming and fun. Distracting. That was the truth of it. He'd been distracting. They had started with a few casual dates, and then, so gradually Anna had barely even noticed, they'd slipped into a relationship that didn't require a lot of effort.

She'd barely stopped to think when he'd proposed. Her work had been going well. Marriage had been a logical step—sometime in the future. Mike had claimed he understood that her hours were crazy, and if she wasn't ready to set a date just yet, that had been fine. But as time passed, it had become less fine.

Time was the one thing Anna had known she needed. And the time had never been right. On some inner level, she must have known her reluctance to set a date had nothing to do with being too busy. She hadn't loved Mike the way that she'd loved Henry. Maybe she hadn't let herself love him like that.

It hurt too much to love with her entire heart. When Henry had left, everything she'd believed about him, about herself, about the two of them together, had splintered into shards. She'd spent her life since seeing the world in fragments, the past, the present, the future she'd believed in all distorted. Loving someone that much had left her wide open to the kind of pain it was almost impossible to survive.

"Waiting for me, doll?" An arm landed heavily around Anna's shoulders, and hot beer breath fanned across her cheek.

Anna froze. Froze in a way she hadn't frozen since she was a child, but then, she'd spent so much of the past few days dredging up things she'd been ignoring too long. Unburying things she'd hidden deep away.

She told herself to move, to wrench away from the man. The signal took too long to reach her brain.

It was the man in the bar with the Aran sweater. A drunk. Nothing more. She stepped forward. The fence blocked her and, when she turned, the man put his arm out to box her in.

"Don't go running off so soon," he said with a happy, drunken smile, as though what he was doing was perfectly all right. "I came out to get acquainted."

Anna turned the other way. He stepped around her.

"Let me go," she said, her voice high and tight.

"Nae, now, don't be getting mad. I liked the way you smiled at me far better, and you wanted me to follow, didn't you? Well, here I am." He pushed in closer, grinning wider.

Anna spun, and he blocked her again. She was tall, but he was taller and broader, and even drunk he moved with surprising speed. The courtyard was empty in the cold night air, everyone inside where the light shone warmly through the windows.

It was stupid to be afraid. She wasn't a ten-year-old girl this time, pulled into a closet backstage at a beauty pageant by a judge—an old man—who pulled her against his crotch and kissed her so hard that her own teeth cut through her lip. She wasn't alone this time. All she had to do was yell, and someone would hear her.

Only then it would be another scene, wouldn't it? Two car accidents and one more stupid mess she'd gotten herself into in front of half the village.

She'd spent her whole life trying so hard to avoid making messes. To avoid unpleasantness. No matter how hard she tried, she couldn't seem to do the right thing.

To heck with it, then. She was done being nice. Done being polite.

Done holding back.

"Let me go," she repeated coldly, "or I swear I'll make you and the children you will never have regret you ever saw me."

He studied her and something in her voice must have finally penetrated his drunken cheerfulness. The grin faltered, and he stepped away from her, his hands raised in surrender.

"No use getting in a flap, doll. I was only being friendly-like."

He turned with exaggerated care and swaggered away. Anna hugged herself, shivering, and watched him go, trying to catch her breath.

Beyond him, Connal was just emerging from the inn. Spotting Anna, his stride lengthened, and he hurried toward her with a muffled greeting to the drunk as he walked past. Anna locked her knees to keep herself from running toward him.

"Are you all right?" he asked as he drew closer. "I was coming out to find you, because Rhona said you'd gone looking for me."

"I'm fine," Anna said, her teeth chattering, her breath still coming fast.

"You're freezing. What are you doing out here?" He studied her more closely. "What happened? That man, he didn't—" Connal glanced back at the door that had just swung shut behind the drunk, and his expression shifted. Puzzled to furious.

He half-turned, shoulders bunching, fingers curled into his palms. But Anna grabbed his sleeve, needing his warmth. Needing not to be alone.

He studied her, shivering himself in the thin sweater he was wearing, and she saw the moment of hesitation before he reached for her and started to rub her arms, trying to warm her up.

Big fires started with a little bit of friction.

He touched her. Looked down at her. They looked at each other. Her heartbeat skittered, and his eyes dropped to her mouth.

This was probably stupid, a stupid thing to do, but Anna clearly couldn't avoid messes, and where had being careful gotten her in life? Henry and Mike and nowhere. . . .

No, not nowhere.

Here.

And Connal had been honest with her from the beginning. He'd shown her his vulnerabilities.

She didn't step away. He had that shimmer around him again, and the electricity in the air concentrated around her into one hard shove, pushing her forward into his arms. He watched her as she fell against him, watched a long moment without moving, and then his hand slid almost reluctantly along the column of her neck and the curve of her cheek, lingering there, a question written on his features.

Do you want this?

Yes. Heavens, yes, Anna thought, though she couldn't have said a word even if she'd tried.

Connal's eyes had gone dark and solemn. Slowly, carefully, he lowered his head, gave her plenty of time to step away, to run. His lips brushed hers with such gentleness, a butterfly's touch. For the first time in her life, Anna came close to understanding chaos theory: how the wings of a butterfly beating could cause a hurricane. Every drop of her blood surged to meet him, every muscle quivered, begging to be closer.

He murmured something against her mouth and tore off his hat. Drawing her closer, he deepened the kiss, made it grow even more electric until Anna thought she would drown with the joyful pain of waking up, of being alive. Her heart beat so fast she couldn't breathe.

She hadn't felt like this since high school. Since Henry.

No, not even Henry.

It was as if every sensation she had ever experienced was all collecting inside her now, a million nerve endings zinging from her lips to her core, every fiber and excited molecule. The feeling was all heat that blurred away thought and plans and calculations, all the hopes she'd tucked away in the dark recesses of herself along with her dreams for the future.

And she let herself fall, because she was surprised and a little drunk and suddenly—inexplicably—oh, so tired of holding herself back, of listening to the voice of reason in her head, of telling herself she wasn't free or alive or enough for this to happen to her yet.

Yet.

Yet was the most tyrannical of words, wasn't it? It almost always came after "not" or was used in place of "but," and it was never said with "yes, please."

Yes, please was exactly what Anna wanted now. What she needed.

She pressed against Connal, met his lips with her own, claimed his tongue, his breath, his pulse that was as erratic as hers. She wanted to feel everything, to be the kind of girl who lived without a three-step program and a plan for the future. A girl who lived for the moment and in the moment.

This moment.

These lips.

This magic that was singing so unexpectedly in her blood.

She kissed him back until she was dizzy, until they were dizzy together, leaning against each other, breathing hard. He rested his forehead against hers, then started to pull back only to be drawn back to her mouth again as though he couldn't help himself, as if his lips were drawn there magnetically. And that was the word for what she felt between them. Magnetism that aligned her neurons to his, her polar north toward him, until every cell of her was aware and melting beneath his touch.

GLAD INNOCENCE

Where glad innocence reign
'Mang the braes o' Balquhidder

ROBERT TANNAHILL, "THE BRAES OF BALQUHIDDER"

I N HER PAINFULLY SUN-FILLED ROOM the next morning, Anna sat fully dressed with her head in her hands. It wasn't only the mild hangover that kept her there; it was the awkwardness of it all.

How was she supposed to face Connal again when she'd practically swallowed his tonsils in the middle of the darn courtyard, probably in full view of half the village? He'd been gracious about it, lovely even. Not that he hadn't seemed to enjoy it—he'd given every sign of enjoyment— but then he'd carefully disentangled her, gone inside and fetched her coat and purse, gently loaded her into his car, and dropped her at Elspeth's with a careful goodnight kiss on the forehead as if he was afraid that he would break her.

She'd lain awake half the night, hot memories of that kiss keeping her company until the effects of Flora's coffees had worn off and cold mortification had kept her from sleep.

Oh, well. What was a little more humiliation? It was becoming a familiar feeling.

No more—absolutely, positively no more—whiskey.

Ever.

But she couldn't hide in her room all day. She had too much work to do before the next meeting about the play that night, not to mention the first meetings of all the other assorted event committees.

With a soft groan, she picked herself up and forced herself downstairs to the kitchen—where she found Connal MacGregor seated at the table wearing another shoulder-hugging sweater. Chatting with Elspeth while eating bacon, sausage, and tattie scones, he seemed to take up all the oxygen in the room. Anna nearly turned around and headed straight back up the stairs.

Except that Elspeth saw her. "Morning, love. You don't look like you slept much at all."

"Blame it on Flora's coffee."

Elspeth laughed. "In that case, have some more coffee. No alcohol. Shall I make up a pot for you?"

"Yes, please," Connal said, "but give us a second, would you?" He got up from the table and came around to push Anna backwards out the kitchen door.

In the hallway, as soon as they were out of sight, he put his hands on either side of her face and looked deep into her eyes. "I'm going to kiss you now," he said. "Are you going to object?"

Anna stared. Couldn't utter a single word. Shook her head.

Connal lowered his head and claimed a kiss. A short, deep, warming kiss.

She hadn't realized she was cold until he'd heated her up again.

"There," he said, pulling away and taking all that warmth back with him.

She blinked, confused and bereft. "What was that for? And what are you doing here? It's barely eight o'clock."

"I got to worrying that you were going to mistake my self-control when I dropped you off last night for reluctance or regret, and I didn't want to give you a chance to talk yourself into making things awkward between us. Maybe, also, I needed to know it hadn't been all fear or Drambuie on your part."

"It wasn't fear or liquor," Anna blurted before she'd taken the time to think that he'd given her the perfect excuse. If she wanted an excuse. Did she want one?

No.

"Regrets?" he asked, his brows drawing together.

She could have lied; maybe she should have. But regardless of how little sleep she'd had, she felt understood and wide-awake in her body for the first time in years. She felt alive and exhilarated and a little bit afraid, not of Connal, but of pain. Of joy. Of allowing herself to feel.

"No," she said firmly. "I don't regret a thing. Except that the news is probably all over the village by now, and that's the third collision I've had here in as many days."

"Oh, a collision, am I?" Connal laughed, his eyes teasing and warm. He pulled her closer. "In that case, let's try colliding again, shall we? I don't think I mind at all."

He bent his lips to hers again.

The magic of those kisses the night before hadn't had anything to do with alcohol or adrenaline or fear. They'd been him and her. Them.

Fire ignited between them now, fire from the very first touch as if the blaze had been banked all night just waiting for a breath of oxygen. But eventually Anna's stomach growled, and they both laughed and stopped to breathe. Anna rested her head against Connal's chest, listening to his heart beating fast.

The scent of coffee and bacon drifted out toward them from where Elspeth was working at the stove, and Connal wound his fingers through Anna's. "Come on. Time for more of this later." He paused and looked down at her. "If you want more?"

She nodded, not sure she could speak.

After escorting her back into the kitchen, he held out the chair for her and dropped a kiss on the top of her head. Smiling mildly at Elspeth, he said, "I'm taking your niece out for lunch later. Just so you know."

Elspeth came and sat, nursing her cup of tea between her hands. "Make it somewhere public, would you? You've won me a hundred quid from Davy Grigg, the pair of you."

"What was the bet this time?" Connal asked, raising a wicked eyebrow.

"The village money was all on Brando when Anna first arrived, but I managed to get good odds after dinner the other night. Thank goodness, too, because once everyone saw the two of you at the pub before the village meeting, I couldn't have gotten in a decent bet. Poor Brando. He never does get a break."

Anna felt a stab of guilt thinking back to her conversation with Brando the night before, though not about herself. He had never been meant for her, and she was sure he knew it. "There's a lot more to Brando than anyone here gives him credit for," she said. "We shouldn't make a joke out of his love life."

Elspeth's lovely smile wavered, and the crease between her brows grew deeper. "Och, we aren't poking fun at him to be mean. We love him"—she tossed a quick frown at Connal—"some of us do, at least. We worry about him without his sister here. It's just our way. And we're proud of what he's made of himself."

"Maybe let him know that," Anna said, glancing over at Connal, too. "He thinks the glen still sees him as a teenage delinquent. Maybe that's why he fought so hard to make certain his voice was heard about the festival."

Connal gave a noncommittal grunt and cut a piece of bacon. Elspeth sat a moment holding her tea, lost in thought. Then she rose with a soft scrape of chair legs on wood and came to kiss Anna on the cheek. "Sometimes it takes someone coming in from outside and shaking things up, showing us what we're too used to seeing to find the truth in it. You're good for all of us. Now, what will you have to eat?"

Bacon and sausage held no appeal, but there was gingerbread left. Anna crossed to the counter and liberated the last two pieces from the domed keeper, set them on a Wedgwood plate, and brought them back to the table. Connal slid a manila file in front of her.

"What's this?" Remembering the last folder she'd gotten while sitting at this table, Anna opened it as if something inside might jump out and bite her.

"Graham went over the play for us last night," Connal said, sitting back in his seat. "Just a few initial scenes to give us an idea of how it might work."

Something tenuous and edgy in Connal's voice brought Anna's head up. "Last night? It was after ten by the time you dropped me off."

"America's hours behind us, and apparently he had time. Take a look and tell me what you think."

Self-conscious while he watched her, Anna began to read. Almost immediately she laughed aloud—and she kept laughing. Graham Connor had managed to translate the play into modern English without altering its character, and the smaller parts were all delightfully more bungling and filled with quirks that would only seem quirkier when played by amateurs. Connal had penciled in notes about who should play what role, and she could almost picture different people in the village playing the parts—because they *were* the parts. All they had to do was draw from their life experience and be themselves.

"Do you like it?" Again there was a thread of anxiousness in Connal's voice.

For the first time, Anna realized the risk he'd taken, the enormity of the favor he had asked of Graham Connor with no guarantee that she—or the talentless amateurs in the production—would be willing to work with what Graham gave them. Let alone do it justice.

"It's genius," she said, "and you're brilliant for coming up with the idea and being willing to talk Graham Connor into writing it. How soon could he have it finished?" Then she had another thought. "But you aren't paying him for it, are you? I don't think the village fund will stretch that far."

"Don't worry about money. Graham likes to tinker. If the production goes off well, he'll either release the modified play for royalties, or he'll write it off as a favor for a friend who's gotten him out of a jam or two in the past." He smiled. "Money's not Graham's concern, and I imagine he can finish the revision in the next couple of days. So, is that settled, then?"

"Gratefully. Although I imagine there will be a few people in the village who feel this hits a bit too close to home. Sorcha, for example. Also Rhona won't be happy."

"Rhona will have to live with it. Victoria is booked, but Vanessa Devereaux is tentatively willing to play both Hippolyta and Titania. She and Pierce Saunders said they could come so long as they only have to be here for the final dress rehearsal and the two performances on Friday and Sunday. And Julian"—Connal paused with a barely perceptible wince—"can't wait to get here. He's finishing up a film and said to look for him in a couple of weeks."

Elspeth had gotten up to get more tea. She turned with the teapot in her hand. "Vanessa Devereaux? *The* Vanessa Devereaux?"

Connal raised an eyebrow, as though that were obvious. "Is there another one?"

"Oh, my goodness." Elspeth's cheeks went pink, and she came over to hug first Connal then Anna. "This is fantastic, Connal. Anna. Only wait until I tell the others! Or you should tell them. You should definitely get the credit."

"I only agreed to do this on the condition that I wouldn't be credited, remember? That's rather the entire point." Connal turned back to Anna, his eyes smiling. "Now. About that lunch of ours. Can I pick you up at noon?"

Working together at the table in the sunny kitchen, Anna and Elspeth knocked as much off their enormous to-do lists as they could before lunch: phone calls to vendors for the main tent and rental chairs, crowd control ropes, velvet curtains for the stage they would need to build, not to mention trophies for all the athletic events and dance events and the piping competition. There were also the craftspeople to contact—renting out booths for food and crafts was a big part of the projected income needed for the Village Hall.

Then there was the matter of a graphic artist.

"Couldn't JoAnne do the posters to save some money?" Anna asked as Elspeth complained about the prices on the websites she'd been studying. "The work she's done for you on the museum placards is beautiful."

"It is, and you should see her portraits. But she's still spitting mad about us making the festival bigger. She's scarcely speaking to me at all, much less ready to lift a finger to help."

"How can she still be mad if Connal isn't?" Anna glanced up from her laptop.

"She's a sweet girl, but a bit of an odd duck. It's herself she's protecting as much as Moira, I suspect. Her own sanctuary here in the glen where she can work on her art in private." Brows drawing low over clouded eyes, Elspeth stared out the mullioned window above the sink. "Her mother's a school friend of mine," she said, "and I thought I was doing her a favor helping JoAnne get the job taking care of Moira. Now I'm not so sure. The girl's got more talent than her father ever had, but she grew up watching the way he swaggered around, convinced the world owed him a living as an artist. JoAnne's afraid to show her art to anyone who matters for fear they'll reject her the way they rejected him. She couldn't love Moira more if Moira were her own, but she's hiding here in the glen, same as Connal. I suppose remote places tend to collect broken souls."

"You think Connal's broken?" Anna asked.

Elspeth smiled gently. "I think every person is lost and broken in some way. Our own ways."

Anna thought about JoAnne and Connal both protecting Moira so fiercely. Not that Moira wasn't worth protecting. Maybe Anna had no right to think so, having known Moira for a few short hours, but it struck her that the girl was stronger than anyone gave her credit for being. Stronger and smarter.

Children were at that age, weren't they? Anna herself hadn't been able to go to the police or the pageant management and report the judge who had tried to touch her, but she could have. She would have if her mother had only let her. Even then she'd known that there were things you shouldn't hide. Things you *couldn't* hide. Maybe if she'd faced those demons then, she wouldn't have spent her whole life trying so hard to be perfect and not ruffle any feathers.

Was that part of the reason she had agreed to marry a man she wasn't head over heels in love with? She hated to admit it, but maybe it had been less painful to say yes to Mike, to go along, than it would have been to have to move out and start all over again, to acknowledge that she didn't want to settle for someone who didn't leave *her* ruffled.

Love was supposed to be messy, wasn't it? Wild and free and a little dangerous. Love was meant to give you the confidence to soar, to fly, knowing there would always be someone to catch you if you fell.

Anna tried not to worry that it was Connal's face she saw in her mind's eye as she had that thought. Connal's face, not Mike's. Not Henry's.

She forced her mind back to her work. Leaving the decision of choosing a graphics firm to Elspeth, she concentrated on the intricate puzzle of matching committees with volunteers and assigning them the most appropriate of the hundreds of tasks that needed to be done. The trick to any successful event, she had learned long ago, was to make everyone involved feel as if they'd been useful and heard and appreciated. She suspected, though, that she'd go deaf before everyone in Balwhither had their say.

Lost in the task, she jumped when Elspeth tapped her lightly on the shoulder.

"I hope you're not planning on going out with Connal dressed like that?" Elspeth said, smiling down at her. "You'll freeze, and he's going to be here in fifteen minutes."

Anna swept the papers back into their folders and charged toward the stairs. On the kitchen threshold, she turned back. "Are you sure it's all right for me to leave you with all this? You're not taking on too much, are you?"

"I'll rest when the festival is over. I'm the one who got us into it, after all, so don't try to use me as an excuse for being nervous about going out with Connal." Elspeth came over and drew Anna into an embrace that smelled of cinnamon, vanilla, and the heather sachets she kept in her sweater drawer. "I'm just thankful you are here. For many, many different reasons, including the fact that we need you."

Anna closed her eyes and felt damp warmth press against her lashes. Honestly, she needed to be here far more than anyone needed her. The chance to bury herself in meaningful work and help others had let her step away from her own problems enough to gain perspective, to discover things about herself. That was the best gift anyone could have given her at this point in her life.

"The gratitude is all on my side," she said, squeezing her aunt back so hard she embarrassed herself. "I don't know what I would have done if I'd given in and gone to Ohio like Mother wanted. Or sat around feeling sorry for myself in my apartment while I sent out resumes to a million law firms that were never going to hire a lawyer someone else had fired."

Elspeth smoothed a strand of Anna's hair and tucked it behind her ear. "Things happen for a reason. I firmly believe that, but sometimes we have to give them a little help. And we have to stop running long enough for the good in life to catch up with us."

Something in Anna's chest split open and inflated like a balloon, something full of hope, longing, and wonder. A red balloon, and she wanted to hold it in her fist and run with it up and down the loch while it caught the wind and flew.

HEAT AND SWEETNESS

I listened, motionless and still;
And, as I mounted up the hill,
The music in my heart I bore,
Long after it was heard no more.

WILLIAM WORDSWORTH, "THE SOLITARY REAPER"

A NNA WORE HER WARMEST COAT and sturdiest shoes, as Connal had requested. The climb wasn't long, but it was steep and required scrambling over sodden ground made more difficult by the half-dormant heather and the low bushes of clustered blaeberries that grew beneath it.

"People confuse them with blueberries," Connal explained, "but they're different. Bilberries, I think, is the proper English term for them."

"And I always thought Gregor Mark was English, but listen to you now."

"Aye." Connal laughed. "My father took us away from the glen when I was twelve and moved us to London. The accent's been creeping back on me bit by bit. Here, mind your step." He caught Anna's elbow when her feet skidded on a wet clump of grass.

Elsewhere in the glen, there were trampled-down paths that would have made for easier walking. Between the museum and Inverlochlarig, there was even a small carpark, deserted now, that gave access to Beinn a' Chroin and Ben More at the far end of the glen and Beinn Tulaichean and Cruach Ardrain, the nearest four of the high Munros that rose above the smaller hills. Connal had no interest in any of those more traveled paths. Hiking trails too often came with hikers, and though he laughed it off by saying he wanted to have Anna to himself if they were going to have a date, even now he wore a cap and sunglasses to screen his face.

Still, the climb wasn't bad. On the worst of it, he was careful to walk beside Anna, steadying her anytime she missed her footing. Otherwise, he twined his hand with hers. Which wasn't steadying at all.

His touch was unnerving. Every aspect of the day and the climb conspired to make Anna feel ready to burst out of her skin.

For once, the Highland drizzle had given way to a brilliant sky. Rain and grass and wildness perfumed the wind, and already on the slope behind Inverlochlarig House here and there a jonquil or a violet bloomed, providing a sharp burst of joyous color that struck Anna like an unexpected gift.

Halfway up the slope, they reached a gully sheltered from the wind. Connal stopped behind her and put his hands across her eyes. "Don't look yet," he said, and then he spun her around, her back brushing his chest and her skin warming beneath his fingers. He took his hands away. "Now open your eyes. What do you think? Was it worth the hike?"

"Oh yes," Anna breathed.

The glen spread out below her: the two lochs, the scattered farmhouses and the harled white stone buildings clustered in the village, the turquoise hotel and, just beneath them, the two gray mansions, Inverlochlarig and Breagh House, though the first dwarfed the latter. Low to the ground, the temperature was dropping instead of rising, a cold front sweeping in. Wraiths of fog had formed on the lakes, giving the whole picture an enchanted appearance, as if any moment a hand with a sword might emerge from the water, or Oberon and Titania might step out from the woods with their fairy hosts, laughing at something that Robin Goodfellow might have done.

"It's magical." She turned back to Connal and found him watching her instead of looking out at the glen.

"I believe it is," he said, his breath hitching just a little. He dipped his head and caught her lips with his own.

Heat and sweetness were instantaneous. Delicious. But Connal drew back after too brief a moment and swung the dark backpack off his shoulders. From it, he removed a red wool tartan blanket, which he shook out onto the ground, and a lighter cashmere one, which he tucked around Anna's shoulders as he urged her to sit. When she'd complied, he produced a bottle of wine, two crystal glasses carefully wrapped, a loaf of crusty bread, several boxes of food, plates, cutlery, and a pair of crisp linen napkins.

"I'll admit, this is a little more elaborate than I was expecting when you offered up a picnic," she said, helping him pop the lids from containers of smoked salmon pâté, Scotch eggs, individual cold beef pies, and golden-brown Empire biscuits with gleaming candied cherries set atop perfect dollops of creamy icing.

The wine gurgled into her glass as he poured, ruby red shot through with sunlight. "This should be champagne, since I told you it was a date. But I have to confess"—he smiled at her—"I didn't make the food. That was Agnes. I'm a little afraid of her, so we'll have to eat every bite, or I won't hear the end of it."

Anna's stomach growled as if on cue. She and Connal both laughed, and they watched each other while they filled their plates and ate amid easy conversation and occasional comfortable silences.

"So do you bring all your dates up here?" Anna asked, lightly but also seriously.

"I don't know if I should admit this, but I've never had a date here in the glen before."

"Never?" Anna let her lashes screen her eyes. "Then what do you do for company?"

"Moira's usually all the companionship I need, though I still have friends to visit. Julian Ashford, for one. I meet up with them in different places. Women, too, occasionally—if that's what you're asking. But I'm discreet. I can't afford to stir up tabloid interest."

"Don't you miss it, though?"

"Miss what?"

"The excitement of acting. Of being a star. Being able to go out in the world—to own the world."

Connal stretched out on the blanket and propped himself on one elbow. "I had the fame long enough to realize that celebrity isn't all it's cracked up to be. I loved being an actor, don't get me wrong. Sometimes I miss that part of it, the chance to put on someone else's skin and see how and why they are who they are, what makes them shift and change and settle into patterns of behavior. I miss the challenge of becoming someone else, and the brief release of not being myself. But honestly? No, I don't miss being Gregor Mark."

"So you'll never go back to it? Not even when Moira is grown and has her own life?"

"Whatever Moira wants, I'll support her with every inch of my being. I'm not an ogre, and I won't try to keep her here a minute longer than she wants to stay, but the world is cruel. I'll protect her from it as long as I can. We like to pretend that we can remake it with speeches of inclusiveness or do-good campaigns. Maybe in a decade or two or three, those ideas will have truly taken root. Realistically, I doubt it. Beauty is still prized too highly, and the lack of it is penalized. Moira's palsy would be less noticeable if the other half of her face was less beautiful than Isobel's. If she weren't Isobel's daughter. And mine."

"Have you decided what you'll do about letting her go to the festival? Can't she go without you? I could hear in her voice how much she wanted to go the Lochearnhead

Games and hear the pipers. And you said yourself it would be cruel to have all the activities here when she can't go."

"People will stare even if they don't know who she is. There's at least one more surgery when she's ready for it—when she makes the choice herself—but she'll never be as perfect in the eyes of the world as she is to me. All I can do for her is keep her away from the attention and tabloids saying cruel things long enough to let her grow into the person she is meant to be. Long enough for her to see who she is instead of what she looks like."

Anna studied him. He was staring down into the wine in his glass as though he could see Moira's future written there. But there was no such thing as a crystal ball. Anna couldn't help thinking how similar Connal's speech was to the things her own mother had so often said to her. With one significant difference: Connal was fighting to protect Moira from the world of superficial judgments until she was comfortable enough in herself to meet it. Anna's mother had tried to mold Anna to fit into that world.

Anna took Connal's hand and brought it to her lips. If she'd tried to speak right then, her voice would have given her away. Connal sat up and shifted beside her. Her legs were folded beneath her, which made her tilt against him. Which wasn't a bad thing.

Not that it was a good thing either. At some point, there was going to be a reckoning for the time she spent with him, and it was becoming increasingly obvious that the bill might be too high for her heart to pay.

Still, she decided to worry about that later. For three years, she had let herself settle for Mike and a nice, safe romance, and where had that gotten her?

Right here, her inner voice answered. Right now.

She was here with Connal, and for once, she was going to fight to stay firmly in the moment. As long as she was here, as long as Connal remained interested, she was going to enjoy every second they had together.

CASTING DOUBT

Lovers and madmen have such seething brains,
Such shaping fantasies, that apprehend
More than cool reason ever comprehends.

WILLIAM SHAKESPEARE, *A MIDSUMMER NIGHT'S DREAM*

R HONA GREWER WAS NOT HAPPY about playing understudy to anyone, not even the famous Vanessa Devereaux. Anna had hoped that having the chance to rehearse opposite tall, dark, and gorgeous Julian Ashford would diminish Rhona's anger. Judging by the stiletto heel thumping furiously against Rhona's chair leg and the hissing whispers she was exchanging with her daughters and Erica MacLaren, the announcement had failed to have that effect. Around them, the inn's green dining room was filled with people, every table occupied. Anna had to raise her voice to be heard over the clink of beer glasses, the rustle of fabric, and the low murmur of conversation. Nevertheless, Rhona managed to make her disgruntled comments audible above the noise.

Standing by herself at the front of the room to read the announcements, Anna had claimed responsibility for the casting decisions. It made sense for her to take the fall for the hard decisions about the festival. Apart from her, everyone else would have to stay and continue to live together after the event was over. She'd known taking the blame would not be easy. Even so, standing up here, she felt like she was facing the mean girls' table in a high school cafeteria. That didn't bode well for the next generation in the glen, either, considering that Sorcha, Fenella, and Erica—along with Moira's nanny—were the only women between the ages of seventeen and twenty-five.

She read off the last of the announcements and wasn't at all surprised when Rhona, Sorcha, and Erica all jumped up from their chairs.

"This isn't *fair*," Sorcha protested. "I auditioned to play *Helena*, not Hermia. I don't *want* to be Hermia."

"And I don't want to play Lysander," Erica said. "Why should I have to play a man?"

"We're having Lysander be a girl, remember," Anna said patiently. "Gender flipping."

Rhona ignored Anna completely. She turned to Connal, pouting. "You can't honestly mean to let *her* push us all out of the very best roles? Who said she should be the one to do the casting? Do something, Connal. This is supposed to be a community play! I've been rehearsing Titania the entire week. Now she's telling me I don't even have a part."

Connal shifted away from the wall where he'd been leaning. His expression managed to be equal parts forbidding and polite. "Despite how Anna has generously tried to take the blame, the casting choices are more mine than anyone else's," he said. "I'm the director, and I made the final decisions after going over the audition notes and input from her and Brando. I factored in what the professional actors are going to do and chose the cast that would give the play the best chance of success. If the three of you are upset about that, I'm sorry, but the decisions are final. Erica, you'll be great as Lysander. Fenella is best-suited to play Helena, and Sorcha, you will shine as Hermia."

Sorcha squinted at her twin and sniffed. "Helena is the better part."

"I wouldn't mind if Sorcha wants to play Helena. It's all right with me," Fenella said, her shoulders hunched beneath the weight of her sister's stronger personality.

"It's not all right with me, though," Connal said more kindly. "No casting decisions are ever going to give everyone what they want. We'll all have to do the best we can and use the fact that we have more female actors than men to make the play a bit more modern."

"What about me?" Rhona demanded. "It was my idea to do the play in the first place. You and Anna never even came back to see my audition. I should at least get another chance before you tell me I'm only to be an understudy."

"You're making our point for us, Rhona love. Don't you see?" Brando smiled at her, charm at full throttle. "The play was your idea, so you've already done a service to the village. Your name will go in the program as . . . creative inspiration." He glanced at Anna and Connal, who both shrugged approval. "Not to mention that it was your idea for Connal to direct. Now that he's persuaded Vanessa Devereaux to donate her time and talent, which will do wonders to bring people in for the festival, we owe you an even bigger debt."

"Then let me play one of the parts. Vanessa doesn't have to be both Titania and Hippolyta."

"I've already explained that," Connal said patiently. "We're using the original Shakespearean idea of doubling the Athenian characters and the fairy court, so Vanessa will play two roles the same way that Julian will be both Theseus and Oberon and Pierce will be Philostrate and Puck. Not to mention that Vanessa has a lot of fans—that's the point of getting well-known actors in for the lead parts. We want to bring in as many people as possible to see the play. Don't we?"

Rhona opened her mouth then closed it again without speaking. She shot Anna a look that could have shattered glass and sank back into her seat with a slow sibilance of air like a tire deflating.

Connal clapped once, loudly, and hurried on. "All right. Good. Now that's settled, everyone, come up here and collect your scripts, rehearsal schedules, and the individual notes I've made for you. Read them over in case you have questions. Starting tomorrow, we'll be moving our meetings to my house promptly at seven for the first rehearsal."

Anna stepped out of the way as the actors all surged forward. Rhona sent her a last poisonous glare and stalked past followed by Erica and the twins.

Brando sidled closer to whisper in Anna's ear. "I'd keep an eye on what you eat and drink as from now if I were you. And don't go near Rhona if she happens to have a knife."

"I'd worry more about Vanessa's health than mine," Anna said, only half-joking. "One bad piece of fish or a poisonous mushroom, and Rhona would get her chance to play Titania after all."

Brando laughed and patted her on the shoulder. "You are naive to the ways of the glen, aren't you, lass? It's not the play alone that's got Rhona glaring daggers. Connal's friendly enough, but he's kept mostly to himself all these years. This was going to be Rhona's big opportunity to impress him. At least that's how she'll have seen it. I'd bet you a dinner that he's the whole reason she suggested doing a play in the first place."

"You're joking?"

Tracing a cross over his heart, Brando shook his head. "I've no doubt Rhona's been dreaming of the two of them rehearsing lines together in front of a cozy fire, himself telling her how he'd never properly appreciated her beauty all these years, how he's sorry for all the time they've wasted. Instead, she's having to watch the two of you making calves' eyes at each other all night. You do know the temperature fair heats up in the room every time you exchange a look?"

"It does not," Anna said with her cheeks burning.

"Aye right, it doesn't," Brando answered, laughing at her.

The thought of watching—speculating about her relationship with Connal, whatever that relationship was or wasn't going to be—made Anna want to sink through the floor. The village was like her law firm or her parents' country club: every bit of gossip treated like currency that bought someone else a few moments of attention at her expense.

"In that case," she said, smiling at Brando, "I'll leave and let the temperature get back to normal. Meanwhile, *you* can finish helping Connal get things organized."

Brando straightened, looking pained. "We need you to referee."

"Actually, you don't." Anna patted him on the arm. "Try acting like grown-ups for a change. I should see how Elspeth's doing with the rest of the committees anyway."

Meeting Connal's gaze above the crowd circled around him, she pointed to herself then the door. He smiled, holding the look between them long enough to make her breath hitch, to make her remember what Brando had said. Connal's smile was like a physical touch, as though he'd reached out to her from across the room.

Rhona leaned in to whisper to Sorcha again. Both of them glared at Anna.

Anna hoped Connal knew what he was doing with those two, that was all she had to say. It was unlike Elspeth to be as harsh about anyone as she'd been about both Rhona and Sorcha that morning in the kitchen.

"Until a few years ago," Elspeth had confided to Anna earlier, "I'd have told anyone who asked that they'd be hard-pressed to find a person in the glen more self-absorbed than Rhona Grewer, but Sorcha has her bested. You watch yourself with both of them. And how we're supposed to choose between Sorcha and Fenella for May Queen, I haven't a clue, but it's between the two of them, Erica MacLaren, and JoAnne, who isn't properly from the glen at all. Anyway, JoAnne is still too furious about the festival to think of doing it. Erica has already done it twice, but she's not much better than Sorcha when it comes down to it. And if we pick Fenella, Sorcha will make her life a misery. The way Sorcha treats her sister, you'd think poor Fenella was as ugly as a toad, when the two of them are as alike as two sisters could ever look. "

"That's probably half of Sorcha's problem right there," Anna had answered, thinking of her own sisters—especially Katharine. "When you have to fight to make yourself stand out, you have to channel extra energy into believing in yourself. Some people start seeing themselves the way they want to be instead of the way they are. They justify a lot of things that shouldn't be excused."

Elspeth had gone silent, studying her across the table. "You're right, and I'm glad you see that. I'm not saying you should forgive your sister for what she did, don't get me wrong, but the longer you carry that emotional baggage around with you, the more you're letting her hurt you. And you know you can't keep avoiding your mother forever, either. Ailsa's ringing my phone off the hook."

"I'm not ignoring her. I email her at least twice every day," Anna had said.

Which wasn't the point, and she knew it, but the longer she went without talking to her mother, the less she wanted to talk to her. Was that so wrong? All right, maybe it was. Maybe it *was* cowardice on her part. Fine.

Just one more day of peace. That was all she needed. Two days, tops.

In the meantime, she needed to be careful not to equate Sorcha and Katharine. Comparing them wasn't fair, but Sorcha had that same look-at-me appearance, the same calculated loudness to her voice, the same flamboyant gestures that called attention to herself no matter what was going on elsewhere in a room. Fenella, by contrast, was quiet and conscientious and did her best to efface herself the moment she realized she'd become the focus of attention.

That couldn't work for long; Anna knew that from personal experience. She'd done the same thing with Katharine. Margaret, older by five years, had always been Katharine's role model, but with just a year between them, Anna had been competition. Everything between her and Katharine had been a contest. Like Fenella, at times, she'd tried making herself smaller, less of a target. It only made things worse.

Connal's casting had just set Fenella firmly in her sister's crosshairs. Stirring up the rivalry between them when they had to play two of the bigger roles in the play might not have been his most brilliant notion.

He might know women, but Anna had a lifetime of experience with her sisters. Every bit of that experience told her there was a confrontation brewing.

Chewing her lip, she crossed into the dimmer light of the pub room. After peering around briefly, she spotted Elspeth in the far corner where several long tables littered with half-filled beer glasses had been pushed together.

Elspeth looked up from addressing the men and two women who had signed up to form the organizing committee for the bagpipe competition as Anna joined them. "Are you all right?" Elspeth asked. "I take it the casting announcements didn't go over well? You're looking a bit pink and bothered."

"It's a little stuffy in here, that's all." Anna nodded around at the volunteers, who had stopped in mid-argument as she came up.

Elspeth introduced the few people Anna hadn't already met. Angus Greer, a slim man with a shock of unruly red hair, unfolded himself from his seat. He rose an abnormally long time, eventually towering over her at what had to be at least six-feet seven-inches as he shook her hand. His pretty wife Kirsty, in contrast, was all of five-foot-two, her hair dark as midnight and her scowl even darker.

"We need some rules for hours of practice," Kirsty said as Anna wedged herself in beside Elspeth at the table.

"Aw, sweetheart," Angus said, "we've been over this."

"You've been over it." Kirsty glowered at him. "I'm not over it. Not by a long shot." She turned back to Anna. "Elspeth says you're the one setting the rules, aren't you?"

Anna leveled her aunt a look. At this rate, she was going to end up being the most-hated person this side of Glasgow. "With advice from the people who know more than I do," she said, "but yes. Since I'm the official event planner, I have to take responsibility."

"Then tell these daft men there need to be set times when they can practice, would you?" Kirsty leaned forward on her elbows. "We can't have them caterwauling at all hours when decent folk are trying to sleep."

"I don't know anything about what it takes to prepare for a competition. Are there usually rules about practicing?" Anna asked.

"There should be. We'll all go do-lally if we have to listen to them wailing about for an entire month."

"How are we supposed to win if we can't practice? The trophies'll all go outside the glen," Erica MacLaren's brother Rory said before taking a sullen sip of his beer. Then he glanced up at Anna with the light shining on the top of his prematurely balding head and revealing the red veins that spider-webbed along the surface of his nose and ruddy cheeks. "This isn't something you've all cooked up to give an advantage to the MacGregor pipers, is it?"

Elspeth rounded on him. "How would setting practice times favor the MacGregors, I ask you? Unless you're implying that they're naturally better given the same amount of practice."

"I'm never saying that—"

"Then hold your tongue, man, and don't be an idiot. I've never chosen sides between MacGregors and

MacLarens in my life where this village is concerned, and Anna's certainly got no stake in doing so."

"She's seeing himself, isn't she?"

"And Connal has never taken sides either, when it comes to that." Elspeth turned to Kirsty. "You want my opinion, lass? Fine. Let the wives tell the men where and when to practice."

"Aw, now then. The likes of Rory'll have a leg up seeing as how there's not a woman born who'd have him," Kirsty's husband said.

"Then he's not likely to get a leg up very often then, is he?" said Iain Camm MacGregor, Angus's shorter, rounder cousin.

Laughter rippled around the table, and Rory turned the color of the deep red tablecloths in the dining room.

Kirsty banged her fist down hard enough to make the glasses rattle. "Treat it all as a joke if you want to," she said, turning to her husband, "but if I have to argue with you for an entire month, Angus Greer, you'll be looking for a new place to live by the end of it—"

"Nine o'clock in the morning to nine o'clock at night," Anna interjected quickly. "That will be the only practice time allowed, and anyone caught practicing outside of those hours will be disqualified. Good enough?"

"But no sneaking off outside the glen anywhere, mind," Iain Camm said. "Anyone caught doing that ought to be automatically disqualified."

"What about the pipers coming in from outside the glen? We'll be practically giving the trophy away," Rory said, scowling at him.

"Speaking of trophies," Anna said brightly, swallowing a groan. "We need a volunteer to order them, and a judge—"

"Judges," Angus said.

"From outside the glen," Rory said.

Iain Camm nodded morosely. "Aye, and not from anywhere nearby either, and no MacGregors or MacLarens."

Anna squeezed the bridge of her nose and shook her head. If the rest of the committees were half as bad as this, it was going to be a long month until Beltane. Maybe she'd been too hasty in swearing off Flora's Highland coffee.

THE HAND OF FATE

All the world is made of faith, and trust, and pixie dust.

J. M. BARRIE, *PETER PAN*

L ITTLE MORE THAN AN HOUR—and seven squabbling committee meetings—later, Connal stopped in front of Breagh House and turned toward the backseat of the Audi where Anna sat. He placed a staying hand on her forearm before she could get out.

"Are you too tired to come back for a nightcap?" he asked.

In the passenger seat beside him, Elspeth said a discreet good night and hurried out of the car. Fingers of ground fog curled around her feet as she walked toward the house, and thanks to the fatigue of the long day and too much time putting strain on her knee, her limp was more pronounced.

"I can't," Anna said, watching her. "I should make sure Elspeth gets some rest. If I leave her alone, she'll stay up going over schedules and trying to get the committees back on track. She's trying to do too much."

Connal's profile was shadowed, the only light cast by the glow of the lamps that trickled in from along the front of the house. "So are you. Don't let the village make you crazy. You'll end up twisting yourself into knots trying to please them all, and the truth is, you never will."

"I want to be fair. Right now, I don't understand the politics yet, and I'm afraid of upsetting people, but overall, I'm having fun. It's like a puzzle, and I'm turning the different pieces this way and that and trying to make them fit. I forgot how much I loved planning events."

"As much as you liked being a lawyer?" Connal turned to search her face, though Anna wasn't sure how much he could see written there amid the shadowed darkness.

It was another question she hadn't stopped to ask herself. There'd been too many changes too fast, too many realizations flying at her—and more kept coming every day.

Was she going to miss the law? The money, living in D.C., having something meaningful to do? Her work had become her identity, but what she'd loved about being a lawyer—the aspects that had drawn her to it in the first place—were the very things she loved about putting an event together. Defining a problem. Chasing research. Framing a story into something that persuaded people. Finding creative solutions. Making people happier.

When it came down to it, though, very little of her time since law school'd had anything to do with happiness.

How had she lost sight of that? She'd been determined to succeed, to climb out of the humiliation of Henry. She'd graduated at the top of her class and gotten good job offers, and she'd taken the best of the best of those— because that was what one did, wasn't it? What was expected. Somewhere in there, had she forgotten to ask herself what she actually wanted to do? Her work as a lawyer had become about winning and losing and billing hours.

Was that what she wanted?

No.

She clasped her hands together tightly. "Brando said something yesterday about the loch finding a way to make things happen for us no matter how we work against it. In spite of ourselves. I don't know about the loch, but it seems like something is pushing me to examine my life lately. To make changes."

Half-turned in his seat, Connal had gone still. "Lately, I feel like that every day," he said, sounding bemused. Then he unclipped his seat belt, got out of the car, and came around to open her door before he spoke again. "I'm trying to come to terms with the realization that all the plans and choices I have ever made have led me to somewhere I was meant to be, as if I never had any choice at all."

"What do you mean?" Anna peered up at him in the yellow glow of the carriage lamps.

He took her elbow and shook his head. "Someday, I'll explain. But it's an humbling feeling. We get puffed up with self-importance, wrapped up in our place in the world, and forget that there are much bigger things out there, things we can't begin to fathom. Things that simply require faith. That's all I'm saying."

Taking Anna's hand, he pulled her to her feet and stood looking down at her, his eyes shining in the light. The moon emerging from behind a bank of clouds cast a silver glow behind him. "You asked me a while ago whether I would ever go back to acting, and I didn't fully answer you. The truth is, I always loved losing myself in becoming someone else. Things were pretty miserable at home when I started acting, and that became a form of escape, I guess. Once I became a celebrity, being an actor was overshadowed. I lost the sense of myself and where I was going. Of what was important to me." He paused and swallowed hard, his Adam's apple bobbing. "When I lost Isobel, I thought coming back here would be what was best for Moira. It never occurred to me that this was where I was supposed to be. But it is. I'm supposed to be right here—"

Something in his voice, in the way he watched Anna, said that he wasn't quite finished speaking. She waited for him to go on. His eyes flickered, and a muscle twitched in his cheek, but then he only lowered his head with exquisite slowness until his lips settled over hers. His hands cupped her cheeks, tilted her head up to meet him, drew her closer.

Kissing Connal MacGregor set Anna's every nerve ending on fire, burned away doubt and her ability to think, made every pore of her skin crackle with heat and life. She lost herself in his kiss and the wide-openness of the glen at night, where the silence was broken only by their own labored breathing, the call of the night birds, and the lap of the water curling up against the shore.

"Come to lunch again tomorrow," Connal said as he pulled away.

"I will." She hugged the indefinable scent of him to herself, musk and spice and promise, as she returned to Elspeth's house. Still smiling, she made her way back to the warm light trickling from the kitchen.

SABOTAGE

I am learning that criticism is not nearly as effective as sabotage.

ANONYMOUS

THERE WAS ALWAYS a fresh disaster to mediate: the never-ending squabbles between Sorcha and Fenella, Rhona's pouting, pipers almost coming to blows over the choice of songs for the closing ceremony, someone stealing posters. But at noon every day, Anna took a break and spent a couple of hours with Connal—and often Moira.

Connal seemed desperate to show her the entire glen. They spent hours walking the braes, flying an incredibly ugly kite that Moira and Anna made together along the loch, visiting the MacLarens' gathering place at Creag an Tuirc, the waterfall, the grave of the Reverend Kirk on the hillside, and the burial places of the "Children of the Mist," the MacGregors in the glen whose clan name had been taken from them.

It was too cold for Moira to come with them the day they went to the cemetery, and too cold for all but the most determined tourists. Connal and Anna wandered alone among the tombstones. The wind blew a lament through the ruins of the old stone church, stinging Anna's cheeks, while out on the hillsides it made the heather bushes dance.

"You should have a thicker jacket." Connal took off his green scarf to wrap around her neck when she shivered despite the many layers she'd worn. "I'm going to make you catch your death dragging you around like this, aren't I? I'm sorry. I'm being selfish."

"I love every minute," Anna said, though mostly she loved seeing him as happy as he was when they were out walking in the glen.

"Do you really not mind? I always feel the clock running out this time of year. Rambling like this, before the hikers and campers are out in force, is the only time I feel free. I want to spend as much of the day outdoors as I can."

Anna slanted a look at him as she burrowed deeper into the softness of the scarf. He had so much energy out here in the glen or when he was directing the play, always moving, circling the actors, repositioning them, demonstrating how to read a line. It was hard to picture him cooped up indoors with only Moira for company, both of them isolated from the world, from life, by a stone wall and a decade of distrust.

"Would you really never go back to acting? I can't picture you rattling around in the house all day. Cutting yourself off from being creative."

His expression went blank. "There's always plenty to keep me occupied. Raising a smart child requires creativity in itself. Not to mention that a house this age and size takes time and effort to keep up, and there are investments. Reading. Music. There's always something. But there's too much baggage with a career like mine. You either give in to the public nature of that, or you stay completely private. Either way, the public and the media think they know you, and what they don't know, the tabloids make up. I was too young and excited by it all at first to realize how much it cost me. Then gradually, I found myself playing a role off-screen as much as on, wearing a mask to protect myself. By the time I lost Isobel, I'd lost track of what was beneath the mask." Tangling his fingers through Anna's, Connal gently pulled her toward him and stood looking down at her. He released his breath, not quite a sigh but close. "When I'm with you, I feel more like myself than I can remember feeling in years." Admitting that appeared to surprise him.

Anna found herself smiling against his lips. She was usually the one who blurted things out to him or Elspeth, as if their conversations lanced open wounds she'd been carrying inside so long they'd festered into abscesses.

Talking to Connal was easy. He listened without judging, but he didn't shy away from the sore spots either. The first night they hadn't had a play rehearsal or a committee meeting to juggle, they sat reading together on the floor of the tower library, their legs stretched out on the soft, worn carpet. A fire crackled in the hearth, and between that and a deep glass of wine, Anna felt warm and comfortable.

She turned a page in the old copy of *Wuthering Heights* she had pulled off the shelf and wondered why she had once loved the book so much. Heathcliff wasn't romantic, merely depressing. Looking up, she found Connal watching her.

"What?" she asked.

He set aside the nonfiction book he'd been reading. "Have you spoken to your mother yet?"

"Did Elspeth ask you to talk to me?" Anna closed her eyes. "I know I should, but I can't. I need to sort things through on my own, find my feet again. She makes me feel like I'm ten years old again whenever I talk to her."

"Parents always do that," Connal said. "It's in the rulebook."

Anna's smile was barely there. "I've felt like the odd one out in the family since I was ten, as if nothing I do is right, and I don't know how to fix that. I wish we could be friends, at least with Margaret and my mother."

"Not your other sister?"

"Katharine? Trust me, that ship sailed a long time ago. I'd sink it in the deepest ocean I could find, given half a choice."

Connal sat up and pulled her to rest against his chest. "Why?"

Leaning back against him, she found herself telling him about Katharine and Henry. "I don't know if I would have seen what he really was if I'd been looking for it; he had me fooled all along. But Katharine—she'd always been a selfish liar, taking anything I had that she wanted and managing to make it seem like my fault I had lost it. Even now, in my mother's mind, I'm the one who's being unreasonable for not making up with Katharine. It doesn't matter how old I get, I can't break the patterns set when we were children."

Connal gathered Anna closer. "Family relationships are hard because you can't get rid of them. Your relatives see you through the lens of the events they've shared with you. Then you grow up and live through new experiences without them. You change, but they don't know that because they weren't there to see it."

"Is that what it's like with your family?" Anna shifted in his arms so she could see his face.

"There's only my mother, and she's remarried to an Italian count, living in Perugia. She sweeps in a couple of times a year, despairs of me ever giving Moira the mother she desperately needs, then flies out again without seeing the irony of that statement."

"And your father?"

Connal rested his chin on the top of Anna's head. "He died when I was twelve. Cancer. But he was a great father. I was heartbroken, losing him. That was the reason my mother let me audition for my first film. It gave us both something to think about other than the fact that he was dying. A way to cope. The odd thing is, she was on the brink of divorcing him when he first got sick, and then she was inconsolable after he was gone."

Anna thought about her own parents, the way they argued constantly, never happy with each other's company. Would they have been better off divorcing? Her father spent most of his time retreating to the office or the golf course, and even when the two of them attended a party together, they would end up on opposite sides of the room. She had always blamed her mother for that, but why had her father never left? Would it have made either of them any happier?

She wished she was stronger when it came to her mother. Typing an email was easy. Picking up the phone was almost impossible.

That didn't keep her mother from calling a dozen times a week.

The phone rang in the study. It could have been someone calling about the festival, or a friend calling Elspeth, but three-twenty in Scotland meant ten-twenty in Cincinnati when Ailsa Cameron was just leaving her morning yoga class and getting into her car. Pointing to herself, Anna shook her head and mouthed, "I'm not here."

Lips thinning, Elspeth picked up the phone. "Hallo?"

Her mother's side of the conversation wasn't audible, but Anna didn't need to hear it.

Elspeth released a pent-up breath. "I have given her your messages, Ailsa. I can't help it that she's not here—the festival keeps her busy. No, she won't turn on her phone. She's doing her best to save money. And yes, I've told her you'd pay for it."

Holding the phone away from her ear an inch, Elspeth waited while Anna's mother, presumably, cycled through the same things she repeated every day. But then Elspeth's expression stiffened.

"Oh, for the love of heaven, Ailsa, don't be silly. I'm not trying to take her away from you. Anna's a grown woman. She makes her own decisions. Maybe if you'd listen to what she has to say once in a while instead of lecturing, she'd be more ready to hear your side in return. Can't you just give her some space? Not everything in the universe revolves around you." Elspeth slammed the phone down and shoved the charging cradle farther away into the corner of her desk, as if increasing the space between herself and the instrument could keep her sister at a safer distance, too.

"I'm sorry," Anna said.

"I'm just going to stop picking it up from now on."

"No, don't do that. It's not fair of me to make you keep putting her off—you've worked so hard to stay friends with her."

Elspeth directed a sharp look at Anna. "How do you know that?"

Anna hadn't thought about it, but it was obvious looking back. "Because you've always been patient with her. You're the one who did the listening, and you're the one who went to Cincinnati every year. Although maybe that's good. I'd hate to think of her getting on a plane and coming to lecture me in person."

"She'd have to face her own demons before she did that, love." Elspeth pulled her laptop closer and clicked the trackpad to turn the screensaver off. "Half the reason your mother spends her time meddling in other people's problems is so she doesn't have to think about her own mistakes. But you are going to have to talk to her sooner or later. You know that."

"Which mistakes?" Anna asked.

Elspeth shook her head, her lips pressed together so tightly it was apparent nothing was getting past them. She went back to hunting and pecking at the keyboard, assigning booth numbers for the festival's arts, crafts, and food concessions.

Anna let it go. There were plenty of other things to worry about. With only a week and a half to go before the festival, the small bits of mischief that had been plaguing them all along had suddenly grown more serious, and she had urgent phone calls to make.

At seven o'clock the next morning, the doorbell rang. The sun was still low in the sky, and the loch was wraithed in mist. Anna answered and found Brando on the stoop, stamping his feet against the cold. "We have another problem," he said, brushing past her. "The posters are gone again. I've replaced the bloody things around the village three times already, and the one on the highway at the glen turnoff as well. What do you want to do? I've only got one left out of the batch I picked up from the printers."

He followed Anna into the kitchen and dropped into a chair as Elspeth said good morning from where she was making pie crust at the counter. Brando blew on his hands to warm them, and Anna huddled deeper into her sweater as if he'd brought the cold in with him from outside as she stood beside him.

"Whoever's behind it is getting a bit more creative," she said. "We've been assuming it was kids, or pranks, but someone called and canceled the order for portable toilets yesterday. I spent an hour calling some of the other vendors last night and found two more who'd had calls asking for changes or cancellations. Needless to say, neither Elspeth nor I are making those calls."

Brando's eyebrows rose. "You think someone's actively trying to sabotage the festival?"

"I don't know what to think. Maybe the posters are actually a blessing in disguise. Are you going back to Edinburgh today?"

"Julian Ashford's arriving this afternoon, but he's driving himself from the airport. I suppose I could run in before that if you needed, though I don't see much point in putting more up if they're going to disappear again."

"No, what I'm wondering if there's a store in Edinburgh somewhere that sells camera traps. The kind people use for photographing wildlife."

Elspeth turned where she was rolling out the dough. "You want to catch whoever it is in the act? I'm not sure that's a good idea."

"Why not?" Eyes narrowing, Brando shifted to study her. "Do you suspect someone? Aye, you do. Who is it, and what do you know that you're not saying?"

Elspeth shook her curls and turned back to rolling out the dough. "I don't know anything. It could be anyone," she said too quickly. "There's still Rhona for one thing. We've suspected her all along, and I wouldn't put it past either Erica or Sorcha to do something sly to get back at us. Kirsty and Angus are barely speaking to each other, and Kirsty blames it all on the festival. They'll end up divorced over the piping competition if he's not careful—"

"You think it's JoAnne, don't you? That's the only person you'd protect," Anna said.

"Now, why would it be JoAnne?" Elspeth asked, her voice rising as she hastily turned away.

"Come on. Kirsty? You didn't really expect to sell us that, and JoAnne's made no secret of how much she hates the festival. She's barely even speaking to you—and you should see how she glares daggers at me whenever Connal and I take Moira out walking with us in the afternoons."

"Plenty of other people have better reasons than that." Elspeth dropped the rolling pin on the wooden cutting board, sending a puff of flour into the air. "Lilieth down at the farm across from the campsite, for example. She's fit to be tied over what the extra campers will do to upset her livestock. Not to mention there's Mackenzie Stewart who's livid because we wouldn't pay to set up concrete pads for caravan sites in his back pasture. Other people are angry that the guest list for the Beltane Ball is smaller because we have to hold it here. It could be anyone."

Brando watched Elspeth a moment longer then gave a barely perceptible shake of his head and turned his attention back to Anna. "If you're serious about the camera trap, I could have a chat with Connal's groundskeeper. Logan's had a camera set to catch poachers at the osprey's nest at the end of the loch, but he might loan it to us for a night or two. Problem is, whatever I tell him will be all around the village in half an hour."

"Aye, that's the truth," Elspeth said. "Man's a terrible gossip."

Anna bit her lip. "I could ask Connal, I suppose. Quietly. If it's JoAnne, he'd have to know sooner or later anyway."

"I won't have that poor girl losing her job over this." Elspeth shook the rolling pin at Anna. "Not when you've no idea whether she's guilty. Moira loves her to pieces, and JoAnne needs the work."

"I'm not saying this has anything to do with how she takes care of Moira, Aunt Elspeth, and Connal wouldn't be unfair to her. He isn't like that."

"The village would be. They've never liked JoAnne much to start with, and they won't tolerate her meddling in the festival—if that's what she's been doing. So much as a whiff of accusation, and they'll as good as convict her for it."

"Which is all the more reason for us to find out who's behind it before anything more serious happens. The longer we let this go, the greater the risk that she'll do something more extreme."

"*If* it's her," Elspeth said. "Which I doubt."

"Yes, if." Anna got up and poured Brando a cup of tea and brought it back to him while Elspeth turned to smooth the pie dough into submission. That, apparently, was easier to wrangle than a mystery. Or the village, for that matter, where everyone saw resistance as their duty and inalienable right.

Brando set the cup and saucer Anna gave him on the table. "Thanks."

"I'll talk to Connal at lunch," Anna said, sitting down on the edge of the chair beside him. "If he'll agree to loan us the camera, could you find time to collect it and set it up by the highway? We want that part to be quiet, obviously, but make a production of setting up the poster. Make sure everyone knows it's the last one we have. Meanwhile, I'll call in to the printer as soon as they open this morning and see how soon they can get us another batch."

Once Brando had gone, she spent the morning helping Elspeth move display cases in the museum in an effort to turn it back—somehow—into a ballroom. Leaving Elspeth to handle the smaller pieces, she went back to juggling finances, making phone calls, and drafting another press release. The bills kept adding up, and the village fund was dwindling, and half the people she called from the long list of suppliers who were providing everything from the tent and the folding chairs to T-shirts and awards were out or busy and needed to call her back.

At eleven-thirty, she handed Elspeth an extensive list of notes about phone calls and helped her aunt lift down a few additional museum exhibits from the walls and tuck them beneath the tables. Then she left to have lunch with Connal.

She didn't love the prospect of confronting him about JoAnne, but she had to admit she almost hoped Moira's nanny was behind the sabotage. At least that way there was a chance Connal could make it stop.

TANGLED WEBS

Oh, what a tangled web we weave . . . when first we practice to deceive.

SIR WALTER SCOTT, *MARMION*

T HE AIR WAS TOOTH-CHATTERINGLY COLD. Occasional swirls of snowflakes drifted out of the gunmetal clouds only to melt before they hit the ground, adding to Anna's worries. What if there was snow for the festival? Staring up at the blowing sky, she drew her hat lower and pulled her scarf up to cover her nose, hoping Connal wouldn't want to go out walking in this weather, much less bring Moira with them. But she hated the idea of disappointing either of them, so she'd prepared herself by wearing Elspeth's winter coat and bundling up in extra layers.

After a quarter mile, the path skirted around the high stone wall that surrounded Inverlochlarig House and veered off toward the carpark and the trail up into the hills. Anna turned the other direction and crossed through a thin wood until she reached a narrow side gate that led onto Connal's property. Using the spare key he'd given her, she let herself inside.

The manor itself sat back from Loch Fàil and Loch Daoine amid landscaped grounds that ran all the way down to the peninsula between the two lochs where the Sighting would take place. The dark blue water on either side glowed like a jewel among the surrounding braes. It was the prettiest scenery in all the glen.

Anna locked the gate behind her and cut through the copse of pale-trunked birch trees, skirted a border of bare rose bushes, and crossed the lawn to the wide front steps. Her hand raised to ring the bell, she twitched in surprise when the door opened before she had the chance.

Erica MacLaren, as blond and pretty as her brother Rory was gruff and balding, took a step toward her, emerging from the darkness. Standing on the stoop, Anna blinked into the dim interior.

"Sorry," Erica said. "I didn't mean to startle you. Lorna's got me in to do the monthly deep-clean today. She's in the kitchen if you're looking for her, and Connal's in the library." Holding the door open wider, she stepped back again in invitation, a feather duster in her hand and the kind of half-smile on her lips that suggested she probably wasn't sorry at all. Instead of relaxing into the role of Lysander as the rehearsals went on, she'd only gotten more resentful, and Anna decidedly was not one of her favorite people.

Anna took off her hat and unwound the scarf from around her head. "Is Moira up in the playroom with JoAnne?"

"No, they've gone out wandering somewhere, the two of them, before Moira has to go back to her lessons. JoAnne asked Lorna to pack a lunch."

Anna glanced back out the open door, not sure whether to be annoyed, or worried, or grateful. But while the snowflakes were drifting down more quickly, they still weren't sticking to the ground, and she reminded herself that Moira wasn't as fragile as she appeared. Anyway, she had no business interfering with when or where JoAnne took Moira. JoAnne and Connal had done a good job with Moira long before Anna had arrived, and Moira was going to be fine once Anna was gone. She needed to remember that.

The thought still made her breath catch. Time was slipping away too fast.

Crossing to the left, she entered the great hall beyond the foyer. Lined by triple rows of long-dead stags, antique refractory tables, and equally ancient oriental rugs, the room was flanked by enormous drafty stone fireplaces on either end that made it feel even colder. She left her coat on and hurried to where a set of narrow stone steps led into the three-story tower that housed the library and Connal's study.

Connal sat at his desk, backed by shelves of books and a cheerful fire. The bluish glow of a laptop screen framed his face, and he appeared lost in thought, chewing the end of a red pencil and frowning down at a stack of printed pages laid out in front of him.

Anna's chest squeezed, a feeling on the cusp of pain and pleasure.

She stole a moment in the doorway for the sheer enjoyment of watching him, but as always, he seemed to know by instinct that she was there. A smile broke over his face, and he jumped to his feet to meet her.

"I didn't hear the door," he said, coming around the side of the desk.

"Erica saw me coming and let me in."

He kissed her then stepped back to study her. "You look worried. Is something wrong?"

"Can we talk for a moment?"

His eyebrows quirked together into a question. "Well, that doesn't sound at all ominous."

"I'm not sure ominous is the right word. More like troubling." Anna shed her coat, scarf, and hat and sank into the deep navy cushions of one of the armchairs that stood in front of the carved antique desk. It was a chair in which Connal sometimes sat to work himself, and it smelled like him: his shampoo and aftershave and the crisp scent of the wind sweeping across the loch and over the heather-covered hills.

She explained about the most recent theft of the posters before confiding the rest. "These latest things may have nothing to do with the posters at all, but taken together it's made me wonder how many other small things that we've been dismissing as bad luck, or simple error, or blaming on kids were just part of a bigger picture. I wouldn't have known about the canceled order for the toilets at all if the company hadn't assumed I'd gotten a better offer and called to suggest a discount. I've had to spend yesterday afternoon and this morning calling around to every vendor and making sure everything is still scheduled for the right dates. On top of that, I found two websites where someone called to have the festival listing taken down, and I haven't even checked all the rest of the websites yet—Elspeth is sending out a follow-up press release today, and we'll have to make more phone calls."

"You have any idea who's behind it?" Connal lowered himself into the chair beside her.

Anna glanced at him then smoothed her scarf out along her lap. "Elspeth suspected JoAnne—she won't admit it, but that's who she has in mind. And I have to concede that makes sense. Everyone else is at least involved in the festival or stands to benefit in one way or another. JoAnne's the only one who still wants to stop it outright. Of course, we can't accuse her now, and I'm not saying there aren't any other suspects. I guess I'm asking for your opinion—that and I'd like to borrow the camera trap Logan has set up by the osprey's nest and try to catch whoever is stealing the posters in the act. Hopefully, it's the same person, and that would solve the problem."

"JoAnne?" Connal shook his head.

"You're saying it can't be her?"

"My first instinct is that it isn't—if I thought she was capable of anything like this, I wouldn't dare have her around Moira, of course . . . "

"But?" Anna twisted the scarf between her fingers.

"But she's not the easiest person to know, and she can fly into a dither if someone so much as looks at her crosswise. Scared as a rabbit, sometimes." Sitting with his legs spread, Connal leaned forward and clasped his hands between his knees.

"So what do you want to do? Can we use the camera trap?"

"Of course, but for the rest, I honestly don't know. I suppose the fact that I can't dismiss her involvement outright means I have a problem. She's protective of Moira, which is good, and maybe a little possessive, which wouldn't be. She knew you were coming today, but she still wanted to take Moira out before the snow came down. I filed it away as something to keep an eye on. You think it's more than that?"

Anna smoothed the scarf again. "I don't know her, Connal. She's barely spoken to me. Moira's sweet and charming once she opens up. It's not my place to meddle, so forget I said anything."

"How can I forget?" Connal asked, his expression stunned. "All I've ever wanted is for Moira to be happy, to be confident. But you're right. It still takes her time to open up when she meets someone. JoAnne doesn't like people much, and I stay away from strangers. I hate the idea that the two of us could unconsciously be encouraging Moira not to trust anyone she doesn't know."

"We've talked about the festival—you know how much she wants to go."

"And I gave in this morning when she pestered me again," Connal said, smiling faintly.

"That's fantastic." Anna leaned toward him, beaming. "I'm so happy you've decided to go."

"I can't go." Connal shook his head. "That hasn't changed. I'm still not sure letting Moira go is the right decision. What if someone says something to her? What if something happens?" Connal stared down at the floor, his face reflecting all the what-ifs he'd already catalogued and feared.

Self-conscious watching him, Anna looked away. His desk was messy, the usual neat stacks of folders tumbled over, a pile of crisp white papers fanned out across the scratched leather blotter, red pencil marks visible on the pages. A name caught her eye, and she drew the paper toward her.

"Are these the final script changes that Vanessa Devereaux wanted?" she asked.

"No!" Connal's hand shot out to grab her wrist.

But Anna had already pulled the paper close enough to see the rest of the title page:

```
                          THE RARE ENCOUNTER
                       AN ORIGINAL SCREENPLAY
                             BY GRAHAM CONNOR
```

```
FADE IN:
EXT. BROWNSTONE APARTMENT (NEW YORK), STEPS - NIGHT
ANGLE ON apartment doorway. It opens and DELILAH
CHAMBERS a
```

That was all that registered before Connal had jumped up to gather the pages together and slip them into a folder. He circled back around the desk, shoved the file into a drawer, and stood looking at Anna, breathing a little rapidly. His face was pale, and his lips twitched as though he was searching for words of explanation.

Anna's heart shriveled as if he'd splashed it with ice cold water. Already part of her was drowning. Disappearing.

She pushed herself slowly to her feet. "So that's why Graham Connor was so willing to be accommodating about the play, I guess. And why you don't mind not having a creative outlet."

"I was going to tell you. I simply haven't found the right moment—"

"Really? What about when I asked you about going back to acting? Or whether you missed having a creative outlet? Or whether you weren't bored rattling around here by yourself? When you confided in me about how much you'd lost your sense of self, how you and Isobel had started acting too young, how you'd been plunged into a world where nothing was real? Or when I told you how betrayed Henry had made me feel, how I've wondered all these years whether our relationship was ever real or whether he'd been acting a part from the very beginning?" Anna snatched her coat and scarf from the back of the chair. "You've been hiding yourself from me, Connal. You didn't trust me. You didn't believe in me enough to share the fact that you were Graham Connor, so how do I know if anything about you is real?"

Even as she asked, Anna realized that whatever Connal answered wouldn't matter. How could she believe anything he said?

"Anna, wait. Please. What we have *is* real. I swear to you—"

"Anna!" Footsteps raced up the stairs, and Moira ran into the room, her hair fanning behind her like a streak of liquid platinum. She threw her arms around Anna's waist with a lopsided grin that made her wind-reddened face look even more as though half of it had begun to melt. "I was coming to find you." She turned back to her father. "Did you ask her yet?"

"Ask me what, sweetie?" Anna smiled. It was impossible not to smile at Moira.

"If you and Elspeth will take me to the games and the trimming of the May Bush and the Beltane Ball for a little while. Daddy said I could go if I went with you, but he won't take me, and he says I can't go to the bonfire because that's past my bedtime."

Anna turned toward the door as Moira's nanny arrived and stopped on the landing outside. "What about JoAnne?"

JoAnne looked at her with startled eyes then quickly ducked her head. Not much taller than Moira herself and dwarfed by a flowing skirt and shapeless sweater, the woman always managed to look fragile and a little scattered. Even her hair, swept into a ponytail, was a corkscrew mass of curls that didn't seem to know which way to go.

"I'm not about to have anything to do with that festival." JoAnne's breathy voice held a hard, sharp edge.

"I've said as much to Connal, and I wish you wouldn't go putting thoughts in Moira's head."

"Maybe this isn't the time to talk about that," Anna said.

Moira scowled at JoAnne. "I've gone every year. I *want* to go."

"It was only the glen then," JoAnne said. "Just us."

Anna sighed. "The glen very much needs the festival to go forward smoothly. For that, we need everyone to pull together, including you."

"You've no right!" JoAnne raised her chin and scowled at Anna. "You've no right to speak for anyone in the glen. All you've done is come in from outside and spoil things."

"You moved here from Glasgow yourself," Connal said firmly. "The rest of the village is grateful for everything Anna's doing to help, and this *isn't* the time to talk about it."

"How can you say that? You know what could happen." JoAnne put a hand on Moira's shoulder. "You know how people are—"

"That's enough, JoAnne," Connal's voice had gone grim and cold, "but just so that we are very clear: you are not to do anything to work against the festival either. No tricks or pranks, however mild."

JoAnne's face reddened, and her feet shifted toward the door as though she wanted to run. "I wouldn't."

"Good," Connal said. "I hope I don't hear otherwise."

Anna wanted him to say more, to tell Moira that JoAnne hadn't meant what she'd said about people—that it was all right for Moira to look forward to having fun. That wasn't her place, though.

And she was tired . . . So tired of all of the holding back. The hiding. His. Hers. Because wasn't she hiding, too? Hiding from her mother? From reality. From herself. What else had these past weeks of pretending there could be anything real between herself and Connal been other than a form of self-deception?

She couldn't look at him. She couldn't pretend that things were the same between them. She needed time to think and process. What had she thought she was doing with a man like Connal—or Gregor Mark, or Graham Connor? Whatever he chose to call himself.

Who was he, really? Did she have any idea?

She'd always thought it was awful when television shows talked about women in bad relationships having a "type"—making the same mistakes over and over with the same kind of men. Was Connal any different than Henry? But what did it matter, when it came down to it? In just over two weeks, she was leaving. Better that she knew what Connal was like now. She'd have two weeks to shore herself up instead of spending all that time deceiving herself with who she wanted him to be.

Her throat ached, and her eyes stung at the thought. At the situation in general.

Still, she couldn't let that show. Moira stood watching all of them with her eyes wide and hesitant.

Anna stopped in front of her and smiled with every ounce of conviction that she could dredge up within herself. "I'm glad you're as excited about the festival as I am, Moira, and Elspeth and I will be happy to have you with us. We'll have an amazing time, the three of us. We'll watch all the games, and the dancing, and the piping competition. But we'll talk more about that later, all right? For now, I need to get back and take care of some things. I was just about to leave when you came tearing in."

"What about that thing you and I were in the middle of discussing?" Connal asked from behind her. There was strain in his voice now, almost a note of fear.

Anna realized she'd forgotten her hat, and she turned and snatched it from the chair. She couldn't help seeing his expression then, white and pinched and worried.

"You and I will have to talk about that some other time," she said, with no intention of discussing it with him again at all. Brushing past JoAnne, she hurried toward the steps.

NEVER LOVED SO BLINDLY

Had we never lov'd sae blindly,
Never met—or never parted—
we had ne'er been broken-hearted

ROBERT BURNS, "AE FOND KISS"

B EHIND ANNA, the front door crashed open and Connal
shouted, "Anna, wait!"

Anna ignored him and rushed on through the copse of
silver-trunked birches toward the narrow side gate. The key
shook in her hand when she worked the lock, and a fresh
flurry of snowflakes brushed her face, catching in eyelashes
wet with tears of fury. Impatiently, she brushed away both
the warmth and ice and slammed the gate behind her.

Connal gave another shout. "Anna, please. Hold up!"

She knew she couldn't ignore him forever. Lately, she'd
been ignoring too many things she couldn't face. She'd told

herself that was part of living in the moment, but all she'd been doing was setting herself up for brand-new heartache.

Nothing good ever came of throwing your heart away. Of trusting blindly.

On the other hand, what had caution ever brought her? A limbo of going to work and coming home, getting engaged to someone she liked—a lot—but didn't love. Not with all her soul. She'd convinced herself she was happy. She had been happy, but it had been a half-asleep happiness that was colorless compared to the wide-awake, pure joy that being with Connal gave her. When had she ever paused to watch Mike for the pleasure of looking at him? It wasn't Connal's looks that took her breath away; it was so much more than that. It was the way the light caught his eyes and made them exactly ten times more alive than anyone else she'd ever met, the way he would pause at the crest of a hill and watch a hawk surfing the wind, his face filled with wonder and longing as if, in that moment, he could imagine himself gifted with the miracle of flight.

God, how could she have been so stupid? Hadn't she learned *anything* since Henry?

She spun to face Connal as his feet pounded on the path behind her. "What did you think I was going to do when I found out?" she demanded. "How did you think I was going to feel?"

"Anna." He raised his hand to cup her face, his fingers trembling lightly with cold or emotion—he hadn't even stopped to put on a coat. She pulled back, and he dropped the hand, fingers curling uselessly at his sides. "Please listen," he said. "When I told you that no one knows I'm

Graham, I meant no one at all. Not one person except my agent, and she has to know. It wasn't something I ever set out to do. I was going stir-crazy when I first brought Moira here, and she never slept. Until she was nearly two, I was up rocking her half the night, so I started sitting at the computer with her on my lap, writing my thoughts out in the small hours. The thoughts turned into stories. Into escapes. I had no idea what I was doing, or whether what I was writing was any good. I never said a word to my agent for a year and a half after I'd finished the first screenplay, and by that time I'd written three of them—"

"That doesn't have anything to do with the fact that you lied to me."

"Please. Just listen." Connal's breath came in hard white puffs, his chest rising hard. "My agent and I came up with the pen name together, not only because the first whiff of anything related to Gregor Mark was going to stir things up again, but also because we were afraid people would always see a Gregor Mark movie in the writing even when it wasn't there. That was the last thing I wanted. We talked about masks a while ago, you and I. Well, Gregor wasn't—isn't—a mask. He's me. Naked and bare and raw, and it's taken me years to understand that. To recognize myself in the words I put down on the page." Lines of sincerity furrowed into Connal's face, as if it mattered that Anna believed him.

How could she tell if he was being honest? If he was real?

He raised his hand, reaching toward her once more, and she took another backward step.

His shoulders tensed again, and he bowed his head. "What I'm trying to say is that I haven't told a soul about my writing. Not even Moira knows, and she's been the most important thing in my life—the only important person in my life until you. I've kept this secret so long, I didn't know how to share it, and around here, a secret spreads like fire. Any little thing is liable to burn down the refuge I've tried to build for Moira."

"Are you sure it's Moira you're protecting?"

"What do you mean? Everything I've done has been for her."

"Yes, and now she's going to the festival, and you aren't. You're still hiding."

"What kind of fun would she have if everyone stared at her because of me? If I was suddenly the center of attention?"

"We're all a product of our parents. Their mistakes. Their choices. Moira's strong. She's kind and generous. Thoughtful. And she's smart. She's seen herself in the mirror. She knows what she looks like. I'm not saying maybe it isn't a good idea to let her experience the festival as her own person instead of as your daughter, but I still don't think you're being fully honest with yourself about your reasons. You're lying to yourself as much as you lied to me. That's even more dangerous—I know that from personal experience."

"So what are you saying?" Connal's eyes glittered, but he looked away and stood hunch-shouldered, fists pushed down into the pockets of his jeans. "Where does that leave us?"

"It leaves us with a lot of work to do until the festival then a quick good-bye when I go home—which is what I was always going to have to do." Anna's voice quivered. "Hopefully, it leaves us friends. You can trust me, though. I won't tell anyone your secrets."

Turning away was one of the hardest things that Anna had ever done. She gathered her dignity and walked on through the flurrying snow and the damp, mildewed leaves left over from the previous fall. Connal didn't follow her, and the more distance she put between them, the more she felt as if she'd reached into her chest and torn her heart out, leaving herself numb and empty.

Shivering a few minutes later, she stomped her feet on the mat at the front door to Breagh House and let herself inside. As always, the house did its best to wrap her in warmth and comfort: the quiet gleam of old wood, the scent of orange oil furniture polish, the slightly dusty odor of antique carpets that spoke of stable decades passing.

She followed the inviting scent of Elspeth's plum crumble pie into the kitchen. The room was empty, so she went on to the rose-colored morning room that Elspeth had adapted into a study. Seeing Elspeth's head bent over the laptop, eyes peering across the top of her reading glasses, Anna felt suddenly like a child again. She wanted to run forward and have Elspeth wrap her in her arms and tell her everything was going to be all right, even if that was flimflam.

Honesty was hard.

Taking one look at Anna's face, Elspeth pushed up from her chair. "Aw, sweetheart. What happened? What did Connal do?"

Not trusting her voice, Anna only shook her head. She'd promised Connal she wouldn't share his secret, and now she would have to keep it from Elspeth, too.

"It's just very cold outside," she mumbled, remaining in the doorway. "Snow flurries. I'm worried about the festival, that's all."

"Don't borrow trouble where none is needed." Elspeth's eyes remained fixed on Anna's face. "And don't try to sell me smokescreens. Did Connal fire JoAnne? He did, didn't he? Tell me."

"Nothing like that." Anna's voice was even tighter. "Although I think we were right about it being her. She didn't quite confess to it, but close enough. Connal warned her off."

Elspeth tipped her head, her eyes too sharp for Anna's comfort. Whatever she saw, she let it go. "Good then, but now the bad news," she said. "I got hold of the remaining vendors, and the order for the volunteer T-shirts had been canceled, too. Not only that, but the tent rental and security rope people rang back to say that someone had asked for the date to be pushed back a week."

"That's clever and even sneakier than canceling it outright."

"Aye, and given that, can we afford to assume it *was* JoAnne? What if it wasn't and the sabotage doesn't stop?"

Anna took a long, hard breath and tried to think. "All right, here's what we'll do," she said a moment later, "I'll phone everyone back again and give them a code they'll have to receive from anyone who tries to request a change. We'll use a unique code for every vendor, and give them out to anyone who is purchasing stall space for the craft fair, too. Meanwhile, would you track down the main websites where the festival should be listed, and make sure it's there and that the information is right?"

"I already sent out the press release, too."

"That's great. Then hopefully, we're back in business."

Retreating into the kitchen on the pretext of not wanting to interfere with Elspeth's work, Anna spent the rest of the afternoon trying to stay out from under her aunt's watchful eye. It was a blessing to lose herself in spreadsheets and telephone calls, but at five o'clock, she straightened, stretched her stiff neck, rolled her shoulders, and closed the file in front of her. Picking up the house phone, she checked to make certain the line was free before phoning Brando to ask him to get the camera trap from Connal at the play rehearsal that night.

"Aren't you coming up to meet Julian?" Brando asked. "You're the first thing he asked about when he checked in. All right, second thing technically—he made certain there was whiskey in his room first, but then he asked about you. 'So where's this girl Connal won't stop talking about?' That's exactly what he said."

Anna pinched the bridge of her nose and shook her head. "Tell him I doubt Elspeth and I will finish with the committee meetings before rehearsal wraps up for the night, but we'll look forward to meeting him tomorrow night instead."

She kept her tone cheerful, but Brando's curiosity trickled down the phone line with a long silence before he spoke again. "You'd tell me if something was wrong, wouldn't you?" he asked. "I've got a willing ear."

"Nothing's wrong," Anna said, "apart from the sabotage. Like I said, please talk to Connal about the camera. I didn't get a chance to finish making arrangements because JoAnne came in, but if you can get that and the poster set up on the highway tonight, that would be fantastic."

She hung up and sat a moment, alone in the kitchen with its sunny wallpaper and the photographs on the Welsh dresser on the far wall. On her way to make a fresh pot of tea, she stopped and picked up her favorite of the pictures, an old black and white of Elspeth and Ailsa pulling a newly-cut pine tree for Christmas between them across a blanket of snow, both of them laughing while they sank knee-deep with every step. They'd been seventeen and eighteen that year, according to Elspeth. Ailsa had intended to go off to university in Edinburgh that fall, although she'd never gone. She'd run off to Ohio with John Cameron that summer instead, and she'd never come back except once for their mother's funeral.

The thought of never coming back to Balwhither hit Anna so hard it was as if someone had kicked her in the chest. Never seeing Connal and Moira, the loch and the hills, Brando, Flora and Duncan, Davy Grigg. Kirsty and Angus. Every one of the people in the village who, with all their quirks and arguments, made her feel welcome and accepted as herself. In turn, that acceptance was letting her find out who she was, who she wanted to be.

The ache of leaving was still with her when she drove Elspeth to the inn a little later for the committee meetings. She slowed the borrowed Vauxhall that Brice at the garage had loaned them, wanting to drink in every wave on the loch and every steep, green hillside. One of the MacGregor pipers stood at the water's edge playing something that managed to be both mournful and full of hope, and Shame, the retriever, sat beside him with his tail sweeping the ground and his golden head tilted as if listening intently. Even Davy's sheep stood turned in the piper's direction, flicking their ears and chewing thoughtfully.

"Everything here is always both joyful and heartbreaking," Anna said. "It's never one thing or another."

"That's the way life is, though, isn't it?" Elspeth turned in her seat and studied Anna's profile. Catching Anna's hand, she gave a little squeeze. "Love comes from interest and joy, and the other edge of that is pain. There's always pain. But you and Connal will work things out—I've no doubt of that. Are you sure you don't want to talk about it?"

"I can't. It's not my secret."

"Meaning there's something you just found out." Elspeth studied her long and hard. "I won't pretend to know what that is, but secrets are funny things. The longer you hold on to them, the harder it is to let them go, and they burrow in and eat away at you. If Connal's shared something with you that he hasn't told the rest of us, give him a little leeway. You two are too good together to give up so easily. Trust me, I know what it's like to be left alone with regrets and could-have-beens. You don't want to live like that."

Tears welled in Anna's eyes in answer to the pain in Elspeth's voice. She pulled onto the shoulder of the single-track road in front of the inn and cut the Vauxhall's engine. "You're not alone, Aunt Elspeth. There are so many people here who love you."

"There's no amount of people who can take the place of that one special person. That's the plain truth of it." Elspeth sighed.

Anna'd always wondered why Elspeth, who was so beautiful inside and out and with so much life and love to give, could have ended up with no one by her side all these years. Was that same loneliness in Anna's future? If the joy she had felt with Connal these past weeks had shown her anything, it was that having a career and her own sense of accomplishment was important to her, but that it was far from everything she wanted in her life. She didn't want to go back to feeling half-alive.

"Who was he, Aunt Elspeth?" she asked, her voice barely audible. "The man who hurt you?"

"He didn't hurt me, love. Not in the way you're thinking. Secrets get in the way of love, and it withers before it ever blooms."

CLIMBING WALLS

Every man dies, not every man really lives.

WILLIAM ROSS WALLACE

ANNA SAT CROSSLEGGED on her bed that night and typed out yet another chatty email to her mother. That was the good thing about the time difference between Scotland and Ohio: she could send out an email last thing at night and turn off her phone again with the perfectly legitimate excuse of having gone to bed before her mother immediately rang her back.

Tomorrow, she promised herself. Tomorrow, she would pick up the phone and sit through the verbal version of what she'd already gotten in a dozen emails, variations on the theme of her own many failings.

At least, in one way, it would be a relief to get it over with. The task of finding excuses for not picking up when her mother called was taxing her creativity.

Dear Mom,

Sorry I couldn't phone you back. The committee meetings ran long tonight, and earlier I was trying to find a way to track down the thief who's been stealing the festival posters and canceling orders with our vendors. On a bright note, Julian Ashford arrived today to begin rehearsing with the actors from the village. Neither Vanessa Devereaux nor Pierce Saunders can arrive until the day before the festival. They'll do only the last dress rehearsal and the two performances, but they're both such pros that I'm not worried. Aunt Elspeth's knee, meanwhile, is much better. I had to talk her out of trying to walk to the inn tonight for the meetings, but fortunately the temperature was so cold that I was able to complain with perfect sincerity that I would freeze on the way back home.

I'm thrilled for Margaret about her Good Morning America audition. So exciting! I know you'd miss her, but think how much fun you two will have shopping when you go out to New York to visit. Will try to call soon!

Love,
Anna

She sent the message and turned the phone off, then crossed the room to plug it in to charge at the spindle-legged writing desk. A faint scratching beneath the windowsill outside caught her attention, and she paused to listen.

The sound came again, too loud for a bird, as if some large creature was scrabbling along the wall. Scanning the desk for something heavy, she found only the brass lamp that stood about twenty inches high. She unplugged that and carried it with her to the window. After easing the sash up, she poked her head out with the lamp raised like a weapon above her head.

"Don't hit me with that," Connal said from three feet below her. "At least not until you hear what I have to say." Toes and fingertips dug into the crevices between the stones, he lifted one hand higher, found a new fingerhold, moved his feet, and repositioned the other hand so that he was about a foot closer to the window than he had been.

Anna's heart kicked into runaway mode, and she sucked in a freezing blast of air. "What on earth are you doing, you idiot? You're going to fall and crack your skull like an egg."

"Great visual. Thanks for that," Connal said, climbing another foot.

"I'm serious. Go back down. Right now."

"It's safer to go down than up at this point, and I'm not going anywhere until we've had a chance to talk. If you don't want me to fall, stand back and let me in."

The thought of Connal falling . . . Panic squeezed Anna's lungs. She stepped back, watching with her heart still beating a furious tattoo until he had grabbed the bottom jamb of the window and swung safely through. Unfolding himself, he dusted his hands against his jeans.

"Well, I haven't done that in a while," he said, breathing heavily. "It's harder than I remembered. I must be out of shape."

Anna crossed her arms to keep from pulling him close in sheer relief. "I take it there was a lot of second-story work in your misspent youth?"

"Nothing that exciting." He looked down at her with a wicked grin. "The studios used to let me do some of my own stunts before the insurance got too high. I managed to learn a few tricks."

"Did you miss learning about the invention of the telephone? I hear it's useful for talking to people—and much safer than climbing the side of a house at midnight."

"It's only useful with people who don't have a history of not picking up when they don't want to talk to someone. And I figured if I waited until morning and came by, it would be unbearably awkward for Elspeth if you refused to see me." Connal closed the window against the cold night air and rubbed his fingers together briskly before tucking them into his armpits to try to warm them.

Anna retreated to the desk and set down the lamp, adding some distance between them. Not that Connal was wrong.

"I didn't set out with the intention of deceiving you, Anna. Please believe me." Connal's voice was so soft she had to strain to hear him. "And hurting you in any way was the very last thing I wanted. I've been going about this entire relationship backward, and I can't tell you how much I wish I hadn't made such a muddle of it."

"Relationship?" Anna shivered and leaned back again the desk.

"What would you call it?" He shot her a look she couldn't read, part sadness and part something else. "It's more than casual. It has been since the moment I saw you, and I hoped a month would be enough to give us a good foundation for seeing where it could go."

"You yelled at me the first time you saw me, remember?" Anna gripped the edge of the desk more tightly. "Maybe I should have stuck with first impressions. I'd be feeling like less of a fool right now."

"I am sorry."

"I told you about Henry. You told me you didn't want to go back to acting."

"Acting and writing are two different things. But you're right: I'm not very good at trusting people. I've been betrayed too often—and so have you. Let me ask you something. If you hadn't told me about Henry, if you hadn't had the experience with Henry, would you have expected me to tell you that I was Graham three weeks into our relationship?"

"I didn't think it was the kind of relationship that dealt in weeks," Anna said.

"It isn't, and right now, I'm afraid of losing you before we find out what we can be together. I can't tell you what my life will look like a year from now, or three years from now, but I know that I want what we have to work. Can't that be enough?" He took a step closer, then two, until they stood a foot apart. He raised his hand and brushed the back of his fingers against her cheek. "Please don't throw it away because I made one mistake. A big mistake, but it was only one. I've been honest with you about everything else. Maybe I was afraid, and I think you're afraid, too. I think that fear is keeping us both from moving forward."

He turned his hand, cupping her cheek, and instinctively Anna pressed her face against his palm. How could she crave his touch so much? She couldn't get close enough. Skin to skin, she wanted to melt into him.

Was he right? Was it easier to focus on his fear than it was to release her own? There was little she hated worse than a hypocrite. Also, she hadn't forgotten what Elspeth had said about regrets and could-have-beens.

"You scare me because you have the power to hurt me even worse than I've been hurt before."

"We have the power to hurt each other. Please don't shut me out." His voice trembled, and there was pain in his eyes.

Taking the last step, Anna raised her face to his, then stood on her toes to meet him as his lips came down to hers. The contact was bittersweet, too much and not enough, and yet a warm glow of happiness and relief started at her core and spread outwards until she thought it would burst through her skin. There didn't seem to be enough space in her to hold it all.

Had she felt half of this for Henry? No wonder she was scared to death. Connal's touch plunged her into a tumble of emotions that went so far beyond those fledgling feelings of childhood memories, hope, and heartbreak that it was like a forest fire burning through everything in its path. She kissed him back, her hands threading themselves into his hair, pulling him closer until he groaned against her lips and drew away.

"I'd better not stay any longer," he said against her hair. "We're not teenagers, even if that's how you make me feel, and I don't think I could survive the mortification of being caught by Elspeth in the middle of the night. Come to lunch with me tomorrow? We can talk some more?"

Anna nodded into his shoulder, but neither of them let go. It felt too much like Connal would vanish if she let go of him, as if she had conjured him in her sleep, and when he stepped back, she felt cold all the way to her bones.

She made him tiptoe with her down the stairs to leave by the front door. Then too keyed up to sleep after he'd gone, she fixed herself a cup of tea and sat in the front parlor in the dark, looking out at the cloud-chased moonlight rippling on the loch. How was she to make sense of what she was doing, of what he'd said, of where the two of them were going? In one respect, he was right, though. At the very least, they needed to know what they had together before it was time for her to leave.

It struck her that every relationship had turning points, the way turning points set the framework of any story. With Connal, she'd passed the point where she'd accepted the call to adventure, the midpoint when she was no longer the same person she had been before. Where did her story with him end? She didn't know, but she couldn't turn back; she knew that much. He had drawn her all the way out of the safe, familiar walls she had built around her heart, and whatever happened between them from here on out, she was going to feel every bruise and bump and bit of joy.

KILLING SWINE

Where hast thou been, sister?
Killing swine.

WILLIAM SHAKESPEARE, *MACBETH*

I N THE GOOD NEWS DEPARTMENT, the festival poster at the A84 junction survived the night, and there was no suspicious activity recorded on the camera trap. Brando stopped by at eleven the next morning to deliver the message along with the new posters he'd picked up from the printer.

"Maybe Connal's warning put JoAnne off, presuming it was her. She has to love Moira more than she hates the festival," Anna said, standing on the stoop holding the front door open while the wind blustering off the loch threatened to rip it from her hand. "Do you want to come in?"

"Afraid I can't. Julian Ashford's turning out to be a bit of a diva. He told me last night he was exhausted after the rehearsal and there wasn't enough whiskey in the world to make up for it, so he planned to sleep until noon. Also would I please do him a brunch for one o'clock. If we weren't desperate to have him for the play, I'd give him sausage and eggs and be done with it."

"We are desperate, though, so sweeten him up with something delicious."

"All right, since you ask so nicely." Brando gave her a wide, boyish grin. "Why don't you come around for lunch yourself, you and Elspeth. Bring Connal, too, if you like. In fact, I'll phone him and demand he comes. You can all keep me from strangling Julian before tonight's rehearsal."

"Was it that bad?"

"*He* was brilliant. Apart from that, Rhona threw herself at him, Sorcha and Fenella fought like cats, and Erica still looks like she smells something foul every time Lysander professes his love to Helena. But we shall persevere. Worst case, we'll have to give out free whiskey in the tent before opening night and hope the audience is too drunk to notice the bad performances."

With a wave of his hand and a scratch of gravel beneath his boot heel, Brando swung himself down the steps and hopped back in the Land Rover to drive away. Shivering in her thin sweater, Anna slammed the door on the cold wind and retreated into the house.

Making her way to Elspeth's study, she had barely crossed the threshold before Elspeth held a finger in the air. "Hold on just a minute, love. I'm trying to snipe a box of museum junk on this auction site," Elspeth said, her hand hovering over the keyboard. She stared at the screen, then suddenly slapped the enter key and watched the screen some more. "Ha." She looked up with a delighted smile. "Who says the early bird gets the worm? I'm the eagle who swoops in and snatches it out of the early bird's mouth."

"That's a terrible metaphor," Anna said, "and don't you have enough junk in the museum already? The room's full to overflowing, which I know for a fact since I helped you move it all."

"This is for the gift shop."

Anna blinked. "What gift shop?" In all the time since she'd arrived, there'd been a total of four people who had stopped by the museum, and she'd never seen any sign of anything for sale other than a carousel of dusty postcards in a corner. "I assumed that was just on the sign to bring people in? I thought you probably told people the sign was outdated or something."

"Of course, there's a gift shop. It's those last two cases nearest the door. I tell people they can buy anything they want from there—for the right price, of course." Elspeth typed a few keystrokes into the computer then shifted back in her chair.

"Hold on." Anna gaped at her. "You can't do that when you're making up stories about where things came from. That's misrepresentation—"

"It's not as though I'm saying something is three-hundred years old when it isn't. I'm only making up a story about who it belonged to—"

"—and if you tell them something belonged to Reverend Kirk or Bonnie Prince Charlie or Rob Roy MacGregor, then you're adding to the value of the thing. That's fraud."

"Fraud-schmaud. I explain that who it belonged to can't be proven. Look at the placards carefully next time you're in the ballroom. They all say 'believed to have belonged to' or 'believed to have been used by.' Which is true. By the time I'm finished telling a story, I believe it myself. Things could have happened exactly the way I say they did, and there's no proving they didn't."

"Aunt Elspeth—"

"Och, love," Elspeth laughed at her. "Let an old woman have her fun, won't you? Wait a wee bit and let me pay this. Then you can tell me whatever you came in to tell me." She turned her attention back to the screen, and Anna, shaking her head, picked up the file of never-ending tasks from the desk and took them back to her laptop in the kitchen where she worked until Connal came by to pick them up for brunch.

Julian Ashford appeared older than he did on screen when they met him at the hotel. He was also a little blurred around the edges, as if too much drink and life had seeped in beneath his skin. But he wielded charm in an opulent, slightly over-the-top way that was both mildly irritating and irresistible.

"So you're the girl who managed to coax Connal out of his hermit's den?" he said, pulling out Anna's chair for her with a flourish as the four of them sat down at a round table that Brando had set up in the living room of Julian's suite.

"Not quite out," Anna said, tucking the napkin on her lap, "and mainly that was Brando—and I suppose we have Rhona to credit, too, since she was the one who suggested having Connal direct."

"*Her.*" Julian raised a dark eyebrow and rolled his eyes. "If someone doesn't murder her in the next few days, I'll be tempted to do her in myself."

Anna sent Connal a wary glance. "I take it the rehearsal was not a huge success last night."

Connal's lips twitched at the corners, and he leaned back to let the server deposit a salad of purple, green, and red lettuces peppered with nasturtium blossoms in front of him. "Rhona's only meant to be there to deliver Vanessa's lines while everyone else rehearses, but she had us stop two dozen times so she could repeat a line because she thought she could do it better. Especially when it gave her an excuse to get close to Julian and look soulfully into his eyes."

Julian nodded, looking both annoyed and amused, the hazel eyes that laughed out at the world a stark contrast against the dark skin that came courtesy of his Nigerian mother. If Rhona couldn't have Connal, she could do worse than Julian.

"Be patient with her, all of you," Anna said. "She's self-absorbed, but basically harmless. We're better off humoring her."

"I reserve judgment on that score." Julian picked a roll out of the basket that the server offered him. "Meanwhile her acting skills render the lines unrecognizable, worse than the brilliant buffoonery that Graham Connor has perpetuated on the script. I suppose the worst of it is that when it comes down to it, I'm no longer the womanizer I like to think myself. I prefer my women to have a little mystery."

"You prefer to have them mysteriously throwing themselves at you," Connal countered, taking a sip of water.

"All right, I don't mind having *choices*, but I wouldn't choose that woman if you paid me. And those daughters of hers. The one takes every opportunity to upstage her sister, and the other one is so busy trying to dodge around her that she looks like Charles Condomine at the end of *Blythe Spirit,* looking for whichever piece of the furnishings is going to get thrown at her next."

"You just did that play at the Gielgud last year, didn't you?" Connal commented with an innocent look. "I heard the critics raved."

"Don't change the subject, Connal. Even my favorite subject—*me*—won't get you off the hook for saddling me with those three, and that Erica woman is no better. She's stirring up trouble, running between the girls and their mother like a carrier pigeon every ten minutes with a new piece of gossip." He waggled his fork at Connal. "All I can say is that I hope you've warned Vanessa, old man, because you've met Vanessa's temper, and so have I. I've no desire to meet it again anytime soon. The only thing you have going for you is this fabulous food, and I must say, I'd put up with quite a bit to eat like this every day."

Anna couldn't disagree. Every course the servers brought out was better than the last, and by the time Brando himself arrived with a delicate rhubarb crumble with whiskey-flavored cream, Julian was in a better mood. Anna was in awe.

"You made all this?" she asked. "It's incredible."

"Well, I do have a little help," Brando said, laughing at her.

"You know what I mean."

"All I can tell you is that I've had worse food at Michelin 3-star restaurants," Julian said, "and if you keep feeding me like this, I'll sing your praises from the rooftops to everyone I know." He raised his glass to Brando in a toast.

A faint wash of red colored Brando's cheeks, and he brushed a few stray crumbs from the white cloth at Elspeth's elbow. "I'm glad to hear it, and of course I'd be grateful."

Although he still wore a kilt, he had changed into black shoes shined to a gleaming finish and a crisp white chef's jacket with a double row of buttons. Not used to seeing him in professional mode, Anna felt another twinge of guilt for having been taken in by his easygoing nature. Each detail of the meal and the hotel was both perfect and surprising, with elegant modern touches and dramatic accents that emphasized instead of taking away from the traditional roots. Like Brando himself, the effect was warm and effortlessly inviting.

"Weddings," she said to him on the way out the door later. "You need to do wedding and honeymoon packages and anniversaries. Events. Lots and lots of events."

"Are you volunteering to organize?" he asked. "Because you're hired."

Anna glanced at Connal, who had stopped ahead at the door to wait for her, but they hadn't discussed her staying. Only that they would see what happened. "If I can't volunteer, then Elspeth should," she said. "Or someone. This place should be full every night of the year."

She couldn't keep from thinking about the hotel, and the glen in general—and how quickly the future was looming—while she and Elspeth worked that afternoon, but she pushed the thoughts aside. As the day wore on, she had no time to worry about anything other than the fresh wave of chaos that descended.

Angus Greer and Rory MacLaren had a fistfight at the edge of the loch and had to be pulled off each other by Flora Macara, who waded into the water and dragged them apart as they were thrashing around the shallows. Then the awards Anna had ordered arrived with Piobaireachd misspelled on the piping trophy and the separate medals for the Shean Trubhais and Reel of Tulloch twelve-and-under dance categories blended into a single medal labeled Shean Tulloch. She double-checked the printout to be sure the error wasn't hers and released a sigh of relief when she found she had typed them all into the form correctly. Still, it meant doing the dinner dishes with the phone wedged between her ear and shoulder while she argued with the manager and talked him into an expedited re-order.

That night's rehearsal went no better. Anna stood out of the way at the back of the great hall where the tables had been pushed aside and tape laid out on the floor to mark the boundaries of the stage. Connal had even marked precisely where Sorcha was supposed to stand, with numbers written on each spot so she couldn't claim confusion. But the moment she was onstage, whenever Fenella spoke, Sorcha still edged around so that she was the one in the audience's line of sight.

Connal finally threw his clipboard on the floor with a clatter that brought every head in the room whipping around to face him. "Sorcha, if you don't stop upstaging Helena, I swear I'll—"

He broke off and shook his head.

Sorcha stared at him, wide-eyed. "You'll what?"

Connal gritted his teeth and exchanged a look with Anna. But there was nothing they could do. There was no one else in the glen to play Sorcha's part. Sorcha, Fenella, and Erica were the only women between the ages of seventeen and twenty-five, and Kirsty and the others between twenty-five and thirty-five were already doing as much as they could handle.

"Or I'll get Anna to play Hermia," he said, gesturing back to where Anna stood. "Now behave yourself, or I swear I will put an earpiece in Anna's ear and cue her the lines myself on opening night. Do you understand?"

Sorcha came as close to stomping her foot as any grown woman Anna had ever seen. "You should have made me Helena," she said. "That's the part I want to play."

"No." Connal pointed to where she was supposed to be standing. "Now stand on your mark, and start again from the top."

THE DEATH OF MUSIC

The music in my heart I bore,
Long after it was heard no more.

WILLIAM WORDSWORTH, "THE SOLITARY REAPER"

F OR A WEEK, the posters all stayed in place, and the
camera trap caught nothing. Anna and Connal hiked to
the area beyond the loch to set it back up in view of the
osprey's nest. One of the two raptors in the breeding pair
took to the sky at their approach and circled above them,
the mottled white feathers of its underside blending into
the clouds as Anna peered up into the noonday sun.

"She's incredible," Anna said and, turning, she found
Connal watching the bird with that same fierce joy she had
caught in his expression once before while he'd watched a
hawk in flight.

"Ospreys were extinct in Great Britain for three
decades, did you know that? This pair settled here about

three years ago, and it feels like a miracle to me every time I see them."

"I didn't used to believe in miracles."

"And now you do?"

"Now I do," Anna answered, smiling.

Swooping her up suddenly, Connal spun her around and around, both of them laughing for no apparent reason, and Anna felt free, like she was flying. Slowly, he let her down, his eyes on hers. Then he kissed her until her every coherent thought melted away.

When he raised his head, leaving her lips warm and swollen, she was left with a sense of *rightness,* as if something that had been missing within her had snapped back into place and made her whole. She let herself fall into the heat and the alchemy of it, and her heart burst open in a rush of energy that knifed between pain and pleasure.

It was at that precise moment she realized she had fallen irrevocably in love with Connal MacGregor. Not the way she had loved Henry, or the way that she had envisioned love. Not in any way that compared to anything else. She simply loved him.

She wanted to tell him and didn't dare.

The osprey wheeled away. Connal watched it fly with his face shining in pleasure and longing. "I'm glad you believe in miracles," he said. "Some things can't be explained. You just have to accept their magic."

She smiled vaguely, and they hurried to set up the camera trap again because she needed to get back.

"Is something wrong?" Connal asked her as he left her at Breagh House. "You've been quiet the last few minutes."

"Slight headache, that's all."

She took two Tylenol tablets from the bottle in her purse after he had gone, and she forced herself to concentrate on making the last of the booth assignments for the craft fair vendors who had sent in deposits. There was a good variety, everything from artisanal cheeses to wall art, including jewelry, kilts, heraldry and genealogy, pony rides, musical instruments—virtually anything anyone might want to buy. She drew in three additional booths, split them in two, and penciled in the number and name for each new vendor, but there was no space left in the flat area they had designated near the village.

Picking up the site plan, she carried it with her toward the ballroom where Elspeth was putting tablecloths on the display cases in an attempt to disguise them as buffet tables. The phone rang as she passed the study.

"Get that, will you?" Elspeth called, popping her head into the hallway.

Anna checked her watch and crossed toward the desk. Ten-twenty on the button in Cincinnati, so her mother would be walking out of her yoga class and climbing into her car. Anna had to hand it to her, the fact that she could use the telephone as a cudgel from thousands of miles away was a testament to her determination. It wasn't as if she didn't know that Anna had been avoiding her. She knew. She simply didn't care, or she simply refused to accept that they weren't all one big happy family. She'd been pretending that all of Anna's life, after all. Pretending her marriage to Anna's father was perfect, pretending Anna's break-up had been by mutual consent, pretending that nothing bad ever happened that might shake her perfectly respectable standing at the country club and in the Junior League. So much pretending and doing things for the sake of what other people thought. Other people who, when it came down to it, didn't matter.

Anna glared at the phone as she plucked it from the charger. "Hello?"

"Anna, is that you?" her mother asked. "Well, it's about time. Are you finally going to speak to me?"

"I've been emailing every day."

"I'm not stupid, darling. Give me a little credit," her mother said with a sniff.

The sniff sounded suspiciously damp, and the thought of her mother crying left an odd, hollow ache in Anna's stomach. But she couldn't remember the last time she'd seen her mother cry, and her emails hadn't hinted at hurt or remorse. They'd mainly projected guilt of the weapons-grade variety.

"Is everything all right at home?" Anna asked. "Anything new?"

"The same as usual. Your father's complaining that the greens on the golf course are in terrible shape, and Margaret is a little nervous about her big audition."

"National television would be a huge step for her."

"But New York is so far away. Already, Katharine's all the way on the other side of the country—and you, I don't know where you're going to end up living. You should move back here if you want to start organizing events. I still think this whole festival idea of Elspeth's is ridiculous, but your sister claims that getting Julian Ashford and Pierce

Saunders to do a play was quite a coup, and people still talk about the Fire and Ice Ball you organized for me. We could get you bucketloads of bookings."

"Margaret said it was a coup?"

"Not Margaret, darling, pay attention. Katharine is beside herself with excitement for you." She paused, and Anna's heart grew loud, ticking away the moments because she had come to know her mother's silences all too well. "You know," Ailsa continued, "I don't suppose you'd have a small part left over for Katharine? She's a quick study—she could learn her lines on the flight over, and she could use a little pick-me-up. It would be a way to make peace between you."

Anna's hands turned cold. She couldn't breathe. "No," she managed to choke out. "We don't have any parts left over. The final rehearsal is tomorrow night, and I don't need to make peace. I'm not the one who did anything wrong."

"You could at least mention her to the actors, couldn't you? Show them a photo of her? Just knowing you had done that would cheer her up, and she's had such a hard time lately with Henry working crazy hours in that crime drama. They may not make it, to be honest, even though I'm not supposed to tell you. Couldn't you finally let go of what happened and do something nice for her? It's been years, and Henry was all wrong for you anyway."

Anna closed her eyes. Took a deep, deep breath.

She almost hung up again, but that hadn't solved anything last time, even if it had felt darn good. No, she had to grow up. She needed to stop being a doormat, and if she didn't gather up the nerve to do that now, she would end up either having to stop talking to her mother altogether—openly and for good—or risk losing any shred of self-respect that she had left. She couldn't keep living like this.

"I'm sorry to hear about Katharine and Henry," she began—then changed her mind. "No, actually, I'm not sorry. If I were a better person, I could manage sympathy, but right now, all I can say is that if Henry dumps her, Katharine deserves what she gets. And Henry? There's no justice in the world if he ends up with a successful career—but then the world is full of selfish witches and narcissistic jerks who people fawn over for no apparent reason."

"Anna! How can you say that?"

"Because every word is true. How do you think it makes me feel when you keep taking Katharine's side? She's a grown woman. You don't need to protect her. What about protecting me for a change? Where was that maternal streak when I was ten years old—"

"I thought we weren't ever going to discuss that."

"Why shouldn't we discuss it? We should have discussed it with the police. All these years, I've kept wondering how many other girls that judge has done that to, or was going to do it to. I wondered if it was my fault, if I'd done something to make him single me out."

"Of course it wasn't your fault, and I sent a letter to the pageant directors—anonymously. He was never asked back to judge."

"That pageant. What about other pageants?" Anna's heart was beating too fast, making her dizzy. She leaned against Elspeth's desk. "And why didn't you ever tell me you sent a letter?" she asked more quietly. "Knowing that might have made it easier for me. At least I would have felt like someone had done something instead of letting it go as if it didn't matter. As if I didn't matter."

Her mother's breathing was the only sound on the other end of the line for a long time. Anna felt her own chest rising and falling heavily.

"I didn't want you dragged through the mud," Ailsa finally said. "You can't imagine how awful it is. I've seen all those television shows. The process isn't fair, and if it's bad now, it was so much worse back then. You don't ever want to have to be the girl who has to stand in court and testify about what some man did to you. Your looks are a gift. They should never be used against you."

Anna's right hand squeezed the phone while her left balled itself into a fist. "You're the one who put us into beauty pageants and made our lives all about the way we look, about dressing us up and showing us off."

"You think you wouldn't be defined by looks one way or another?" Ailsa's voice trembled. "I'm sorry if you think I didn't do the right thing, but I did the best I could for you. Where men still hold all the cards, looks give you power. Sometimes they're the only thing that gives you power."

"Power comes from inside, from the confidence of knowing that you're loved. You stripped that confidence away from me the minute you told me not to tell. You made me feel ashamed, as if I'd done something that was my fault. And you made me feel like a coward for not being able to go back out on that stage, knowing he would be out there, sitting and watching me. Looking at me. You made me feel like I wasn't as good as Margaret and Katharine. Like you didn't love me as much as you loved them."

"You don't think I love you? You never gave me the chance to show you—"

"I gave you every chance, and every time, every single time I needed you to approve or just be happy for me, you made it clear my choices were wrong or that Katharine and Margaret made better choices. Even when Katharine ran off with Henry, you didn't shut her out. You tried to make me pretend that what she'd done wasn't horrible, that I wasn't devastated. That I'd get over it. Only you don't get over not being able to trust someone you love. And that's the bottom line. I can't trust Katharine not to destroy me, and I can't trust you to defend me, to support me the way I am. When you love someone, you don't try to change them or make them different. That's one thing that Katharine gets that it's taken me too long to figure out. She never let you guilt her or change her. She's always been the one you weren't sure about, the one who might not love you if you didn't give her what she wanted, so you keep trying, keep making excuses for her. Even today you weren't thinking of me. You weren't loving *me*. You were thinking about what I could do for Katharine, to make sure *she* kept loving *you*."

Without waiting for her mother to respond, Anna replaced the phone very gently in the cradle. She stood beside it, shaking. Not crying. She didn't have any tears left for either her mother or for Katharine, and she hadn't said anything that wasn't true. She didn't regret a word.

Looking up, she found Elspeth coming toward her, and she walked forward into Elspeth's arms. Elspeth drew her in. Held her close. "I'm sorry, Anna. I'm so sorry about your mother and Katharine, and I'm sorry that happened to you with the judge. I had no idea—Ailsa never told me."

"She didn't tell anyone, but I'll never be sure that was for my sake or to save herself embarrassment. I was lucky, really. It was only a kiss and a grope in a closet he pulled me into, and I kicked him and ran away. That doesn't sound like much now, but at the time, it felt dirty and shameful, and I've always wondered if it was worse for some other girl because I didn't do anything to stop him."

Surprisingly, even then she had no tears left to cry. She stepped back and wiped her hands on her jeans and tried to gather the pieces of herself back together.

"You're shaking like a new-shorn sheep," Elspeth said. "Let's get some sugar in you and a nice hot cuppa." Taking her hand, Elspeth pulled her to the kitchen.

Anna stood in the doorway with her arms hugged around herself while Elspeth filled the kettle and set it on the stove. Watching her aunt, it struck her how different she was from Ailsa. Not that Anna was anything like Margaret or Katharine, either, but now she wondered if she would have been more like them if what had happened hadn't happened. Her priorities, her focus, her entire life would have been different.

"What happened to my mother before she left the glen?" Anna asked. "What made her the way she is?"

Elspeth's hand shook, and she spilled dry black tea leaves off the spoon onto the counter. "If I could explain your mother, maybe I could fix her. We all make choices we have to live with."

She brushed off the counter and dusted the spilled tea into the sink before measuring out more leaves into the pot. Anna dropped sideways into a chair at the kitchen table.

"Did something awful happen to her?" Anna asked. "Something like what happened to me?"

"Lord, no! Is that what you've been thinking?" Elspeth shook her head. "Och, I suppose I can't blame you for that, but I'm afraid it's nothing that awful—or that simple. It was the loch. Remember I told you that not everyone sees something they like? Well, Ailsa had a Sighting of her true love the year before she was meant to go to university."

"My father?"

"Brando's father. But Ailsa had no intention of becoming a farmer's wife, spending her whole life here in the glen. She wanted more for herself." The soft whistle of the kettle grew insistent, and Elspeth grabbed the handle with a dishtowel. Only when she'd made the tea, did she turn back to Anna with her face formed into sharpened planes. "She always had big plans, did Ailsa. She was going to study journalism and be a television presenter and go to London. What she saw in the loch scared her half to death, because Brando's father was never going to do anything but farm the land his family's been farming for generations. She barely knew him, but she knew that much, so she jumped at the first opportunity to get away. She's been trying to convince herself ever since that she's happy with the choices she made. Every time you make different choices, she feels it like a judgment on herself."

Anna sat back, her spine stiffened into an exclamation mark of fury. "You're saying she married Dad because her subconscious conjured up the face of a man she was afraid to love?"

"The loch has nothing to do with your subconscious." Elspeth's hands trembled carrying the teapot to the table.

Anna jumped up and took it from her, then went back to get the cups and milk and sugar while Elspeth sank gracelessly into a chair.

"Are you all right?" Anna asked, sliding a cup of tea into Elspeth's hand. "Here, drink this."

Elspeth's eyes were bruises in her shadowed face. "You'll have to swear on your life you'll never tell your mother what I'm about to tell you."

"Of course." Anna held her own cup in both hands and nodded. "I promise."

"The Sighting is real. If it wasn't no one could ever see a total stranger—and that's exactly what I saw the same year your mother saw Brando's father." Pausing, Elspeth took a sip of tea, winced, and added a teaspoon of sugar to the cup. "At the time, I didn't put much stock into what I saw. I was already signed up to do a work-study program on an archeological dig in the Hebrides that summer, and that was as far into the future as I was willing to look. Then because of what she'd seen in the loch, Ailsa didn't want to stick around that summer, so she charmed her way into a volunteer slot in the same program. I didn't want her to come, and we had a horrible argument, but then I fell and broke my arm. She ended up going by herself, and she was there from June to August. When she came home, she brought your father with her, and she was pregnant, so they were getting married."

Anna's hands went numb. "That's impossible. Margaret wasn't born for two years after they were married."

"There was another baby before Margaret. He was stillborn at seven months."

"No." Anna shook her head as if she could shake the words away.

"I'm sorry, love, but there's more as well. The man Ailsa brought home was the stranger I had Sighted in the loch."

"What?" Anna froze, staring at her. "My father? Are you saying that *my father* was the man you were supposed to love?"

"I think so. The loch thought so."

Anna shook her head again. "Did you ever tell her? Were you—are you—in love with him?"

"There wasn't anything to say. Your father and I both felt the connection when we met. It doesn't take long. You find yourself aware when someone is watching you, and you can't stop watching them. You feel like the world is brighter when they're around. You touch them, and it's magic. I still feel that electricity every time I see your father, but it was already too late for us before we'd ever met. Ailsa's my sister. I could never have hurt her like that."

Anna had forgotten how to breathe. Questions and memories and odd, disjointed connections from her childhood spun through her brain, making it ache trying to keep up. The worst was how broken Elspeth appeared now, sitting across the table, how small and old and frail. Worn out.

She picked up Elspeth's hands and clasped them between her own. "I'm so sorry, Aunt Elspeth. I can't even imagine how you've felt."

"Actually, I think you can," Elspeth told her gently. "I think you know exactly how it feels."

"No." Anna pulled away. "You've been able to forgive. I haven't."

"You were about to marry Henry, and Katharine knew how much you loved him. Ailsa had no idea what had happened, and I've made sure she's never suspected. That was the difference. It wasn't Ailsa's fault. And even so, don't think it's always been easy staying friends with her. She takes the devil's own patience and a lot of work." Elspeth used two fingers to lift up Anna's chin. "Listen to me, Anna. I'm not telling you any of this to have you feel sorry for me. I'm telling you that your mother threw away true love for social standing and a life outside the glen, and she's spent her life pretending that she's happy so she doesn't have to admit she's miserable. You rejecting the way she lives makes her fight harder to justify her own decisions. That's how she's always been. It doesn't mean she doesn't love you."

"Her idea of love is different from mine."

"We all love the best way we can," Elspeth said. "That's all we can do. The more generously you love, the more fiercely you can feel it."

Anna wondered if that was true, but she didn't know how to love any differently. Loving someone was risky, dangerous. Maybe it was supposed to be like that. If you tried to protect yourself, even a little bit, didn't you limit how much you could feel?

BURNING BRIDGES

Our subject leads us to talk of deadly feuds . . .

SIR WALTER SCOTT, *A LEGEND OF MONTROSE*

THE ARRIVAL OF VANESSA DEVEREAUX and Pierce Saunders plunged the final dress rehearsal into chaos. In person, Pierce was a smaller presence than he was on screen, a slim, sharp-featured man who arrived wearing jeans, scuffed loafers, and a Notre Dame sweatshirt with a stain below the collar. His mobile expressions and slightly gangly limbs made him perfect for the parts of Philostrate and the mischievous fairy Puck. Vanessa, on the other hand, swept in trailing a scarf and an expensive scent and caught every eye in the room.

On the stage inside the enormous tent set up beside the inn, she dazzled. She and Julian Ashford seemed cordially professional until they stepped into their roles, but when they played opposite each other as Hippolyta and

Theseus or as Titania and Oberon, their chemistry sizzled with love and opposition.

Behind the rented curtains, Anna stood by with the script, ready to call out cues for any lines the actors needed help remembering. She grew breathless watching Vanessa and Julian together. Breathless and relieved, because for the first time, with the major players there and the costumes and the painted sets, the magic and humor Connal had envisioned all came together.

"I don't see what makes Vanessa Devereaux all that great," Rhona said to Sorcha, standing behind Anna in the wings. "Look at her. She's dull. Titania is supposed to be queen of the fairies. She should be sexier, more animated. More."

"She looks even older than you do," Sorcha said loud enough for a few of the others backstage to turn their heads.

Anna sidled closer. "It's better not to talk back here— and better not to say anything at all that might upset people."

Sorcha rolled her eyes, but she glanced over at Connal, who sat in a folding chair watching the rehearsal from the front of the tent. At the other side of the stage, Duncan Macara—as Nick Bottom newly enchanted by the fairy Puck—entered wearing a donkey's head. His fellow actors screamed and ran away at the sight of him. The lighting shifted to a dim blue, darkening the stage and turning the twisted papier-mâché trees malignant and macabre.

Stumbling around, Duncan tried to make sense of what had happened. "I see their trickery: this is to make an ass of me, to frighten me if they can. But I will not stir from this place. I will walk up and down here, and I will sing so they'll know I'm not afraid!"

He began to bray out a song. Being the center of attention and forced to carry the whole play in his hesitant tenor at that moment, he managed to hit the perfect mixture of fear and bravado all mixed together with a creditable imitation of a donkey.

A spotlight shone over to where Vanessa, dressed in a fiery red wig and scandalously cut gossamer gown, lay asleep on a nearby bed hung with vines and flowers. Woken by Nick Bottom's snorting and braying, she sat up and peered around, managing to become Titania, Queen of the Fairies, from the very first movement of her head. Enchanted by her husband Oberon to fall in love with the first vile thing she encountered, she sat up and turned toward Duncan. "What's this? What angel wakes me from my flowery bed?"

Sorcha's laugh was loud enough that Vanessa spun to look at her.

"Sorry." Sorcha shrugged and raised her hands. "I'm sorry."

Turning back toward Duncan, Vanessa rose from her bower and floated toward him as if she couldn't help herself. She made the magical pull between them palpable. Anna could almost see the attraction dancing around her, the way she always felt herself drawn to Connal. But wasn't all love magic? What else could make a person entrust their whole heart to someone else?

Vanessa raised a trembling finger toward the face of Duncan's donkey mask, then turned her palm and cupped his cheek. "I pray thee, gentle mortal, sing again. Your music is as beautiful to my ears as your features are beautiful to my eyes."

Sorcha snorted, the sound loud and carrying. Erica poked her in the ribs while Anna held a finger to her lips in warning.

"I do like that wig on her, though," Sorcha said, turning to Fenella. "Help me put my hair in little braids like that for when I'm May Queen, would you?"

"Why are you assuming you'll be May Queen? It could be me again—or Fenella," Erica said.

"Fenella? Who'd vote for *Fenella?*"

Anna squeezed her wrist. Hard. "I might, for one. Now be quiet, all of you, and pay attention."

The wings went quiet after that, but Sorcha and Erica continued to glare at each other, and they drifted farther apart until they stood backstage with several feet of flattened grass between them. There was also suddenly a calculation that Anna didn't like in Sorcha's expression as she snuck glances at Erica and Fenella.

That calculation worried Anna enough that she decided to bring it up when she and Connal sat working together by the fireplace in his study late that night. She set aside her last-minute checklists and glanced over at him.

"I wish you were coming to the play tomorrow night. Couldn't you at least come stand behind the curtain?"

Connal glanced up from reading the director's notes on his latest screenplay. "You and Brando can handle anything that goes wrong. If anything goes wrong."

"I'm not so sure about that. Sorcha's all worked up about being May Queen, and she's plotting something. But even if she manages to restrain herself, aren't you curious to see how the play turns out? This is your accomplishment from start to finish."

The firelight flickered across his skin and reflected in his eyes. "It's only an accomplishment if it turns out well, and I'll have the video that Angus is making." Leaning forward, he kissed the top of Anna's hair. "Don't worry. It will all work out." He set the pages of the screenplay on the floor and pulled her toward him. "You know that, don't you? Everything will be fine."

"I'll be gone in six days. That doesn't seem fine at all," she said, hoping he would contradict her. That he would finally say something about the future, about staying. About them.

"I know you want everything to be settled, but there's time. I—" He stopped himself and smoothed her hair where he had ruffled it.

Anna waited, hardly breathing.

"You *what?*" she prompted when he didn't go on.

"Nothing." He turned her toward him. "Just will you trust me, Anna? There are things I need to say to you, but not until the festival is over and things settle down. It wouldn't be fair to discuss things now."

She swallowed her frustration. "Fair? I don't understand."

"I know you don't, and I'm sorry for that. Please, just trust me."

She wanted to trust him, but trust couldn't take care of the purely practical matters, like the fact that she had a plane ticket that said she was leaving two days after the festival was over, and an apartment that she was paying rent for, and a bank account that was slowly dwindling. She'd been doing her best not to worry about those things, but she couldn't help it. And whatever happened between them when the festival was over, it had to be on terms that left her self-respect intact. She couldn't gamble her entire future on Connal, on any man, especially when he let things remain unsaid because—why?

Yes, why?

She couldn't think of a reason, unless he hadn't decided what he wanted. Or he *had* decided and wanted to wait to let her down gently at the last minute so she didn't have to stay around to face him afterward. He was an actor, he could pull that off, and he was kind enough to try to do that for her.

He smiled, a beautiful, almost wistful, smile. "Come here, Anna." Rolling her gently onto her back, he spread her hair out on the soft carpet and propped himself on his elbow looking down at her. "Do you know how beautiful you are? You try so hard at everything you do. You worry so much, watching people, trying to figure out what they're thinking, what they want, what they need. I would love to throttle your mother and Henry and your sister for making you believe that love is that conditional. But I have to balance your fear against what's fair to you. Do you understand?" He shook his head. "Of course you don't. How could you?"

"You're talking in riddles."

"I am, aren't I?" Connal sighed. "Maybe I should stop."

He bent his head slowly and kissed her, and she let herself melt against him, let herself kiss him back with an edge of desperation brought on by the knowledge that their time together was drawing to a close.

"I wish you would at least come to the ball," she asked as he helped her back into her coat to walk her home a few minutes later. "Moira would love that—and so would I."

"As much as I'd love to dance with you both, Vanessa invited a London critic up to see the play. He's booked in at the Braeside for Sunday night, and Van's already invited him to the ball as her guest. I can't argue against that because he could make a big difference for next year's festival. But you could skip the ball and come here instead. Or skip part of it. We could have our own ball here, you and me and Moira."

Anna thought of the three of them alone, pretending to have a ball in the cold, empty room downstairs, dancing by themselves surrounded by walls and gates designed to keep people away. She swallowed down a hard lump of sadness. Or maybe the ache in her chest was caused by the thought of the festival going on again next year, possibly without her.

It was ironic that the one man who had made her strip her heart of all protections and made her fully alive was himself living a life so constrained he was barely living.

She'd been thinking of asking Elspeth if she could stay a little longer, but was there any point? What kind of a future could there be for the two of them if Connal couldn't open himself up to the world? How could she be sure he would open himself up to her? How would she know how much was pretense? That wasn't the way she wanted—or deserved—to be loved.

He hadn't even said the word. She hadn't said the word.

She needed to start putting the pieces of her own heart back together.

It was time for her to prepare to say good-bye.

Queen of the May

I'll have grounds
More relative than this—the play's the thing
Wherein I'll catch the conscience of the King.

William Shakespeare, *Hamlet*

F RIDAY MORNING BEGAN with rain. A flood of rain.
Fortunately, the tent where the play was to be performed had already been set up for the last rehearsal, and the booths for the craft fair were also set and ready. Everything would be dry that needed to be dry, Anna assured herself, and they could finish putting up the signs and final touches once the rain had stopped. Even so, she lay in bed awake as the clock ticked on toward four o'clock. The rain sheeted down the panes of her window. Had they closed the tent up securely when they'd left the night before? Was the plastic sheeting anchored with sandbags the way it was supposed to be fastened? If the rain got

inside behind the stage, they'd have a muddy mess to soak into costumes and put everyone at risk for slipping.

So many things could still go wrong. She didn't need this new extra bit of worry.

She pulled herself out of bed, dressed hurriedly, and retrieved a flashlight and the keys to the borrowed Vauxhall from the kitchen. After scrawling a hasty note in case Elspeth woke up and came downstairs, she dashed outside to the car.

On the way to the village, water splashed in brown sheets from the tires. The high beams let her see only about a foot in front of her, and with the moon behind the clouds, the glen was an angry black. Only an occasional outdoor light shone here and there to reveal where a dwelling stood, but at least the road was mercifully obstacle-free. Brando had instructed Davy Griggs, on pain of never casting another wager for anyone in the village, to keep his bloody sheep penned up for once.

Anna parked as close to the tent as possible. With the hood of her jacket drawn tight around her head, she switched on the flashlight and walked the perimeter of the huge white structure, checking extra carefully near the back where the stage and dressing areas were set up behind rented velvet curtains all ready for the performance. She found three places where the extra tenting material had been draped awkwardly, leaving thin rivulets of water running down inside, but she adjusted the flaps and kicked the sandbags back in place.

On returning to the house, she found herself wide-awake. There was no point going back to bed, so she wrapped herself in a quilt against the cold that had seeped into her bones, made herself a cup of coffee, and went back over the schedules and tasks one last time to make sure she'd thought of everything.

"Don't tell me you worked all night?" Elspeth asked, coming downstairs at seven o'clock.

"No, I just got up early," Anna said, repressing a yawn, and she dragged herself back to the sink to put on a second pot of coffee.

Working through the task lists went more quickly with Elspeth's help. Shortly before noon, Anna drove them both through the drying mud to the village where they spent the afternoon setting up the folding chairs, making sure the booths were correctly numbered, supervising the other volunteers, and doing as much as they could to get a jump on the prep for Saturday's Highland Games events. Visitors began to trickle in, a steady stream of cars splashing through the puddles on the single-track road and pulling either into the parking lot at the inn or continuing on to the camp site or caravan park.

At six-thirty, Vanessa, Julian, and Pierce swept into the tent. The rest of the community actors trickled in. In a fit of caution, Anna had bought bottled water, diet sodas, packaged Tunnock's Tea Cakes, and sealed packets of cheese at the store and left them in the dressing area with strict instructions for someone to watch the food every second—and not to allow any other food or drink to be brought in. Just in case.

At a quarter to seven, she left the tent and hunted for Moira and JoAnne, who should have arrived already.

Peering past the people standing in line for play tickets, she searched the courtyard of The Last Stand, but there was no sign of them or Connal's Audi.

She stopping beside the table where Davy Grigg's wife was selling tickets. "Have you seen JoAnne or Moira, Lissa? They didn't come past here, did they?"

"Not that I've seen." Lissa shook her head and frowned up at Anna from beneath a frizz of blond curls that were doing their best to escape the bun that was meant to contain them. "But I was going to send someone to find you. We've near sold every ticket if you count what we've held back in the front for the VIPs. Want me to start selling the ones for Sunday?"

Anna squinted up at the—thankfully—cloudless sky. It promised to be a spectacular sunset, so she decided to take a risk. "The weather's good, and we've still got the sixty extra chairs we ordered for the Highland Games. Let's open the sides of the tent and add extra rows of seating. You can sell those at a two-pound discount, and we can try to save some more of Sunday's seats."

"Fine by me," Lissa said.

"Good. I'll go find some help to get the chairs set up. If you see JoAnne and Moira, ask them to wait here for me, would you?"

Lissa nodded and turned her attention to selling tickets to the young couple next in line, and Anna hurried off toward the inn. At The Last Stand, the pipers were gathering in the courtyard to begin the procession that would mark the festival's official opening. On the bright side, none of them, including Angus and Rory, had killed each other yet.

But the night was just beginning.

At Elspeth's suggestion, the MacGregor pipers were at the front, and the MacLaren pipers were in the rear, and the now familiar kilt patterns were separated by several rows of pipers from unrelated clans wearing an assortment of different tartans. Under the direction of one of the outside judges, they launched into a practice piece as Anna hurried past them. The first notes sounded like a bag of cats being tortured, but then the notes of "Highland Cathedral" emerged and a row of tattoo drummers at the rear joined in.

Chills erupted along Anna's spine. She paused briefly to watch, then ducked through the door of the inn, and by the time she emerged again with a half-dozen volunteer chair-wranglers, the call of the drums and pipes had begun to work its magic. Carrying across the water and echoing off the braes, it drew people from the campground and caravan park on the left side of the loch as well as the B&Bs, the inn, and the hotel.

But there was still no sign of Moira, and Anna needed to get back for the opening ceremony. Checking her watch, she gave an impatient sigh and went to borrow Elspeth's phone to dial Connal's number.

He picked up with a brief, "Hallo?"

"It's me," Anna said. "Has JoAnne left with Moira yet?"

"About twenty minutes ago. Isn't she there yet? That's odd. Let me try and phone her. Give me a minute, and I'll ring you back."

Anna wandered back outside, shading her eyes to search the groups who had gathered along the fence and in the courtyard to watch the pipers, but there was still no sign of Moira's small blond head or purple jacket. When the phone rang, the screen showed Connal's number. She picked up eagerly.

"I swear, I'm going to kill that woman," he said, his voice icy. "She stopped to feed the wild swans down the loch."

"Are they coming now? The pipers are about to start." Anna whipped around and skirted the wall to head down toward the water.

"Go take care of whatever you need to do. I told JoAnne to bring Moira straight to you, and I'll follow up to make sure she does—"

"Hold on," Anna said as a shout erupted from the back of the inn as the door flew open. In a blur of yellow fur, Shame tore outside with a steak in his mouth and Flora, red-faced, right behind him. Dashing into the crowd of pipers, the dog scattered them like dominos while the music deteriorated into a cacophony of wails and sadistic notes.

"Shame, you idiot! Come back here," Flora shouted.

Shame paused to grin back at her, tongue lolling, then ran and hopped over the three-foot wall, raced past Anna, and bounded like a deer through the shallow water along the side of the loch. Honking in alarm, a pair of swans who'd been swimming near the shore took flight, their wing spans wide and graceful. As if that had been his aim all along, Shame flopped to his belly at the feet of a child in a purple jacket who stood beside a taller figure dressed like a scarecrow in layers of skirts and scarves and sweaters.

"Don't worry about calling JoAnne again," Anna said. "I've found them."

Moira wiggled out of her jacket, and Anna took it from her and draped it over the back of the chair beside Elspeth's in the front row of the tent. As the last of the bagpipes died away, people started drifting in to find their seats, but the VIP section around them was still mostly empty. Even so, Moira seemed more drawn in on herself than usual as she dropped into her chair and stared down at her sneakers, which someone—likely JoAnne—had hand-painted with unicorns and tiny fairies.

"Are you going to be all right here with Elspeth, Moira?" Anna asked, exchanging a glance with her aunt. "Because you don't have to stay. I can call your dad, and JoAnne can come back and take you home."

"JoAnne said I shouldn't want to come. She said that people wouldn't be very nice. They might say things about me."

"JoAnne said that just now?" Anna's nails dug into her palms, but she took a breath and crouched down as Moira gave a solemn nod. "You listen to me, all right? People are people. Some are nice, and some aren't, and not everyone is nice all the time. That's just the way the world works. We can't stop people from saying or doing things that we don't like, but when they do, it's up to us to decide how much we're going to let that hurt us. When something bad happens, we always have the power to remember the good things in the world, the things that make us happy, and that lets the bad things hurt a little less."

"What kind of good things?" Moira stared at her, one-half of her face so beautiful that it physically hurt to see the other side.

"Unicorns and fairies, for starters," Anna said, tapping Moira's shoes, "and having a dad who loves you more than the moon and stars. Having the loch as your front yard and all these hills to play on. Knowing that Elspeth loves you— and I love you, and JoAnne loves you. All the people in the glen love you. Does that help some? Can you try to remember that?"

Moira gave a nod. "Some people stared at me when I walked in, but I know they can't help it. Even JoAnne and Daddy stare sometimes when they think I can't see them."

"Do you mind that very much?"

"I wish my face was the same on both sides." Moira rubbed one thumb against the other. "Daddy says it's what's inside a person that matters, but I think people mostly say that when a person's outside isn't very pretty."

Anna caught Moira's hands in her own. "You listen to me, okay? How you look has nothing to do with *you*. How you look is about your DNA, your parents and grandparents and things outside your control. But how you act, whether you make other people happy or unhappy, that's the only thing you can control, whether you make the world a better place or a worse place. Sometimes that's as simple as smiling at someone and showing them that they matter. If they don't smile back, it's usually because there's something in their own lives that's making them very unhappy. But that's about them, not about you, okay?"

"Okay." Moira blinked at Anna and smiled as fully as she could. As if that one word could change things. As if it was as easy as a smile.

Anna's chest hurt and her eyes stung, and she exchanged a look with Elspeth. Then she left Elspeth and Moira to watch the play together and headed backstage to watch from the wings.

The play went well. By the third act, Anna should have been breathing a sigh of relief. Instead, she edged closer to the curtain as the second scene began, because that scene had always been a problem.

It didn't take long for trouble to start.

Erica, playing Lysander, had been in love with Sorcha's Hermia character throughout the play, but now she had been enchanted by the fairy Puck and had fallen in love with Helena. And Demetrius had been in love with Helena all along.

Sorcha clearly hated that. Despite all of Connal's warnings, she wouldn't stop getting between Fenella and the audience whenever Fenella spoke her lines.

Anna and Brando tried to wave her back. Fenella ducked around her for the fourth time, then quickly had to move again. Finally, she stomped all the way to the front of the stage, leaving Sorcha nowhere to go. She threw her sister a triumphant look, and Erica as Lysander and Donald as Demetrius moved up beside her and stood on either side, protectively, as they delivered their own speeches, arguing about their love for Helena.

Sorcha paused and stared at the audience, her face gone red. Then as if she had suddenly reached a decision, she walked over to Erica and, on her next line, grabbed Erica's buttocks in both hands, leaning in to kiss her with a sexy pout.

"What in bloody hell is she doing?" Brando asked, shifting over to stand beside Anna.

"Nothing good," Anna said.

Erica tore Sorcha's hands away and pushed her back, looking more genuinely revolted than she had ever managed to in rehearsals. "Hang off, you cat, you burr! Vile thing, let loose or I will shake you from me like a serpent."

Sorcha ran her hands around Erica's waist and up her back. "Why have you grown so rude since you left me this morning, my love?" she said, low-voiced and far sultrier than anything she'd done before. "Sweet love—"

"*Your* love? Get off me, you Tartar! Your company is like bad medicine I've been forced to drink." Lip curling, Erica shook Sorcha off again and stepped closer to Fenella.

Sorcha followed her, snaking her hands under Erica's defenses and running them up Erica's chest as she gazed deep into her eyes. "This is all a joke, isn't it? You couldn't truly love Helena."

"Now the joke's on you," Fenella said, pushing in between them.

"What are you doing, my love? Leave her." Sorcha wrapped her arms around Erica's waist and pressed her cheek against her shoulder. "Am I not Hermia? Are you not still my Lysander? I am as beautiful as I was when we went to bed last night when you loved me still, but this morning you were gone. Why would you leave me to go to *her*?"

Brando turned to Anna. "That's not the right line? What is she doing?"

Anna scanned the script. "She's combined two speeches and skipped ahead."

"Why?"

Anna shrugged. Donald and Erica, who should both have had lines in between, looked off stage at Brando, their expressions confused. Anna rolled her hand for Erica to jump ahead and mouthed the beginning of the line Lysander was supposed to have after what Sorcha had just said, "By my life, Hermia . . . "

Erica nodded. "By my life, Hermia, I never want to see you again. Don't hope for me to change my mind, don't question, don't doubt. Nothing is truer than the fact that I hate you and love Helena." Erica tried to pull away from Sorcha, and when Sorcha clung, suddenly stomped on her toe, crying, "Let me go!"

Sorcha, limping, spun around and pushed Fenella with both hands. "You thief of love! How did you come by night and steal my love's heart from me?"

Fenella shoved her back. "Do you hear yourself? Have you no modesty, no maiden shame, no touch of bashfulness? You want to force me to speak the truth? All right. You're a faker, a puppet!"

"Puppet? Why? Because you think you're better than I am? You think you've *won* Lysander from me? You think she's fallen in love with you because I'm not worth loving? How low am I, you painted maypole? Speak. How low am I?" Sorcha stepped forward, her fingers curled into claws. "I am not yet so low that I can't scratch out your thieving eyes!"

Fenella stepped behind Erica while the audience laughed again. "I pray you, Lysander, even if you're mocking me with a pretense at love, do not let her hurt me. I don't have her skill at insults, or her sly cat's tongue. She's always played low and dirty."

"Low? That again!" Sorcha's hand clipped Fenella across the cheek, and Fenella tumbled backward over a prop log that had been set out on the stage and landed on her hip behind it. The audience gave a shout of laughter.

Erica rushed to help her up. "Don't be afraid," she said, thinking quickly and jumping ahead another half page in the script, "I won't let her hurt you."

"*I* won't let her hurt you," Donald delivered the next line as Demetrius, rushing to pry Fenella away from Erica.

Without bothering to speak any lines at all, Fenella tore herself free of them both, leaped over the log, and rushed at Sorcha with her fists raised and her lips twisted into a snarl. Donald caught her and spun her around, and Erica jumped to grab hold of Sorcha.

"Let me go," Sorcha snarled at Erica, fighting to get free. "Let me at her."

Brando flipped frantically through the pages on his clipboard.

Erica shoved Sorcha even harder. "Leave her alone, you dwarf."

Sorcha fell to her knees on stage amid a roar of laughter from the audience. Her cheeks pale beneath the lights, she turned her head and squinted out into the rows of chairs. For a moment, she froze. Then hands covering her face, she jumped to her feet and ran off stage.

The remaining three actors in the scene watched her go, then they slowly turned to Anna and Brando, clearly lost. Silence had fallen across the tent.

"Come off," Brando mouthed at them, frantically beckoning while Anna waved for Julian and Pierce to get on stage and jump ahead in the script.

Fenella ran straight to Sorcha who was stalking back and forth in the curtained off area reserved for actors. "You can't ever let me have one single thing without trying to take it away from me, can you?" Fenella screamed at Sorcha. "You try to take away everything!"

"What do you have that I could possibly want?" Sorcha asked, her chin rising like a flag.

"Lines? Talent? An ego smaller than a train?"

"Shhh!" Anna and Brando both ran toward them. "Be quiet," Brando snapped. "The audience can hear you!"

The audience was ignoring Julian and Pierce, both of whom had calmly restarted their lines on stage. Every face had turned toward the wings, heads craned to hear the fight between Sorcha and Fenella.

Sorcha poked Fenella in the chest with her index finger. "You're delusional, aren't you? Daft and delusional and mousy. No wonder no one ever wants you around."

"Me? What about you? You're only jealous that Erica and Donald like me better."

"In the play," Sorcha snapped. "That's where you're confused. It's not real life, is it?"

"Shut up, the pair of you," Brando hissed, physically shoving them both deeper into the wings, trying to get them out of earshot while Anna waved at Julian and Pierce to speak up. But like the audience, they had fallen silent and turned toward the drama that was happening between the twins.

"You're both horrible." Donald ran up to Sorcha and Fenella, his slightly pudgy face and mild blue eyes close to Sorcha's, and his skin a mottled, angry red. "You too," he added, pointing at Erica. "You're all three of you mean and vain, and I wish none of you were in the play. I wish you didn't even live here in the village." Stalking away, he went off to slump into a chair with his head in his hands.

Inside the rest of the tent, there was utter silence.

"Donald's right, don't you think, Miss Elspeth? None of them are very nice." Moira's voice dropped into the lull. "I wish none of them had to be the May Queen."

FATE'S STEADY MARCH

Nothing else with such slaughtering feats can compare,
To win manly applause, or the smiles of the fair.

MARION BERNSTEIN, "MANLY SPORTS"

I T WAS A TRUTH universally acknowledged that a man competing in a Highland Games should always wear a kilt.

Which was not a bad thing, Anna thought while rushing around the glen on Saturday morning after yet another near-sleepless night. In fact, a kilt may have been the only thing that had saved them the previous night after the Sorcha/Erica/Fenella disaster. Vanessa had stalked offstage without even waiting for the applause to die down after the final curtain call.

"Where's Connal? Where's my bloody phone? If he thinks I'm going to do another bloody performance with this lot, he can bloody well hold his breath," Vanessa had fumed. "This is my *reputation* I'm staking on this. I've never been more embarrassed in my life."

"As if you haven't given more than your own share of tantrums over the years," Julian had said. "Come off your high horse, Van. You remember what it was like to be eighteen."

"I had some bloody *talent* when I was eighteen. I wasn't some no-name upstart—"

"Well, I for one can't imagine anyone doing a better Titania than you just did," Brando had said, swooping in with his charm turned up to maximum. "That was a brilliant performance, and I guarantee that's all anyone will remember when they talk about tonight."

Vanessa had eyed him up and down, taking in the kilt and the snug black T-shirt, not to mention the muscles and the smile and the jawline. "Did you think so?"

"Aye, and anyone who doesn't has no idea what they're talking about."

Vanessa's shoulders had relaxed an inch, and she'd taken Brando's arm when he offered it and gone back to the Braeside Hotel with him for a "bit of bubbly by way of celebration," but she'd turned back to Anna after gathering up her things.

"You and Connal had better figure this out. If you can't guarantee those . . . *girls* . . . will behave on Sunday, you can find yourself someone else to do my parts."

Brando excused himself briefly, leaving Anna to walk Vanessa and Pierce out of the tent while he and Julian went back and threatened to draw and quarter Sorcha and the rest of them if they didn't pull themselves together and behave like grown-ups. And judging by the expressions the girls all wore when Anna got back, no one considered that much of an exaggeration.

Anna and Elspeth had both echoed his threats, and then they'd set out to concentrate on damage control. Between then and this morning, they had handled a dozen brief interviews with reporters from various newspapers and websites, many of whom had stayed on to cover the games. Down on the field now, there was even a video crew from an Edinburgh television show filming the caber toss where contestants were competing to see how far they could throw a tree trunk.

Muscles, like kilts, were in plentiful supply.

The air smelled of grass, spring, and frying grease from the food concession booths, and Anna hurried from one event to another, making sure they ran on schedule, making sure the volunteers were where they were supposed to be and that they had plenty of water to drink, lugging boxes of trophies and awards. She tried to keep Elspeth sitting down and taking it easy, giving her Moira duty to restrict the amount of stress and walking she had to do. But by noon, Elspeth's nearly non-existent limp had become noticeable again. As Davy Griggs prepared to compete in the haggis-hurling competition, Anna coaxed Elspeth off to the information tent on the pretext of relieving his wife, who'd been there all morning answering questions.

"Don't think I don't see right through you," Elspeth said, but she sank gratefully into the chair.

"Consider it payback for bringing me here to take care of you under false pretenses."

"Have I thanked you for that yet?" Elspeth asked, her smile fading into something more serious.

Anna bent and kissed her cheek. "I'm the one who should be thanking *you*, remember?"

"I hope you'll still feel that way when all of this is over. Now away with you both, or you'll miss the chance to watch Davy lose some money. Unless he was smart enough to bet against himself."

Moira had followed Lissa as far as the edge of the tent and stood there bouncing impatiently, peering around as if afraid to miss anything that was going on outside. "Davy's next," she said, coming back to tug at Anna's fingers. "Can't we go?"

Her cheeks were flushed, and her eyes shone, and she'd stopped ducking her head when she caught strangers looking at her. Or maybe there was just too much going on for her to pay attention. Anna let herself get dragged over to where Davy had heaved himself up on top of a whiskey barrel with the haggis—a medium-sized round pudding made of sheep hearts, livers, lungs, and sundry other unmentionables encased in a sheep's stomach—poised in his hand. Winding himself up while trying not to tip the barrel over, he sent the haggis flying and visibly held his breath until it landed without splitting open. A cheer went up.

Anna shook her head. "I still haven't tried haggis," she confided as she and Moira clapped their hands. "This isn't making it seem more appetizing."

"Daddy says it's a taste you have to grow into. I don't think I'm old enough," Moira said, wrinkling her nose.

Anna laughed. "That must be my problem."

"Daddy's, too," Moira said, laughing with her. "But that's a secret. He says if we tell anyone, they'll think we aren't proper Scots."

They ate fried everything for lunch, chips and fish and deep fried Mars Bars for dessert—after which Anna felt vaguely disgusting and suspected she'd have been better with the haggis. Moira, skipping ahead and coming back again, herded her toward the field where the contestants were lining up for the tug-of-war, MacGregor kilts on one side and MacLaren on the other, along the length of rope that lay like a snake across the grass. Men and even a few women associated with either the MacLarens or the MacGregors had apparently come from all over Scotland and England for the event, thanks to the happy coincidence that the Balwhither Highland Games had turned out to be the first one of the season.

"Who do you think is going to win?" Anna asked, catching Moira's hand as the crowd grew more dense around them.

"*We* will, of course," Moira said with no small amount of satisfaction.

"Of course," Anna said. "Shall we put a wager on it?"

Moira nodded, and Anna handed her a five-pound note to give to Davy who, apparently undaunted by not having thrown the haggis farther than half the other competitors, was walking up and down the sidelines collecting bets. Moira hesitated only briefly before going toward the group of people clustered around him.

Davy collected the money and solemnly wrote Moira's name into his betting book. "That's on the MacLarens to win, is it?"

"No!" Moira shook her head. "MacGregors, silly."

"Och, is it now? Well, all right then. We'll have to see if you are right."

Standing at the edge of the crowd, Anna put her hands on Moira's shoulders and looked around with no small sense of achievement while they waited for the event to start. While not a huge crowd, for a month of preparation it wasn't half-bad. Just under a thousand people had paid the general entry fee, and with the additional charges for participating in events and extra for admission to the play, not to mention the booth rental income, they'd already taken in over twelve thousand pounds—almost fifteen thousand dollars. A good start on rebuilding the Village Hall, as long as the village all pitched in with labor and Connal kicked in the rest.

Down on the field, Brando stood on the sideline with Iaian Camm MacGregor, the two of them set to referee. "Ready," Brando said, and the competitors bent to pick up the rope. "Set." Everyone braced themselves. "Pull!"

The MacGregor side gave an enormous heave that forced the MacLarens two feet toward the midline before they managed to dig their heels in. The competition sawed back and forth, inches to the MacGregors then inches to the MacLarens in turn. Grass ripped beneath their feet and the mud-spattered T-shirts and socks and disappeared into the dark colors of the kilts.

Cheers split the crowd every time the momentum changed. The MacLarens leaned on the rope, using their body weight, their legs almost parallel to the ground as they fought for the last inches that separated them from defeat. But another MacGregor surge of muscle dragged the feet of the first MacLaren over to the MacGregor side of the line painted on the grass. A roar of approval went up as the MacGregors dropped the rope. The MacLarens tumbled to the ground with the release of tension. Another shout went up, nearly drowned by the groans on the MacLaren side.

Moira jumped up and down, then spun toward Anna with her face glowing. "You see? We always win."

"Always?" Anna raised an eyebrow at her.

"The last three years at the Lochearnhead games." Moira's half-smile fell. "I didn't get to see them, but people told me."

Anna worked to hold her own smile despite the pressure building behind her eyes. "But you're here now, and that's good, right? Are you having a good time?"

"The best." Moira threw her arms around Anna's waist, and for Anna, the field and the loch and the braes all suddenly went blurry. Her heart ached.

How was she supposed to say good-bye to this? To Moira and Connal and Elspeth—the whole village? These hills that had become the landscape of her heart?

She swallowed down a wave of misery and concentrated on taking things one event at a time.

For the most part, the day was going more smoothly than she'd hoped. There were a couple lost children, a few squabbles between competitors who'd had a bit more beer than was good for them, one concussion, a broken arm, and a minor traffic accident that resulted in the victims heading off to the pub together. But overall, going to collect Moira from Elspeth again later, Anna had to admit things could have been worse. On the other hand, the day was far from over.

Her hand tucked in Elspeth's, Moira stood watching the Married Ladies' Race, which Flora Macara won handily by throwing her ample chest across the finish line just ahead of a MacLaren cousin from outside the glen. Moira and Elspeth shouted along with everyone else. Then, spotting Anna, Moira came running to hug her. "Did you see Flora win?"

"Who knew she was that fast?" Anna replied, putting an arm around Moira's shoulder.

"I'll bet she's fast from chasing Shame," Moira said.

"I'll bet you're right. And speaking of bets, did you figure out what you want to do with your winnings from the tug-of-war?"

"I want to buy a present for Daddy since he can't be here. Will you help me pick one out?"

"Everything all right?" Elspeth asked, studying Anna's stricken face.

Anna and Moira wedged back in beside her to watch the unmarried ladies line up at the starting line for the Spinsters' Race. "Sure," Anna said. "Of course."

Brando called everyone to their marks again, and the race was off with sixty-three-year old Jenny Lawrence— who had apparently run the circuit around the lochs every day since she was twelve years old, rain or shine—taking the lead straight off. Jenny also finished twenty-third overall in the hill race that climbed steeply up to Creag an Tuirc, the ancient rallying point of the clan MacLaren, and continued roughly two and a half miles around the glen.

Leaving Moira and Elspeth again briefly, Anna returned at five o'clock, and the three of them ate meat pies and sticky toffee pudding from the concession booths and wandered around looking at the art and jewelry and trinkets for sale while, in the background, individual pipers competed with their slow laments, salutes, and gathering pieces for the piobaireachd. Moira bought Connal a leather-covered notebook and a pencil shaped like a tree branch, and Anna's attention caught on the gleam of polished silver in the adjacent jewelry booth. She lifted a small bracelet with a unicorn out of the tray.

"What do you think, Moira? Do you like it?"

"I love it," Moira said, her eyes going wide as Anna knelt in front of her to fasten it around her wrist. "For me? Why?"

"For remembrance," Anna said, and then she realized she'd said too much when Elspeth whipped her head around and stared at her. She turned toward the loch where a piper was playing something beautiful and dignified. "Quick, Moira, what's that song? Do you know it? It feels sad, doesn't it?"

"A little." Moira waited for Anna to pay for the bracelet then folded her hand in Anna's while Anna and Elspeth checked at the booths to make sure the vendors had everything they needed.

An hour later, the awards for all the pipers had been handed out. None of the group trophies had gone to the glen, but Iain Camm MacGregor claimed the win in the piobaireachd, and Rory MacLaren won the individual strathspey and reel competition. Angus Greer and an outside piper tied for the trophy for the individual march, and Angus picked up Kirsty and swung her around. She laughed down at him with her black hair tangling around her face and kissed him soundly as if all the arguing of the past weeks had never happened.

The sun went down, and the pipers all gathered together to play "Scotland the Brave" and "Amazing Grace."

Echoing around the glen, the music brought chills to Anna's skin again along with another pinch of pain. She and Elspeth and the villagers had staged every aspect of the festival for maximum theater and romance, but she hadn't realized how those moments would become bittersweet as they passed, each one a once-in-a-lifetime memory that brought her time in the glen closer to its end.

"We'd better go back out to the road," she said, tightening her grip on Moira's hand. "JoAnne will be here any minute to pick you up."

"Do I have to go already?" Moira looked up at her, her expression pleading. "I want to find out who's going to be May Queen and Winter King. And there's the song night. Anna, please?"

"JoAnne's probably on her way already, so you'd have to talk her into staying a little while."

"She won't." Moira shook her head. "She doesn't think anyone is nice. It's like Shame and the other dogs, isn't it? Shame jumps all over everyone and wants to lick them, but Brice at the garage has one who growls and comes straight at you with his fur standing all on end. JoAnne's more like Mrs. Lawrence's dog who stands back and barks and barks and barks, but if you walk toward her, she runs away and hides."

"You think JoAnne doesn't want people to hurt her?" Anna asked.

"I don't think her daddy was very nice to her."

Anna watched JoAnne coming toward them a few minutes later, wearing another shapeless sweater and with her long skirt blowing against her legs. Stoop-shouldered, she avoided eye contact with anyone, and with her face bare of make-up and her hair scraped back in a ponytail, it was as if she was doing everything humanly possible not to be noticed.

Moira tugged her hand free of Anna's and ran to meet her along the fence outside the inn. "Can I stay a little long longer, JoAnne? Please? Please?"

JoAnne frowned and drew Moira in tight against her side. "I don't think that's a good idea."

"I'm not tired, I promise, and I want to hear who's going to be May Queen and Winter King."

"You can find out in the morning."

"No." Mouth set, Moira tilted her head and stomped her foot. Standing in the light of the heat lamps the volunteers had set up around the tent and the courtyard of the inn, half her face was her mother's, but she had

Connal's eyes. Between her parents and JoAnne, she didn't stand a chance of having a normal life unless someone else stepped in.

"I'll tell you what," Anna said, "let me call your father and see what we can work out, all right? Maybe you and JoAnne can both stay for the announcement."

"Don't bother," JoAnne said bitterly. "He'll agree to whatever you want. He always does. I'll go wait in the car until Moira's ready to leave."

The lamps around the courtyard provided warmth for the spillover crowd that didn't fit inside the pub. Campers, villagers, and those who had driven in from the local area for the games all lingered, singing hammy versions of "The Braes of Balquhidder" and "Flower of Scotland," and warming themselves on beer and Flora's fresh pub food, sweets from Grewer's, and the specialty pastries that Brando had brought from his shop in Callander. Rhona, Erica, Sorcha, and Fenella sat at a table slightly ahead and to the left of where Anna found two empty seats and squeezed herself in beside Elspeth with Moira on her lap.

Flora Macara, looking flustered and wearing a different ugly brown sweater and even uglier skirt than the one in which she'd run the Married Ladies' Race, came to stand in the open doorway between the courtyard and the pub. With the ballot box in which she and Duncan had been collecting votes from the villagers tucked beneath one arm, she waved the tally sheet above her head.

"Quiet down, everyone!" she shouted. When that didn't work, she placed two fingers in her mouth and gave a piercing whistle.

"Wow, that's a trick I need to learn," Anna said to Moira. "Can you do that?"

Moira shook her head. "I can almost whistle. I've been practicing."

"Good for you. I should practice, too. It seems awfully useful."

Flora waved the paper again. "There's been a wee delay with the May Queen voting. We'll announce the winner in the morning instead, so go on back to enjoying your evening, everyone."

"What?" Sorcha stood up at the table, and Rhona and Erica also jumped to their feet. "The voting's over. Read the count."

Flora folded the paper and ran her fingernail absently along the crease. "Check back here tomorrow morning at ten o'clock."

"What about the Winter King?" someone shouted from the front.

"We'll announce both together," Flora said firmly. "Tomorrow."

Rhona and the three girls advanced on her, still arguing. Flora turned away from them and crooked a finger at Elspeth and Anna instead, looking as if she wished she could disappear.

Anna swung to her feet. "We'd better go try to save her."

Holding Moira's hand, she wove through the crowd with Elspeth behind her. At the last minute, Elspeth veered off and planted herself in front of Rhona and the girls so that Anna had an opportunity to pull Flora aside.

"What's going on?" Anna asked.

"All I can think is that people must have heard Moira in the tent yesterday," Flora said, bending to whisper in Anna's ear, the sound competing with the drunken singing that had started up again around the courtyard.

The whisper evidently wasn't quiet enough. Moira shuffled her feet and stared down at the ground. "I said I was sorry."

"I know you are." Flora smiled at her. "And you're not in any trouble, I promise."

Anna pulled Moira closer and wrapped an arm around her. "I don't understand. What's the problem?"

"Apparently, everyone agreed with Moira. Almost no one voted for Sorcha or Fenella or Erica as May Queen."

"They picked JoAnne?" Anna turned to the street where Connal's Audi was double-parked, and the light was on inside showing JoAnne's profile as she sat reading. "She'll say that she won't do it—and I don't think we'll be able to change her mind."

"It wasn't JoAnne."

Anna blinked in surprise. "Then who? It has to be someone between seventeen and twenty-five, doesn't it?"

Flora leaned forward to speak into Anna's ear once more, but again she misjudged her volume. "It was Moira," she said too loudly. "They picked Moira for May Queen and Brando for Winter King, and Connal's going to have a fit."

Moira gave a squeak. And as the shock registered, Anna found Rhona, Sorcha, and Erica all staring at Moira, their faces white and stunned.

Dancing with Wolves

*He often felt that too many people lived their lives
acting and pretending, wearing masks
and losing themselves in the process.*

Nicholas Sparks, *The Choice*

O NCE THEY ARRIVED back at Inverlochlarig and Moira,
bouncing in excitement, told her father, Connal
waited only as long as it took JoAnne to bustle the girl away
toward the carved mahogany staircase out of earshot
before he turned back to Anna. His eyes blazed cold with
fury. "Absolutely not. I knew it was a bloody stupid idea to
let her go to the games. I should have listened to my better
judgment instead of giving in to the pair of you."

"She had a wonderful time, and nothing happened."

"This happened, and what are people thinking? They
love Moira. Or I thought they did—why would they do this
to her?"

Anger made Anna hot, and she shook off her coat and threw it across a chair. "Maybe they're doing it *for* her. Have you ever thought of that? A misguided attempt to give her confidence. Or a swift kick to show you that she's not Rapunzel to be locked away in a fairytale tower."

"Rapunzel? What are you talking about? Never mind. She can't do it, and that's the end of it. I'll call Flora myself."

"But I want to do it," Moira said, running back around the corner toward them, evading JoAnne who rushed after her calling for her to stop. "I get to wear a crown and everything and walk behind the May Bush, and I get to be the first person to wash my face in the loch for the Sighting."

Connal caught her arms and knelt in front of her. "Do you really want to do those things? They'll wear you out, and you've already had an awful lot of excitement these past two days. Also, you don't like it when people stare. That's half the point of being May Queen, for people to look at you."

"Even you stare sometimes, Daddy. Anna says that's people not being happy with themselves, and I don't want to be afraid of people, like a dog barking. Anyway, you said I'm pretty on the inside, too. Isn't that enough for May Queen?"

"Of course, it is. You're beautiful inside and out." Connal squeezed her tightly, but over her head, his eyes met Anna's. Everything he felt was written in them, love and pride and pain and fear. Releasing Moira after another long moment, he stood up with his hands shaking visibly. "I'll tell you what, duck. You go get ready for bed, and we'll talk about it some more when I come tuck you in. But I think we should probably both sleep on it, all right?"

Moira studied him suspiciously. "You're going to say no, aren't you? You always say you'll think about things when what you mean is no." Frowning at him, she went to Anna and hugged her hard. "Thank you for today," she whispered. "I had the best time ever."

Anna closed her eyes as JoAnne led Moira away. "I don't know what to say, Connal."

"Tell me I'm right in telling her she can't do it."

"I can't tell you that. If she's brave enough to want to try, then don't you have to be brave enough to let her?"

"I'm her father." Connal rubbed his temples and shook his head. "It's my job to protect her so that she doesn't have to be brave. No good could come of this! She'd be the center of attention, people judging her, staring at her. That's a heavy weight all pressing down on her shoulders, and she's just a little girl. How can she bear up under that?" He paced back and forth, the light from the two crystal chandeliers dangling from the twelve-foot ceilings of the great hall spilling over him like water.

Anna loved him, she realized all over again. She loved him. She was in love with him, and she loved Moira, too. But loving him didn't make her blind.

"Are you sure it's fear for Moira that's making you want to hide her away? Or is it fear for your own sake?"

"How can you say that?"

"Because I remember how cruel the tabloids were after Isobel died. I know you don't want all that dredged up again."

"It was the tabloids that drove Isobel to drink—" Connal cut himself off and ran a hand over the back of his neck. "No, that's not entirely true. If she'd been stronger, she could have handled it better. We were both too young when we started acting. Too young when we got married. I knew she wasn't happy, but I didn't know how to help her. Isobel had always been—extreme, living life on the edge, on a pendulum. When she was happy, she swept everyone around her in a wave of joy, and when she was drawn in on herself, the sadness was like an anchor threatening to pull the people around her under along with her. I've wondered since if she wasn't bipolar, but people didn't talk about mental health as much back then, or maybe I just wasn't old enough to know enough about it. Not that that's any kind of excuse."

Anna went to him and pressed his hand against her cheek. "You're punishing yourself, and you can't do that. There were a lot of other people who should have caught her, not just you. Ultimately, she made her own choices. But however much you try to protect Moira, nothing will bring Isobel back. You can't keep her from living life, Connal. She's strong. She's beautiful inside and out, you said it yourself, and anyone who doesn't see that is an idiot."

"The world is full of idiots. Well-meaning and otherwise."

"Yes, and I'm sure the village meant well in picking her as May Queen, but at this point, their intentions don't make any difference. It's the reality you have to deal with. How could you refuse when she wants to do it? What would you say to her? That it's because of her palsy? Because the world is cruel? Because of her mother and the tabloids? Any one of those things are as bad as having a few people staring at her, and I watched her last night and all day today. People weren't unkind. They stare because they're not sure what they're seeing. The palsy isn't something obvious like a scar. It's the subtle sense of something being off that make people need to look a little longer. She handled it well."

"She wasn't the center of everyone's attention then." Connal raised his head, his expression pinched. "Don't you see? I failed to protect Isobel, and I can't fail Moira. I can't."

"The way I see it, the only person you're failing right now is yourself. You're refusing to live your life, and you're refusing to let Moira live it with you. If you want my opinion, you should let her be May Queen if she still wants to after she's slept on it. Trust her to know herself."

Connal clenched his jaw and closed his eyes. When he opened them again, he placed his hands on Anna's shoulders. "If I let her do this, you'll have to promise me you'll watch her like a hawk. If anything happens to upset her, promise me you'll bring her home."

"You seriously wouldn't come with her? Even now?"

"You know I can't."

"You *can*. You choose not to. Imagine how she'd feel if her own father wasn't there to see her crowned. To be proud of her."

"To ruin her moment. Don't you see? That's just another reason she shouldn't do it in the first place." A muscle ticked in Connal's cheek, and he straightened and turned away. "Good night, Anna. Thanks for taking care of her today."

Anna stiffened and picked her coat back off the chair. "Is that a no or a yes about Moira?"

"It's a maybe. I'll phone you in the morning," he said, but his expression was closed.

Tears welled in Anna's eyes, making the shape of him blur. But maybe that was simply the man she had thought he was—or could be—melting away in her mind.

Her hands shook on the steering wheel as she drove the borrowed Vauxhall back to Elspeth's house. Why did she do this over and over again? Make assumptions about men without seeing who they really were? With Henry, she had believed in the mask he had shown her, but Connal hadn't done anything he hadn't promised all along. Connal had stripped his mask off for her. Even so, she had convinced herself there was something in him that wasn't there.

It wasn't that what he'd said about ruining Moira's moment wasn't rational. Anna didn't doubt that he thought he was protecting his daughter, but that wasn't his only reason for not wanting Moira to be May Queen.

And wasn't that exactly the technique Henry had always used? Henry had managed to twist things so that the selfish reasons for his behavior somehow appeared to be entirely selfless. She'd let him get away with it. She'd made excuses for him. She'd enabled him do it.

Henry's grades hadn't been good enough for an Ivy League college, so she had let him talk her into giving up acceptances from Brown and Yale to go to Ohio State because—he'd claimed—a long-distance relationship would have been too hard on *her*. Then college had been a continuation of high school, where she'd spent countless nights helping him study, helping him with his papers and reports. Her own studying, going out with her roommate, having fun with friends, all of it had revolved around Henry's schedule. When he had other plans, she was the one who'd had to make adjustments or sit in her dorm alone.

He'd always had a perfectly plausible explanation. "I know you hate drinking beer with the guys, so I don't want you to have to come along and spend the night feeling awkward. Go be with your friends." Or, "Why don't you put off law school applications until after we get married? A wedding takes so much time to plan, and I don't want you having to worry about all that on top of studying. Plus we should have a year or two to ourselves before you have to start working around the clock again, don't you think?"

Even Mike had made similar arguments. Why wait to get married? She could take a bit of time off from work or dial back her workload. She'd given in on most things that he'd asked, but she hadn't given in on that. Then he'd left her.

Maybe men were all the same.

No, that wasn't fair. Connal wasn't Henry. She knew that. His deception wasn't aimed at her as much as it was aimed at himself. Maybe she was the problem. Maybe she was so starved for love that the more someone withheld it, the more desperately she tried to win it. The more she tried to sweep away the obstacles.

She parked the Vauxhall and walked tiredly up the steps. Letting herself in quietly, she found Elspeth rushing to meet her in the foyer.

"What happened? Are you all right?" Elspeth asked, her face puckered into lines of worry. "What did Connal say?"

"The exact wrong things for the exact right reasons," Anna said. "He's thinking about letting Moira do it. Even if he does, he won't come to see her crowned. I hoped this would break him out of his rut, but it won't. And I'm leaving in three days, and now we're barely speaking."

"Don't put all that on him, love. That's you leaving. Your choice, not his."

"You've already paid for my ticket. I'm not going to waste the money to change it."

"Are you sure Connal's the only one of you who's running scared?" Elspeth tipped her head to study Anna. "How hard did you fight to keep your job? To keep Mike? It takes effort to stay. Running away is easy."

Running away? Anna examined that thought later as she lay in bed unable to fall asleep. Was she running away? Her mother had accused her of that, too, and she hadn't wanted to hear it then. It was true that she'd convinced herself Mike was coming back because she didn't want to face the reality that she'd have to fight for him, to marry him, if she wanted him. She hadn't given any thought to fighting for her job—she'd been too mortified and guilty over the meltdown, over missing the filing. Going back to the partners might not have done any good, but she hadn't tried. Or maybe she hadn't wanted the job that much in the first place.

You fought for the things you couldn't live without. That was the simple truth. She loved Connal. She loved what she thought they could have together. So shouldn't she stay and fight for that? For Moira?

Or was it too soon to take that kind of risk? Was Connal worth the risk at all?

The wind gusted through the village and rattled the sides of the rented tent, doing its best to blow away the suggestion of summer even as the festival celebrated its approach. Music from the ages twelve-and-under Highland dancing competition drifted out from the tent in fits and starts, carried in by the wind then swept away again. Standing in the crowd gathered outside the inn, Anna huddled deeper into the collar of her jacket with one arm around Moira and the other in her pocket.

"There it is! They're coming!" Moira bounced on her toes and pointed up the track that led across the main road and up the hill. "I can see the May Bush."

A small hawthorn tree slung across one shoulder and dragging almost to the ground, Brando came around the bend and raised the axe he carried in his other hand as he saw the crowd. The crowd responded with a cheer, the sound echoed by the thirty or so villagers and visitors who had braved the windswept hillside to go with him to find a tree to cut. Brando pushed through the gate into the inn's courtyard with his kilt swirling, revealing a long, ugly scratch along across one knee, as if the tree had offered up a protest at being made a sacrifice.

It was just on the cusp of full bloom, buds mixed in among the white, sweet-scented blossoms. Brando carried it to the corner of the courtyard where, at least somewhat sheltered from the wind, he jiggled it into the stand that Duncan had set up earlier.

When it was secure, he turned and held out his hand to Moira. "Ready, Mo?"

She nodded with her eyes huge, taking the hand he offered as he helped her up onto the small raised platform beside the May Bush. Cheeks red and eyes roving nervously over the crowd, she held her head high, her long fair hair streaming in the fingers of wind that snuck even into the sheltered corner. Brando knelt to accept the crown of hawthorn leaves that Duncan settled around his head, then he stood and crowned Moira in turn with a wreath of hawthorn blossoms. He led her forward, presenting her to the crowd.

The cheering was louder this time, mixed with catcalls and whistles. And Moira, who had been so determined, visibly trembled as she stood there, looking even smaller beside Brando's height and bulk. Edging behind him, she nervously hid the damaged half of her face, but when he whispered for her to smile and wave, she raised her hand

and wiggled her fingers. When the applause died down, she jumped off the platform and ran back to Anna.

Anna hugged her fiercely. "You did great, kiddo."

"But you aren't done yet," Brando said, coming up behind her. "The May Queen gets to hang the first offering, remember?"

"Here, I brought a ribbon for you," Elspeth said, producing a lavender silk scarf from the pocket of her coat. "I thought lavender was a good fairy color. What do you think?"

Moira nodded and clutched the scarf in a white-knuckle grip.

"Off you go, then. Go hang it on the tree. Brando will help you," Elspeth said.

Moira watched them over her shoulder as Brando walked her toward the tree. Back on the platform, he caught her around the waist and raised her high enough to tie the scarf at the very top while her hair blew across her cheeks.

"I hope we're doing the right thing," Anna said. "It's not my place to meddle when it comes down to it."

"A little late for that sentiment, but it's high time somebody meddled if you ask me. We've all been half-asleep, not seeing that Connal needed a nudge to help him," Elspeth said, digging in her coat pocket to extract another bit of ribbon. She pressed it into Anna's palm.

Anna was surprised to feel cold metal against her skin, and she raised her hand to find a small necklace with a silver cross. The chain was wound through with a thin lavender ribbon, and the cross was etched with a lovely pattern.

"You can't mean for me to leave this on the tree?" Anna said. "It's too valuable."

Elspeth gave her a wistful smile. "There's no point in a sacrifice if it doesn't have any value. Go on. Make your offering. Then take a bit of blossom to carry the luck home with you."

Anna wound the ribbon and the chain on a branch and broke off a small flowering sprig in exchange. Luck, though? That wasn't what she needed.

She needed the ability to make a logical decision.

Stay or go? Take a chance or give up before she risked more pain?

If the May Bush had an answer for her, it wasn't ready to share it yet.

She turned and found Rhona and Sorcha approaching with painted egg shells hung on slender satin ribbons and Fenella and Erica right behind them. Sorcha glared at Moira, her head tipped toward her mother's as she whispered something that Anna couldn't hear. Still, the message was clear enough.

Moira tucked her hand in Anna's and bit her lip. "They're not very happy with me, are they?"

"They're not very happy at all, sweetie, but remember what I told you? That's their problem. People have to find happiness inside themselves. Some people never understand that, and they spend their whole lives looking for other people to make them happy. It doesn't work very well."

Moira studied her, her face tilted up and intent. "Are you happy?"

"*You* make me happy. That's a promise. You made me very proud today, and you make lots of other people happy." Wrapping one arm around Moira's shoulders, Anna squeezed her close then let go. "I'm going to have to leave you with Elspeth until the play, though. All right? I've got to see if the dance competition is going smoothly, check something at the campground, and run back to the house and make sure things are all set for the ball."

"Shouldn't I stay for the whole ball?" Moira asked. "The May Queen always goes to the bonfire."

"Nice try, but don't push your luck. You'll be so worn out by then that you'll be happy to be in bed. And I'll be jealous because I'll be exhausted, too." Anna squeezed Moira's hand. "Now off you go with Elspeth, all right? I'll see you when the play is over."

Moira threw her a grin and slipped her small hand into Elspeth's larger one.

Anna watched them walk away a moment, and then she ducked into the tent to make sure the junior dancing competition wasn't running late. Next, she borrowed the phone at the inn and rang up Julian to make sure neither Vanessa nor Pierce had snuck back to London instead of staying for the second performance of the play.

"I've been feeding their egos, and Brando's been feeding their taste buds. Between us, so far they haven't threatened to mutiny yet," Julian said. "Vanessa hasn't called off the critic from *The Times,* either. Did you see the review on *The Scotsman* website, by the way?"

"I haven't exactly had time to surf the Internet," Anna said dryly.

"In that case, allow me to share. 'Witty, sparkling, and ironic performances by Vanessa Devereaux, Julian Ashford, and Pierce Saunders against a backdrop of amateur actors so terrible they could only be poking fun at Shakespeare's intentions.'"

"Connal must have loved that."

"You should make sure he didn't miss it."

"Or you could call him yourself. What are you up to, Julian?"

Julian was silent a moment before he spoke again. "He confessed that he yelled at you yesterday about the May Queen fiasco. He feels terrible about it, but he's never been at his best when he's feeling guilty. He's a bit of an ass when he's feeling guilty, to tell the truth, so don't let that put you off. You've been good for him, and he needs you. Whether he knows it or not."

"He needs something, but I'm not sure it's me. Anyway, I'm going home in a couple of days."

"Don't. If he hasn't had the good sense to ask you to stay, stay for yourself. We're men, darling. The stupider sex. We don't know what's good for us until you hit us over the head with it. I'll supply the bludgeon if you need one."

Anna laughed as she hung up, but she couldn't help wondering if it could be that easy. Could she decide to stay?

Her expression grim and her mind racing, Anna searched the crowds in the village until she found Sorcha, Fenella, and Rhona standing at the back of the tent watching a boy Moira's age doing the Highland sword dance, his toes coming down perilously close to the crossed blades laid out on the stage.

"Where's Erica?" Anna asked. "I need to speak with all four of you."

"Is there something else you want to take away from us?" Sorcha snarled. "Let me guess, you're going to have Moira do Erica's part today? Or maybe you and Moira want to play *all* the parts."

"What I'd like is for the three of you to behave like adults and worry about what you have instead of what you don't. In spite of you, the reviews haven't been total disasters so far, and Vanessa's had a big critic from London lined up to come for today's performance. If you and Erica and Donald can all manage to work together, it could mean big things for the festival next year."

"Which critic? Do you know what he looks like?" Rhona peered around, scanning the faces in the dim interior of the tent. Between those seated in groups among the rows and others standing in clusters near the back, there were a hundred people, most of them strangers.

"I don't know, but he'll be staying for the ball, which would be an opportunity to talk to him. One more slip-up from any of you, though, and I'll make sure none of you will be at the ball."

"You can't do that," Rhona said.

"Elspeth can, since the ball is at her house. And I'll make sure none of you get past the door."

Sorcha and Rhona glared at her, and Fenella dropped her eyes with a sullen pout.

Anna started to walk away, but after a few steps she turned and went back again. "One more thing: If I see so much as a cross-eyed glance from you in Moira's direction, or I hear a whisper of any of you being unkind to her, you'll be dancing here in the village with the visitors tonight instead of at the ball. I don't care how unfair you think the vote has been. I don't care about your egos, or your squabbles between yourselves. She's a little girl, and you are supposed to be grown women."

"It's a joke, you know that, don't you? Her being May Queen," Rhona said. "The village wanted to have a laugh."

Sorcha's mouth twisted. "The joke's on them then."

Anna's hand itched to slap her. "Actually, the joke's on you. Moira never asked to be picked for May Queen. You still don't understand what everyone was trying to tell you, do you? Your own behavior made it impossible for the village to choose you, and being snippy to Moira is only going to prove that they were right."

OF CROWNS AND CLOAKS

To ... wear a crown is a thing more glorious to them that see it than it is pleasant to them that bear it.

QUEEN ELIZABETH I

T HE AUDIENCE LAUGHED at all the right places in the play. Warmed by body heat and the brilliant sun that had finally emerged from behind the clouds, the tent had grown stuffy by the time the performance culminated in the final scene, and the air stank of sweat and perfume. Despite that, not even the children watching were squirming in their seats. The actors from the village overplayed their parts, just as Connal had meant them to, and Sorcha mostly behaved herself. Fenella, Erica, and Donald were like completely different people. As if the scene on Friday night had shown them what the script was all about, they highlighted the comic elements of the parts that Connal had designed for them with his small rewrites of the original lines.

By the last scene, Anna found herself standing beside Elspeth and Moira backstage with her fingers crossed, hoping they'd all managed to pull the production off without any more disasters. As if he'd read her mind, Brando grinned at her and looped his arm around her shoulders. "I can't believe we've managed to make this work."

"Don't count your chickens," Anna said.

"True enough," Elspeth said. "Sorcha's liable to lop their heads off."

Anna peeked back out at the audience. They were still enthralled, quiet in their seats as Pierce Saunders stood at the edge of the stage and began the fairy Puck's final monologue:

> If we shadows have offended,
> Think but this, and all is mended,
> That you have but slumber'd here . . .

Slumber'd here.

Though she'd heard the speech a hundred times in rehearsals and on Friday night, standing there now with Brando's arm around her, the words abruptly took on a more personal dimension. A few minutes ago, she had been thinking that Erica, Fenella, and Donald had discovered the key to the play within their own lives. How had she missed its meaning in her own?

The whole past month had been a dream, an interlude—time outside of time. She didn't want to wake up. She wanted to stay here and pretend that she could have this, have Connal and Moira and the glen, forever. But now the curtain was coming down, both on the play and on her visit. If she wanted the dream, she had to decide.

Puck spoke his final words, and the audience jumped to their feet, clapping and whistling their appreciation. Slightly drunk on adrenaline and relief, the actors went out to take their curtain call. Then Anna sent Vanessa, Julian, and Pierce out together to take their individual bows, before the rest of the cast from the village went out again. Friends, family members, and total strangers cheered even louder. Anna scanned the stage and audience. So many familiar faces. She wished Connal was there beside her, to take credit if nothing else.

Once again, Brando had to go stand in for him to accept the audience's applause. Not that he didn't deserve it in his own right. His Winter King crown still resting across his forehead, Brando executed a sweeping bow, and the whistles and cheers grew piercingly loud. He flushed red, his carefully constructed mask slipping to show anyone who cared to look how much that show of respect mattered to him.

Anna clapped so hard her palms stung. Brando turned and called for her to come and join him. She shook her head, but Elspeth gave her a shove, and she grabbed Elspeth's hand and Moira's and brought them both on stage along with her. They stood with the actors, talking and laughing, as out in the tent the audience began to gather their things and exit the rows of chairs, turning on phones that glowed and beeped in the gray light that streamed in through the waterproof plastic overhead.

Moira bounced beside Anna as they headed back behind the curtain. "I want to be in the play next year, Anna. Do you think I can?"

Anna's lungs squeezed closed. "I hope so, honey. If you still want to."

Elspeth cleared her throat and threaded her arm in the crook of Moira's elbow. "You know what I was thinking? The temperature will cool again by the end of the procession, so I thought maybe you might like to wear that green velvet cloak that Titania was wearing in the play. You could decide if you want the hood on or off, or throw the whole thing over your back and wear it like a superhero cape."

"Yes, please," Moira said.

Elspeth caught her hand. "Then let's go find Vanessa and get it from her."

When Moira had skipped off with Elspeth, Brando came back over. "I would have laid odds against us making it through to the end without anyone getting killed or at least dismembered."

"Maybe your threat kept them in line," Anna said, laughing. "Drawn and quartered? Really?"

He smiled at her ruefully. "I happen to like history, and as gruesome punishments go, that one makes a good deterrent."

"Threats aside, you did a fantastic job with everything. I hope Connal tells you so, too."

"I'll be sure to wait until whenever he gets around to watching the video. It was his loss, though for not being here, wasn't it? I never thought I'd hear myself say it, but I feel sorry for him. Not coming to see Moira—" He shook his head and cut himself off as Moira and Elspeth returned. "Ready for a long walk, Mo?" He held out his arm, and Moira put her hand on it regally, then walked out with him with her head held high in her crown of hawthorn blossoms and the green velvet cloak that trailed behind her on the ground. They exited the tent together and moved across to the courtyard of the inn while people stared and snapped photos. Anna smiled as, walking behind them, she noted that Brando distracted Moira with chatter all the way.

Outside, the pipers and line of tattoo drummers had assembled again. The bagpipes squealed the first notes, and people streaming in from the village and all around the glen hurried their steps—at least those who weren't glued to their phones or texting.

"Are you ready?" Brando smiled at Moira. She nodded, and he lifted the May Bush from its stand and hoisted it up in front of him.

The pipers exited the courtyard and formed up in the street. Brando and Moira lined up behind them, with Anna and Elspeth one row back, followed by the Highland dancers who had been competing earlier that day and many of the actors from the village still in costume. It seemed to Anna that most eyes were fastened on Moira now, more so than earlier, nearly everyone snapping pictures on their phones or with their cameras. Moira's cheeks were pink, and her eyes darted around, taking in the attention without seeming to mind too much. Tucked close to Brando's side, she glanced over at Anna and Elspeth every few minutes for reassurance, but she left the hood of the green cloak streaming down her back.

"Will you let me use your phone?" Anna asked, leaning in to Elspeth.

"Are you going to try to phone Connal?" Elspeth pulled the phone from her pocket and handed it over. "He should be here to see her. At least he should come as far as the hotel so that he sees her before we turn around."

"That's what I was thinking."

The wind had picked up again, the temperature cooling beneath a brilliant sapphire sky dotted with cotton ball clouds that cast their shadows onto the loch. Anna's fingers hovered over recent numbers in the phone's memory, then she stopped and shook her head. "No," she said. "I'm not going to do it. If I call and nag at him, he won't have changed anything even if he does come out. He needs to decide for himself. It needs to mean enough to him for him to come of his own accord, and if I love him, I'll give him that choice."

"He's not wrong, though, you know. It would be harder—much harder—for Moira if he came."

"Do you really think she'd care? Or would she just want her father to be there and be proud of her?" Anna handed the phone back again as the procession moved out to the brave wailing of the pipes.

Then three things happened almost simultaneously: Connal himself strode around the corner of the road with a cap pulled low on his forehead, the door of the inn banged open and Flora Macara ran out with Shame bounding out behind her, and several people around Anna suddenly shouted, "That's him, isn't it? That's Gregor Mark!"

Connal's head shot up. He stopped in the middle of the road, then hastily stepped out of the way of the approaching line of pipers and squeezed himself against the fence. Shame darted onto the track and made a beeline for the May Bush, leaping and snapping at the colorful ribbons and decorations streaming from the hawthorn's branches.

Brando raised it higher. "Shame, you blasted nuisance. Stop it. Someone grab him, can't you? Where's Flora?"

Moira and Elspeth both dove at Shame, trying to catch him, but Flora had run straight to Anna. "You need to get Moira out of here. Get her back to Connal. We have to warn him," she said, obviously not noticing Connal ahead by the fence. She waved the screen of her phone in front of Anna's eyes. "Someone sent a picture of Moira and Connal to the *The Sun,* and the article says they're both here in Balwhither. It says Moira is May Queen—and the rest of it makes my blood boil."

Anna snatched up the phone, but behind her, women were weaving through the procession, heading in Connal's direction, their own phones raised to snap photos of him. Anna found herself pushed aside as she tried to focus on the screen.

Her breath stopped as if someone had kicked all the air from her lungs. The image beneath the tabloid headline wasn't a photograph at all; it was an illustration of Moira and Connal laughing together, and the expression put the contrast between the two sides of Moira's face in stark relief. Above it, the text read:

WHAT'S GREGOR MARK BEEN HIDING HERE IN SCOTLAND?

Anna's hands went cold. Her throat burned with an icy rage, but what was she supposed to do now? What were *they* supposed to do? Stop the procession? That would only make the situation worse.

"Help me, Flora." Catching at Flora's sleeve, she darted ahead to follow the women who had started rushing at Connal. She stepped in front of them while Flora did the same and waved them back. "Stay in line, everyone."

"But that's Gregor *Mark*," said a pale, sturdy woman with washed-out skin and brilliant blue eyes. She tried to shove past Anna.

"And that's his daughter in the procession," Anna snarled. "What if your daughter was in a recital or a performance at school? Would you want someone making a fuss and spoiling her big moment? Gregor Mark isn't going anywhere. You can get your photos later. Let the procession go on ahead."

She hoped she was telling the truth as she stared the women down.

Reluctantly, they fell back in line, and Moira, her back stiff and her hand wrapped tight in Brando's, continued walking behind the pipers. She had almost reached Connal, and she turned and waved as she passed by, her smile so wide that it made Anna's stomach ache. Anna and Flora shooed the remaining fans away and dropped back to walk protectively behind Moira again, Connal falling into step beside them with his face grim and his hands fisted in his pockets.

"I didn't think I'd be recognized that fast," he said to Anna before stooping to speak into Moira's ear. "You look beautiful, little duck. I like that color green on you, and I'm very, very proud of you."

"It's Titania's cloak," Moira said. "She was the fairy queen."

"Just like you." Connal's gaze lifted as he turned the corner onto the main road that followed along the loch. He scanned the rows of faces in the procession fanning out behind them.

"You weren't recognized by accident," Anna said. "Someone sent a picture to *The Sun*. Someone deliberately told them where you were." She waved for Flora to come over, and watched with her breathing ragged while Flora, still gripping Shame by the collar, handed the phone to Connal.

Connal squinted at the screen, and Elspeth edged around his elbow to peer down as well. Both of them went pale simultaneously. Connal's hands shook as he read the rest of the article beneath the caption. Almost at the same moment, both of them said a single word: "JoAnne."

Anna wasn't quite so convinced. She walked backward as the rest of the procession came around the corner, searching the people in the back for the three Grewers and Erica MacLaren. Not spotting them didn't necessarily mean anything, but it gave her a chance to think. She and Connal and Elspeth had all fallen behind Moira and Brando now, but she lowered her voice anyway, as much as she could while still making herself heard above the wailing of the bagpipes.

"I don't think we should be too quick to accuse JoAnne."

Elspeth lifted her chin, bright spots of color burning on her cheeks. "Don't bother trying to defend her. That's JoAnne's drawing. I've seen it in her sketchbook. You warned us, you warned *me*, and I'm the one who didn't see this coming."

"The posters and the phone calls, those were almost certainly JoAnne. I don't dispute that. But what would she gain by sending her own sketch to the tabloid?" Anna asked. "It doesn't make any sense."

"Nothing that girl does makes sense. Only now her artwork's been noticed, hasn't it?" Flora said. "That picture'll be famous, and you mark my words, she'll be claiming credit in a day or two, coming out with lots more sketches."

"I'm the one to blame if we're going to blame anyone," Connal said. "We had a big argument about Moira being May Queen this morning, and I told her that if she didn't like my decisions, she was welcome to leave. I never dreamed she'd do anything like this. But I should take Moira home. If *The Sun* put this out on their website, they'll have people on the way here already. They could be here practically any minute."

"No!" Anna cried. "You've promised to let her be May Queen. You can't stop her from finishing the procession now, not unless she wants to stop."

Flora grabbed Connal's arm. "Let the poor child have her day, Connal. I'll take Duncan and some of the others, and we'll block the road here at the intersection. No one will be able to get down the glen until after the procession gets back here, and then you can whisk Moira straight off home, safe and sound, if you want to."

"All right." Connal's nod was terse. "Thanks, Flora."

"Flora, wait," Anna called. "Keep an eye on Erica and the Grewers. Maybe I'm biased, and it's not that I'm particularly fond of JoAnne, but she does love Moira. I can't see her doing anything to hurt her. Sorcha and Erica, on the other hand, they have plenty of malice between them, and Erica could have photographed that sketch anytime while she was cleaning at Connal's house."

"Erica's sneaky enough, I'll say that much for her, but she wouldn't have thought up something like this all on her own." Flora's lips tightened, and her eyes narrowed. "Don't you worry. If she and Sorcha are the ones behind this, they'll get what's coming to them. I'll see to it personally." She hurried off, an avenging angel in sensible shoes and an ugly puce-green sweater.

The procession followed the road along the loch, pausing now and then to let someone who had come down from a farm or house hang a ribbon or painted egg shell on the bush in exchange for a bit of blossom. Connal had pulled the hat lower on his head, and his eyes constantly searched the edges of the road with the wary expression of a dog who had been kicked too often. It wasn't a lack of courage, that reaction. It was a lack of trust—and who could blame him? Look what had happened the moment someone wanted to lash out at him.

Anna hadn't taken the time to read the whole article Flora had waved in front of her, but she'd seen enough. Kindness didn't sell newspapers or advertising, and too many people were willing to make money from someone else's work or effort or fame. She'd seen plenty of that working as a lawyer, but she'd thought it was different here in the glen. She'd convinced herself that Connal was wrong to be afraid.

She was the one who'd been mistaken all along.

"I'm sorry, Connal. This is all my fault." She edged closer to him as they rounded the bend with the rowan tree and passed the fence where, ears twitching, Davy Grigg's black-faced sheep had lined up along the road to watch the procession pass.

"How do you figure that?" He slanted an evaluating look at her then dug a hand out of his pocket to wrap it around her fingers. "I'm the one who hid from myself too long. The only way that I managed to keep off the radar until now was by not getting involved in anything. Moira lived in the village more than I did. Brando was right: I wrote out checks, hoping to bribe people into wanting to keep us around and keep our secrets. That's not what I want to be teaching Moira about how to live her life. Look at her, walking up there, waving at everyone. I don't want this to break her, and it may do just that by the time the tabloids dredge up all the old accusations, half-truths, and outright lies they printed about me before. But what you said earlier made me think. I wasn't going to be able to protect Moira from the ugliness forever. It was all going to come out eventually, and she was going to have to hear about it. I think that's what I've been dreading most. That she'd see what the tabloids wrote and wonder if it was true. I've been stupid. If I'd let the tabloids run with the stories about her palsy while she was younger, it would all be a less intriguing story now. I've only made things worse for her."

"You don't know that." Anna watched Moira take a skipping step to catch up with Brando, not because the procession was moving too fast but because she was stopping often to talk or smile and wave. She didn't speak to everyone, but she was friendly, and she chatted with the people she knew well as they hung their ornaments and took their blossoms. "We don't know how big the story is going to be, not yet, and whatever Moira hears, you have to know she's going to believe in you. She trusts you. That's who she is, and that's how you've raised her."

"Trust can disappear overnight, can't it?" Connal said softly, watching her. "I asked you to trust me, but I left all the explanations until it was already too late."

Anna fought to keep on breathing. "Nothing is ever too late, Connal. Don't retreat. Don't pull Moira away."

"I need to get her home."

"What about the ball?" Anna stumbled to a halt. "And the Sighting? She'll be heartbroken if she doesn't get to go to those."

"I don't know what to do," Connal said, looking lost and broken.

Anna opened her mouth, but what right did she have to suggest anything? Hadn't events already demonstrated how wrong she had been?

Maybe there was no right answer in this situation.

Her heart leaden with guilt and doubt, she let Connal walk in silence along the rest of the route that led up the long drive to the Braeside and down again then past Elspeth's house. They turned around in the small parking area at the trailhead between Breagh and Inverlochlarig House.

Flora, true to her word, had organized a roadblock at the end of the road along the loch by the time they returned to the village. A green tractor, two Land Rovers, and a hay wagon barred anyone from driving farther than the inn, but the barrier also made it impossible to see what was waiting for them.

The first row of pipers approached, and one of the Land Rovers reversed away to reveal a white panel van with Braeside Bakery written on the side and a fading red Toyota Hilux parked across the intersection holding back a small line of cars that had driven up from the highway. Several of the vehicles stood with their doors open, and a huddle of people with phones and cameras shouted questions Connal pretended he couldn't hear over the music of the pipes.

The procession turned back along the narrow track toward the inn. More people lined the shoulders, their cell phones raised. One of the reporters to whom Elspeth had spoken on Saturday stood snapping a continuous stream of photos with the large camera slung around her neck.

Anna moved to ask her to stop, but Connal grasped her arm and shook his head. "Don't bother. I know from experience that you'll only make things worse."

"That reporter was smart and professional yesterday. I thought maybe she'd be reasonable."

"Reasonable to you and me doesn't allow them to do their job. Do you know what paper she's with?"

"*The Edinburgh Evening News,* I think," Anna said.

Connal studied the woman a moment, as if sizing her up, as if debating something within himself. Then he caught Anna's hand and held her back as the procession ground to a halt and everyone milled around. "Will you keep Moira with you until I come to pick her up?"

"Where are you going?"

"If that reporter was even halfway reasonable, I'm going to take advantage of it. Maybe if I give a couple of interviews to legitimate papers, I can get my version of the story out to the public and hope for the best."

SHATTERED IMAGES

. . . the longest day at last bends down to evening . . .

JOHANN WOLFGANG VON GOETHE, *WILHELM MEISTER'S TRAVELS*

THE BALLROOM GLOWED with white candles and vases of hawthorn blossoms set atop white tablecloths, all lit by chandeliers and strings of delicate white fairy lights. Anna ran a last check of the room: the long tables of small bites and desserts along the far wall, the punch bowl and the display case doing double duty as a table filled with wine, beer, and assorted whiskeys. She shifted a branch of blooms from one side of a vase to the other and stepped back to check the symmetry as a quartet of folk musicians—keyboard, accordion, fiddle, and drums—set up at the head of the room.

"You need to stop fretting," Brando said, coming up behind her. "Unless all that fidgeting is helping to calm your nerves." He wore yet another kilt with a black shirt and a short formal black jacket with silver buttons. His hair was swept back from his face, revealing the firm line of jaw and chin and making his eyes brighter as he smiled down at her. "Elspeth says you haven't stopped rushing 'round since Connal left with Moira."

"I'm too furious to stop. And sad."

"Aye, and you're also beautiful," Brando said softly, "and this is still a ball. That's a spectacular dress. You should try to find some pleasure in it."

"Trust Elspeth to have a secret stash of designer gowns tucked away in her closet." Any other day, Anna would have had more fun dressing in vintage Dior that made her feel like Audrey Hepburn, but now she only wished the long night would end.

"Elspeth was young once, too, you know," Brando whispered into her ear.

Anna stepped back to look at him. "She's far from old now. I only wish she wasn't so alone."

"She still has you." Brando quirked an eyebrow at her. "Or have you definitely decided to leave?"

"For now, I've decided," Anna said, "to go stand by the door and help Elspeth greet the guests as they arrive."

She did precisely that for the next twenty minutes as people from the glen trickled in. Women came in long gowns and men in kilts and short, dark jackets. Even Julian had scraped up a formal kilt somewhere in a Black Watch tartan, double rows of silver buttons gleaming on his chest and up his sleeves, and Pierce had opted for a Royal Stewart that matched the striking red of Vanessa Devereaux's gown.

"Connal has no idea what he's missing," Julian said, stopping beside Anna at the edge of the foyer and looking her over with appreciation as he took both of her hands in his and kissed her cheek. "I take back what I said about all men being idiots. He's got the market cornered."

"Have you talked to him? How is he? He didn't say anything about the interviews—or anything else—when he came for Moira."

"He's busy kicking himself for being a fool, and it remains to be seen how hard the press is going to push him. Right now, his main concern is keeping Moira out of the mess as much as he can."

"She was so disappointed not to stay for the ball, it broke my heart."

"With luck, most of the interest will die down quickly. I can't say I know what I would have done in Connal's shoes. There's no such thing as right and wrong when it comes to parenting. There's no final exam, no study guide. The script and the stage keep changing, and all we can do is improvise."

"I didn't realize you had children," Anna said.

"I keep it quiet—for some of the same reasons that Connal didn't want Moira growing up in the public eye. The world can be ugly. When you have children, you want to give them the fairytale. You want them to believe in midnight and glass slippers, and most of all, you want them to believe that wicked stepmothers and jealous sisters get punished, and the good people in the world get their due rewards. There are too many people like Sorcha and Erica. Did you hear *The Sun* paid them for that photo? Flora snatched the phone right out of Erica's hand and gave it to the police. The idiot girl apparently wasn't even smart enough to try to hide her tracks. Of course, she confessed that Sorcha put her up to it. They wanted to get back at Connal, maybe get him and Moira to leave."

Anna started to ask what would happen to them, but when it came down to it, she didn't care. Julian was right. There would always be people like Sorcha and Erica—and Katharine. Like Henry.

Did she still hope for the fairytale herself? Prince Charming? Was she holding out for a storybook hero when real people were flawed and complicated and the world didn't have clear-cut rules?

Connal wasn't perfect. The truth was, she didn't care about that either. She loved him. She loved him and Moira with all her wounded and mended heart. It didn't matter if loving them was messy and complicated, she realized suddenly. Wherever they were, that was where she wanted to be.

But for now, she was stuck at the fairytale ball, and they were both alone. Was there more she could have done for them, instead of letting them go off by themselves? More she should have been doing *for* them?

The six pipers Elspeth had hired from outside the glen lined up and began to play, calling everyone who'd been milling around the front rooms into line behind them. With Brando as her escort, Elspeth took her place at the head of the queue behind the pipers, and they set off for the ballroom in a dignified procession.

Julian held out his elbow to Anna. "May I take you in?"

Anna looped her arm through his. "I'll warn you, I should come with hazard lights. I've no idea what I'm doing."

"And I'm a creature of bright lights and big, anonymous cities. Buying a kilt is as far as I've gotten into the culture up here, and frankly, after a few dances, I fully intend to stake out a vacant stretch of wall and nurse a series of whiskeys while observing the evening with a jaundiced eye."

Brando snorted. "Fine for you, but Anna will be having none of that. She'd better be prepared to dance until her feet ache."

The line reached the ballroom, and the pipers slow-stepped across it to the far side and took their places near the other musicians. Once everyone had entered the room, the quartet took over. Bagpipe music was a true reflection of Scotland: no matter the tune, there was an edge of tragedy and dignity and mourning beneath the notes. In contrast, the fiddle and accordion of the dance quartet set off at a lively, joyous pace that sent almost everyone out onto the floor.

Anna did her best to keep up, but after three dances with Brando where she didn't know the complicated steps and felt like she was constantly behind, she pleaded off and went to stand with Julian at the edge of the room while Brando went to dance with Elspeth.

The lights sparkled overhead. Julian brought her a glass of Scotch. "Here, down this," he said, pressing the glass into Anna's hand. She threw the drink back in a single swallow, and Julian laughed. "I suppose you deserve that after the day you've had. Here, have mine as well."

Anna sipped that a bit more cautiously before going off to chat with the other guests, moving through the crowd with Julian or Elspeth or Brando by her side. Eventually, she even managed to find the courage to let Brando lead her out onto the floor again and talk her through the complicated progressive patterns that formed as couples came together and separated, changed partners, and shifted around the room. She wasn't sure she would have managed to follow the dance even without the alcohol and the distraction, but her mind kept wandering outside the confines of the room. The truth was, she longed to be somewhere else.

When the dance was over, she thanked Brando and excused herself, heading back to where Julian stood along one of the few stretches of wall not already occupied by tablecloth-draped display cases, groups of pikes and claymores, or sundry other weapons.

Her back was to the room when the sound behind her underwent a subtle change as the dancers stopped and shifted even though the music had continued. Julian's chin came up. "Well, this is unexpected. You might want to have a look, darling. I believe someone's come back for you."

Anna turned slowly, and her eyes went straight to Connal who, with Moira beside him in a pink satin dress, had stopped to speak with Elspeth. Seeing Anna, he went still. Wearing a kilt and jacket with a crisp white shirt and bowtie, he strode toward her, his eyes locked on hers while the dancers on the floor moved to give him room.

Anna's face went numb, so numb she didn't know what expression she was wearing, and she fought the urge to press both hands to her cheeks. Her heart gave a thud of hope. Connal had brought Moira back, and he was here, and he was coming toward her with a stubborn set to his chin, and his eyes still fixed on her as though he was afraid she was going to turn and run.

"You came," she said when he stopped in front of her, the words squeezed small by the tightness in her throat.

"A smart woman once asked if it was fear for Moira that had been holding me back all along or fear for my own sake. I wasn't clever enough then to know how to answer her."

Anna's throat grew even tighter. "And did you figure it out?"

Connal searched her face, his eyes resting on her heated cheeks. "With help. A very intuitive young lady I had badly disappointed told me that it was all right if we didn't go to the ball because I had come to the procession. She told me she worries about me when I don't let myself have fun. And she asked me if I was skipping the ball because I was afraid if I danced with you I'd be even sadder when you went away. My ten-year-old daughter isn't supposed to be worrying about me. She's certainly not supposed to be smarter than I am."

Anna stared at one of the buttons on his jacket so that she didn't have to meet his eyes. "Would you be sadder if you danced with me before I went away?"

"I'd be miserable and stupid if I let you leave at all," he said. Taking her hands, Connal pressed them flat between his palms and raised them to his chest where she could feel the thudding of his heart. "Before all this mess today, and all the complications, I had promised myself that I wouldn't say anything to you until after the Sighting. I told myself that it would be unfair to you to say anything—that it was all too fast—and what if you didn't see the same thing I had?"

Anna's eyes flicked back to Connal's face. "What same thing?"

He swallowed visibly, and a corner of his mouth kicked up. "I saw you in the loch when I was seventeen. Not only you—you and me and Moira together, the three of us. Moira exactly as she is now, and you exactly as you are. I'd almost forgotten about that image until Moira was born. The more she looked like herself, the harder it became to ignore what the Sighting had shown me. If she was real, then I couldn't help starting to believe that maybe you were real as well. I told myself it had to be some sort of déjà vu, my mind playing tricks. How could I have seen Moira without Isobel? How could I have seen anyone besides Isobel when it was Isobel I loved? None of it made sense. Not until I walked up to your car window that night a month ago and saw you sitting there looking up at me, every bit as beautiful as you'd been when I saw you in the loch. That's partly why I was so horrible, I think. I was in shock."

"You saw me?" Anna repeated. "And Moira?"

"Which seems to mean that, at least for Moira and me, everything in our lives must have happened exactly how it was meant to happen. Even Isobel. The accident and Moira's palsy. Coming here. All of it."

Anna suddenly felt light inside, as if someone had filled her with air and pushed away the anxiety of the last few weeks. The last years. Maybe deep down, everyone wanted to believe in miracles.

The idea that two strangers could discover each other, like two puzzle pieces waiting for the missing part of themselves, had to be miraculous.

"I'm not sure that anything about love is meant to make logical sense," she said, her heart hammering in her ears. "From the first moment you trust your heart to someone else, everything is a leap of faith. It could be the whole purpose of the Sighting is to remind us that some things are gifts and we shouldn't take them for granted."

Connal smiled at her, that wide smile of his that telescoped the world down to the two of them alone. He drew her even closer, and she felt herself open and bloom beneath the heat of his expression, felt herself expand until she was as wide and full as the entire glen and the high green braes around them.

"I walked down to the inn today," Connal said, "thinking that I would see Moira and show you both that I was ready to take a leap of faith back into the world. I meant to invite you both to come to the ball with me. The tabloid article caught me by surprise. The ugliness."

"The ugliness sells newspapers. That's not your fault."

"Will you dance with me?" he asked, tucking her against his side.

"I will always dance with you," Anna said.

EPILOGUE

All, everything that I understand, I understand only because I love.

LEO TOLSTOY, *WAR AND PEACE*

T HE DRESS WAS PERFECT, more silver than white, the Leavers lace so delicate the stitching in the intricate hawthorn pattern was barely visible. From a simple neckline, the bodice hugged her figure then fanned out to a graceful skirt with a sweeping train. Peering into the oval mirror in the master bedroom at Inverlochlarig House, Anna still wondered whether she had picked the dress because it reminded her of the image she had seen in the loch a year ago at the Beltane Sighting, or whether the loch had simply shown her a snapshot of a day a year into the future.

She hadn't expected anything when she'd leaned over the water to wash her face with Elspeth beside her and at least a hundred other people crowded along the water's edge. Reporters had milled around, hoping for a glimpse of Connal and Moira, and the dawn had been cold and clear, fog curling up off the water.

"Are you ready?" Elspeth had asked her.

Anna had been a little nervous given what Connal had told her. What if she saw someone other than Connal? Not that she had believed in the Sighting. Not completely. But she had wanted to believe.

The top of the sun, yellow-orange as an egg yolk, had peered over the Highland hills. Everyone bent at once, hands plunging into the loch, faces stinging as they brought the water to their cheeks. Anna's breath blew a haze into the air, and water dripped from between her fingers. She hadn't seen anything when she bent down, nothing except her own reflection and those of the people all around her. But as she pulled her hands away from her eyes, the drops of water that fell back into the loch rippled out as smoothly as if she stood there all by herself, and in the water, she had seen Connal and Moira on the peninsula with her, Connal in his kilt, smiling at her with love in his eyes, and Moira in a glittering silver dress holding a basket of lacy hawthorn petals.

The dress Anna has been wearing was this one, exact down to the last detail, that she and Connal had found on a mannequin in a bridal store window on a whirlwind trip to Edinburgh just four months ago. How could the loch have shown her that? Maybe it was wishful thinking, Anna admitted as she stood looking in the mirror. Maybe the dress was only similar. Perhaps she would never know for certain, but deep down, she believed.

"You're so beautiful, love, you hurt my heart," Elspeth said, coming up behind her. "Have I ever told you how happy I am that I flimflammed you into coming for the festival?"

Anna turned and kissed Elspeth on the cheek. "Many times, but that was the best story you've ever told."

A knock sounded on the door to the corridor, and they both turned a little warily. "We're all ready," Anna's sister Margaret called. "How are you doing?"

"Coming now," Anna said.

"Just one second." Elspeth pulled out an embroidered handkerchief and unwrapped it to reveal a pair of sapphire earrings that were a near match to the necklace that Connal had given Anna earlier, the blue the same color as the loch, the same color as Connal's eyes. "These were your grandmother's earrings," Elspeth said. "I know Ailsa already gave you her own bracelet as something old, but I wanted to give you something, too. I hope that's okay. Your grandmother would have loved you so much, so very much. As I do."

Anna wrapped her arms around Elspeth fiercely. All her life, Elspeth had been the mother Anna had wanted, the mother she wished she had. But Julian had been right. Parents did the best they could. Anna's own mother was down on the peninsula with the other wedding guests, sitting beside Katharine and Henry, because there had been no keeping those two away. You got the family you were dealt, Anna had decided, and you had to make the best of it. If you were lucky, you found an Elspeth along the way as she had, and that became the family you really needed.

"You are the best person in the world, Aunt Elspeth," she whispered. "I'm so happy you're a flimflam artist. Have I ever told you that?"

"Just consider me your fairy godmother, my girl. Wishes and white lies have never been that far apart."

Smiling, they followed Margaret downstairs, past the great room already set up for the Beltane Ball that would double as a wedding reception later, and through the foyer to where Moira waited in her sparkling silver dress beside Anna's father. His gaze drifted between her and Elspeth while they walked toward him, as if he didn't know where to look. Anna couldn't decide if she wanted to hug him or slap him and tell him to go get a divorce already instead of spending more years being miserable. Except that wouldn't solve the problem. If he divorced Ailsa, Elspeth would never take him.

Anna stooped to kiss Moira's cheek. "You look lovely, sweetheart."

"So do you," Moira said, smiling the crooked half-smile that lit her eyes. "We're like fairy princesses, aren't we?"

Anna's father smiled down at both of them. "Yes, you are." Still tall and handsome and kind after all these years in an unhappy marriage, his hair gray and his face lined with both strain and laughter, he smiled down at Anna. "You look happy enough to float away."

Anna hugged him harder. "I wish you could be as happy as I am."

"You're making me the happiest father in the world by being happy yourself. That's all any parent could ask for."

Swiftly, almost gruffly, Anna's father stooped to kiss her cheek.

Down by the loch, the first notes of "Braes of Balquhidder" sounded from the bagpipes: Ian Camm MacGregor and Rory MacLaren playing together, Rory because he was still trying to make amends for his sister Erica, and Ian Camm because there couldn't be a MacGregor wedding in the glen without a MacGregor piper. Beyond the gates, a crowd of festival-goers and tabloid reporters jockeyed for position, all trying to catch a glimpse. There were even boats bobbing out on the water with camera lenses flashing in the sunlight, and a helicopter hovering overhead making the water choppy on the loch. Anna didn't care. Nothing was going to spoil the day.

Moira picked up the small silver basket of hawthorn petals and went down the front stairs sprinkling them along the path. Elspeth and Margaret fell in behind her, walking the long path toward the peninsula where rows of chairs were set up for the wedding guests and where Connal and the minister waited.

Anna's father handed Anna the bouquet of lacy white hawthorn wound through with silk ribbons in deep blue and palest green.

The "Braes of Balquhidder" changed to "Highland Cathedral" with the drums and flutes of the band chiming in. On her father's arm, Anna walked slowly toward the peninsula where, a year ago, she had glimpsed her future. Now that future stood there waiting for her, looking exactly like the image that she had seen reflected in the water during the Sighting: Connal in his kilt with the MacGregor sash on his shoulder, and Moira in her glittering silver dress. Anna's mother and Katharine, Henry, Brando, JoAnne, Flora and Duncan, Kirsty and Angus, Davy Griggs and his wife, and all the other people from the village were also there with them, smiling.

"I love you, Anna," Connal whispered, his heart in his eyes and the light dancing around him like magic as he took Anna's hand with their family and friends looking on. Moira came to help him raise the thin veil from Anna's face, and when he slipped the ring on her finger, Anna felt the click in the fabric of the world in every cell within her body.

The wedding vows they had written for each other were meaningful and heartfelt, but in all those words there were only seven that truly mattered: I will love you forever and always.

Those seven words mended hearts and reshaped lives, Anna thought, looking around at her big, messy family, old and new alike. She'd been lucky enough to find love, and that in its many forms was what made life worth living.

AUTHOR'S NOTE

Dear Reader,

I was driving in the Highlands of Scotland years ago and came across a rusting black-and-white road sign pointing to Rob Roy MacGregor's grave. Now, being a sucker for Scottish history, Sir Walter Scott, and Liam Neeson in a kilt (not necessarily in that order), I had to take the detour. Right? No choice at all. And I fell utterly in love with the Balquhidder Glen.

The location itself was beautiful, of course, in that wild way of Scottish glens with steep-sided, heather-covered braes and lochs glittering silver beneath an endless sky. But it also had an aura of something magical.

In addition to the grave where Rob Roy, a "MacGregor Despite Them," lies buried beside his wife and two of his sons, the glen houses the ruin of an old stone church where a soberly Presbyterian minister, the Reverend Robert Kirk, preached in the seventeenth century. While engaged in said preaching, he also reportedly wandered into an enchanted world. Years later, according to legend, instead of dying, he was taken back to that Otherworld to become the chaplain to the Fairy Queen.

As if that wouldn't have been enough to fire my imagination, I also had an encounter with a flock of meandering sheep, a lonely horse bit the side mirror of my rental car when I tried to stop petting him, and a shaggy Highland bull charged over to lick my camera lens while I was trying to take his picture. (I have the photo of his tongue somewhere, I swear.) Add to that a lovely meal and a passionate conversation with a Scottish nationalist, and it was a day I've never forgotten.

I always knew I would write about the glen someday. Of course, it's changed some since I visited that first time. And because it has changed, and because my story is fiction which has resulted in some alterations to the landscape, while I'm keeping much of its history and the names of the clans who've traditionally resided there, I am calling it Balwhither instead of Balquhidder. For what it's worth, Balwhither is how you pronounce the name anyway, and it's also how Robert Louis Stephenson wrote about it in his books.

If you've been to Balquhidder, you'll find yourself a little disoriented. The people, places, and events that populate my glen are fictitious, and even the historical events and figures, actual geography, and landmark businesses in the glen are fictionalized. But I hope I've captured the beauty of the place, and I hope it inspires my readers to go and see it for themselves.

In case you're sad to leave the charm of small-town life in a magical setting behind when this story is over, keep an eye out for additional free-standing books in the Celtic Legends series centered on Celtic legends and holidays. And if you like Scottish food, try the recipes included here. Maybe they'll turn out well enough at your house to help persuade your own man to try a kilt!

Anyway, please enjoy!

Happy reading.
Martina

APPLE BUTTERSCOTCH PIE

As with most things historically Scottish, the origin of the term butterscotch is shrouded in controversy and heavily Anglicized through a long history of war, destruction of records, and the suppression of Scots Gaelic in favor of English.

The Keillers of Dundee, manufacturers of the famous Dundee Orange Marmalade, may have made butterscotch confectionary as far back as 1797. The first literary reference comes from Nottingham in 1847, and a nineteenth century article in The Doncaster Archives claimed that a sweet-maker there was making "butter-scotch" as early as 1817. This makes sense if the recipe was originally from Scotland and moving southward. Other sources argue that the "scotch" part of the word comes from "scorching" the syrup, or "scoring" the sweets as they cool for easier breaking.

Whatever the origin of the word, the brown sugar and butter caramelize deliciously over the apples in the baking. Add a dollop of plum jam and a meringue topping, and this mouth-watering dessert will quickly become a favorite for any romantic evening.

For Filling

Ingredients:

Basic pastry crust (see
    recipe or store-bought)
4-6 cups favorite pie apples
1/2 cup plus one tbsp
    granulated sugar
1/3 cup Demerara sugar
    (light brown)
2 tbsp plum jam

2 tbsp flour
2 tbsp cream
1 egg
2 egg whites
pinch of salt

Step-by-Step:

1. Line a 9-inch fluted metal flan tin with pastry dough.
2. Preheat oven to 425°F
3. Peel, core, and slice the apples thin. Layer until they fill the crust completely.
4. In a small bowl, beat the whole egg with one tablespoon of cream.
5. In a separate bowl, mix brown sugar, flour, and salt.
6. Combine wet mixture with dry.
7. Spread combined ingredients over the apples in the tin and bake at 425°F for ten minutes.
8. Reduce oven temp to 350°F and bake for 20 additional minutes or until the apples are soft.
9. In a clean, dry bowl, whip egg whites at medium-speed with an electric mixer until firm peaks form. Beating constantly, add granulated sugar to form a smooth, thick, and glossy meringue.
10. Spread plum jam over the apples.
11. Cover with meringue topping and use the flat side of a knife to swirl the meringue into pretty peaks.
12. Bake at 350°F for 15-25 minutes or so until the meringue is lightly golden. Chill and serve cold.

For Pie Crust

Ingredients:

1 cup all-purpose flour
8 tbsp unsalted butter
2 tbsp caster (fine-
    granulated) sugar
1 egg yolk

1 tbsp iced water
1 tbsp butter
Pastry weights or 1 cup
    dried beans or rice

Step-by-Step:

1. If pre-baking, preheat oven to 350°F.
2. Using a pastry brush, coat a 9-inch pan with melted butter.
3. Sift the flour into a large bowl and crumble in the butter. Combine butter and flour until the mixture forms large crumbs.
4. Add the sugar, egg yolk, and water. Stir to form a fine, soft dough.
5. Press the dough into a ball, then roll it out between two sheets of plastic wrap, until it is 1/8-inch thick, turning frequently to get a round shape big enough to cover the base and sides of your pan.
6. Remove only one side of the plastic wrap and gently ease the pastry into the tin. Press the plastic wrap coated side firmly into the bottom and flutes of the tin, then trim off the excess at the top.
7. Remove wrap and vent pastry with a fork. Refrigerate 20 minutes.
8. If pre-baking, line the crust with wax paper, distribute weights, rice, or beans evenly on top, and bake for 35 minutes.

CHICKEN BONNIE PRINCE CHARLIE

Despite a rocky history with the Stewart kings since James I took away their right to officially use the name MacGregor, the MacGregors of Balwhither were staunch Jacobites, supporting every rebellion from 1689 to the last failed attempt to put Bonnie Prince Charlie on the throne. The recipe for the Drambuie liqueur used in this mouth-watering recipe was reportedly given to the McKinnon family of Skye by the Prince when they gave him sanctuary following the disastrous defeat at the Battle of Culloden.

Ingredients:

4 boneless, skinless chicken
   breasts
4 apples (semi-sweet)
1/2 cup chicken stock
1 cup heavy cream
6 tbsp unsalted butter

1/3 cup flaked almonds
4 tbsp Drambuie liqueur
1/4 cup all-purpose flour
1/2 pinch of pepper
pinch of salt

Step-by-Step:
1. Rinse chicken, pat dry, and pound until even thickness with the flat side of a frying pan.
2. Season chicken with salt and pepper and dredge in flour.
3. In a large skillet over medium high heat, melt 3 tablespoons of butter and heat until it begins to sizzle.
4. Add chicken, reduce heat to medium, and lightly brown on both sides.
5. Sprinkle with 2 tablespoons of Drambuie and chicken stock, cover, reduce to low, and cook for 10 minutes without lifting lid.

6. Core, peel, and thickly slice the apples. Melt 3 tablespoons of butter on low and cook apples until soft.
7. Turn heat off on chicken, but do not move from burner. Leave chicken to sit 10 additional minutes in pan without lifting the lid.
8. Remove chicken from pan to serving dish and warm in oven.
9. Add 2 tablespoons of Drambuie to pan drippings and gradually stir in cream. Turn burner to medium and heat, removing before sauce comes to a boil.
10. Cover chicken with sauce, sprinkle with almonds, and top with softened apples.

Serves four.

FRUITED GINGERBREAD

Nothing is as comfortingly soul-soothing as gingerbread. It smells like Christmas and the best memories of home and family. Add dried fruit before baking and a generous dollop of freshly whipped cream before serving, and it's an instant I-love-you for any occasion.

Ingredients:

3 cups flour	1 cup brown sugar
1 tsp baking powder	1 tsp baking soda
3 tsp ground ginger	2 tsp cinnamon
1 tsp allspice	1 tsp orange zest
1 tsp orange extract	pinch of salt
1/2 cup butter	2 eggs
1 cup molasses	1 cup boiling water
1 cup apricots	1 cup golden raisins

Step-by-Step:

1. Preheat oven to 325°F, and line a 7-inch metal pan with greased wax paper.
2. In a medium pan, melt butter gently over low heat, then remove from heat and add in sugar and molasses until blended. Set aside to cool.
3. Sift the flour and dry ingredients together into a medium bowl.
4. In a small bowl, beat eggs.
5. Add both wet mixtures to the dry mixture and mix until smooth.
6. Stir in orange zest and fruit.

7. Pour into pan and bake for 60 to 65 minutes until firm to the touch.

8. Remove from pan to cool and store in airtight container for at least two days before serving.

Makes 16 squares.

SCONES

Properly pronounced "skon" to rhyme with "gone," legend has it that these tasty Scottish quick bread cakes trace their origin to the Stone of Scone, or Destiny, on which Scottish kings were crowned. Their popularity for tea at Buckingham palace certainly proves they're fit for royalty.

Ingredients:

1 3/4 cups all-purpose flour
5 tbsp unsalted butter
1/2 cup currants or raisins
1/4 cup granulated sugar
1/8 tsp salt

4 tsp baking powder
1/2 cup + 1 tbsp milk
1/4 cup sour cream
1 egg

Step-by-Step:

1. Preheat oven to 400°F.
2. In a large bowl, sift together flour, baking powder, sugar, and salt.
3. Cut in the butter and rub until dough resembles pea-sized crumbs.
4. In a small bowl, combine with sour cream, milk, and dried fruit.
5. Add to other ingredients and lightly mix until well-blended.
6. Wash and dry the small bowl, then add egg and 1 tablespoon of milk. Beat until blended and frothy.
7. Liberally flour your hands and, on a floured surface, roll dough out into a 1/2-inch thick square. With a sharp knife, slice the dough into quarters, then slice each quarter into two triangles.

8. Place on greased cookie sheet, brush with egg wash, and let rest for 10 minutes.
9. Bake for 10-15 minutes until tops are golden brown.
10. Cut or break each scone in two. Serve warm with butter, jam, and clotted cream.

Serves eight.

SCOTTISH COFFEE

The common wisdom about whiskey (from uisce beatha, the water of life) is that the Irish invented it and the Scots perfected it. Compared to Irish whiskey, Scotch has a smokier, sexier flavor, which lends a different character entirely whether you drink it straight up or add it to your coffee when you need a less guilt-inducing nerve-smoother in the middle of the day.

Ingredients:

1/2 oz good Scotch whisky
   or Drambuie

1/2 oz Cointreau, Grand
   Marnier

1 tsp Demerara (light
   brown) sugar

Fresh, dark coffee
Heavy cream to taste
Whipped cream

Step-by-Step:

1. Pour hot water into selected glass or cup and let stand 30 seconds.
2. Empty and thoroughly dry the cup.
3. Fill the cup two within 1 inch of the whiskey or Drambuie and coffee.
4. Add sugar and stir until dissolved.
5. Deflecting cream along the back of a teaspoon, add it gently so that it drifts across the top of the coffee, sinking no more than one half-inch. Adjust to your liking.
6. Top with whipped cream.

Serves one.

SPECIAL OFFER!

If you've enjoyed *Lake of Destiny*, please order the next book in the Celtic Legends collection, *Bell of Eternity*, available in hardcover, trade paperback, and e-book. Look for it at your favorite retailer, and order early to get exclusive introductory e-book pricing!

Want even more men in kilts, quirky villagers, and magical settings? Keep an eye out for additional books coming soon!

To stay on top of all the news, special offers, giveaways, and more romantic Celtic recipes, sign up for my newsletter at MartinaBoone.com/index.php/find_me/ and stay connected.

Bell of Eternity

Does Love Last Beyond the Grave?

Emma Larsen put her life on hold after the accident that left her mother paralyzed and cost a man his life. For four long years, Treave Nancarrow, the deceased man's son, has often been the only friend she could lean on. But when he suddenly proposes marriage after her mother's funeral, Emma can't help being dismayed. She's already trying to decide between transforming her home cooking hobby into a profession or going back to college. She can't afford to jump from one commitment to another before she's had a chance to find out what she really wants. Still, when Treave begs her to accompany him to a wedding at his family's castle in Cornwall so he can show her how compatible they would be, how can she refuse?

She falls in love with the romantic Cornish coast, a world rich with legends, hauntings, and ancient superstitions like the one about the ghostly bell that tolls only when a pair of lovers are destined to be together forever. When a tragedy rocks the small community and everyone pitches in to help, though, Treave seems like a different person, one Emma begins to fear. Then, too, there's Brando MacLaren, the handsome, kilt-wearing Scotsman who helps her reconcile her rocky past and makes her feel adventurous and alive. But Brando has his own healing to do. He also has a secret, one he's keeping from her. Can Emma trust him with her heart? Can she trust either of the men? An ancient Cornish legend might help guide her choice between them--if she can find the courage to believe in herself.

ACKNOWLEDGMENTS

Once again, thank you to my family and my amazing husband for their unwavering support and daily words of encouragement. Huge thanks to Erin Cashman, beloved friend, critique partner, co-conspirator, and all around incredible person, and to Sandra Waugh, generous spirit and source of reason and inspiration, without whom this book would never have come to be.

Boundless gratitude also to Susan Sipal, Leslie Sulli Rose, and Lisa Gail Green for their friendship, eagle eyes, and hand-holding, to Wendy Higgins and David James for encouragement and advice, and Jodi Meadows for patiently and endlessly listening to my growing pains. And finally, enormous thanks to Laura Kemmerer for her tireless editing, Kalen O'Donnell for a beautiful cover, Rachel and Joel Greene for a lovely interior, and everyone involved at Mayfair who made all this possible.

ABOUT MARTINA BOONE

Martina Boone is the award-winning author of the romantic southern gothic Heirs of Watson Island series for young adults, including *Compulsion*, *Persuasion*, and *Illusion* from Simon & Schuster, Simon Pulse, and heartwarming contemporary romances for adult readers beginning with *Lake of Destiny*. She's also the founder of AdventuresInYAPublishing.com, a three-time Writer's Digest 101 Best Websites for Writers site and on the board of the Literary Council of Northern Virginia.

She lives with her husband, children, Shetland Sheepdog, and a lopsided cat, and she enjoys writing romance set in the kinds of magical places she loves to visit. When she isn't writing, she's addicted to travel, horses, skiing, chocolate flavored tea, and anything with Nutella on it.

http://www.martinaboone.com/

Made in the USA
Lexington, KY
09 November 2017